I0657396

DAMNNEARBROKE

DAMN NEAR BROKE

GARY ALEXANDER

NEW ATLANTIC LIBRARY
is an imprint of
ABSOLUTELY AMAZING eBOOKS

Published by Whiz Bang LLC, 926 Truman Avenue, Key West, Florida 33040, USA.

Damn Near Broke copyright © 2017 by Gary Alexander. Electronic compilation/ paperback edition copyright © 2017 by Whiz Bang LLC. Cover painting, *Girl at a Window* by Salvador Dali, 1925.

All rights reserved. No part of this book may be reproduced, scanned, or transmitted in any form or by any means, electronic or mechanical, including photocopying, recording, or any information storage and retrieval system, without permission in writing from the publisher. Please do not participate in or encourage piracy of copyrighted materials in violation of the author's rights. Purchase only authorized ebook editions.

This is a work of fiction. Names, characters, places, and incidents either are the product of the author's imagination or are used fictitiously, and any resemblance to actual persons, living or dead, businesses, companies, events, or locales is entirely coincidental. While the author has made every effort to provide accurate information at the time of publication, neither the publisher nor the author assumes any responsibility for errors, or for changes that occur after publication. Further, the publisher does not have any control over and does not assume any responsibility for author or third-party websites or their contents. How the ebook displays on a given reader is beyond the publisher's control.

For information contact:
Publisher@AbsolutelyAmazingEbooks.com

ISBN-13: 978-1945772320 (The New Atlantian Library)
ISBN-10: 1945772328

Dedicated it to Rebecca, Michelle and Tracy

DAMN**NEAR**BROKE

Chapter 1

BUDDY

Martha and me, we're sardined in the cattle car section of a 747 I may've riveted skin onto during my 31-years at Boeing. She's snoozing, her pillow pressed into my shoulder. I'm looking out at the twilight over Greenland. Nothing down there except ice and snow. It's beyond me how the polar bears get by.

Martha found the ad for this tour online. She's the computer whiz in our household. Price's not cheap, but not too god-awful neither. We can afford it. Our financial ducks are in a row. At just the right time, we lucked out and attended a seminar run by a financial genius by the name of Charles Murganzer. We signed up for his program. Lock, stock and barrel. Our nest egg is running on all cylinders, paying us a steady seven percent every single month, direct-depositing it like clockwork.

You're thinking Ponzi, too good to be true, right? No way. We checked Murganzer Stable Fund up, down, and inside out. It's clean as a whistle. If not for MSF, we'd have to keep working at the Lazy B two more years, me on the 737 wing line and Martha as a tool room clerk, both of us moving into our mid-sixties.

Vegas, where we usually go, was costing us a bundle. I sit down at a roulette table, all the math I ever learned falls right out of my noggin. Martha on the slots, it's a chore and a half to pry her loose.

Martha said she was sick and tired of giving our money to gangsters and the Disney people, and we've never really and truly been anywhere. She decided that since this is a special trip celebrating our retirement, we should "broaden our cultural horizons."

I voted for Branson, Missouri. Martha said Branson did not qualify as culture. So Spain it is, us and 15 or so complete strangers.

Janine's handing out more of her informational handouts. Janine's our tour leader. Janine's got sad eyes and thick ankles. She's as old as our daughter and there's no ring on her finger, poor girl.

I shut my eyes and hear over the hum of the turbines Janine telling the couple in the row ahead of us, "Not to worry, be proud to be an American, not everybody hates us."

~ ~ ~

Two-hour stopover at London-Heathrow. The clock says noon. My aching head and butt say middle of the night. Ed and Ted, friendly rosy-cheeked grocery checkers in their thirties we met waiting to board at Seattle, they're perched on barstools, researching if Guinness in jolly old England tastes the same warm as it does at home cold. Martha says not to encourage them.

Janine scoops us up like a den mother, warning us for the umpteenth time not to get separated after we land at Madrid. We're a yawning, bleary-eyed mishmash, demographical-wise across the board. A whiny yuppie couple, a shutterbug whose hand is grafted to his point and shoot, a gal even older than us who beelines into every gift store in sight.

Martha's taken a liking to these two college professors. They wear beards and those trousers with pockets up and down the sides. They teach philosophy, a real useful subject. They're just as sharp as a tack and one of them has already lost his passport. It was found on top of a vending machine where he'd put it while fumbling for change that won't work in England machines anyhow.

Martha's given up bingo and playing cards at the local senior center. She's taken courses at the community college on brain aerobics and herbalism and feng shui, which in English means how to rearrange your furniture whether it needs it or not.

She's signed up for watercolor class when we get home. The last month, she walked around the house with earphones on listening to Spanish language tapes. I had to yell when I wanted her attention.

What's gotten into my Martha?

Is change of life repeating on her?

~ ~ ~

Madrid's a scenic old town with big gingerbread buildings from way back when. The natives drive like scalded apes, everybody smokes, and I've yet to see a vacant parking place. Our bus doesn't show, so we gotta hoof it from the hotel to this museum. Janine, she has got us on a cultural death march and I'm not at my chipperest.

Martha hit the hay early last night, so I snuck downstairs to the bar and had me a libation with Ed and Ted. They were crying in their suds about how they used to go on cruises or to Club Med, the idea being to get lucky.

Ed and Ted realized that they'd passed their prime as Romeos and that the bikini set was literally out of reach.

They signed up for this Spain tour, hoping to score on, as they put it, repressed librarians.

The pickings are slim. There is this librarian couple along, both stocky ladies with short hair. They would not be receptive to anything these boys have in mind. After the fourth or eighth round, I lectured them, saying grow the fuck up and capitalize on this once-in-a-lifetime learning experience, which I, myself, was gonna try my goddamnedest to whether I like it or not, or something to that effect.

Ed and Ted must not've remembered me shooting off my mouth because they're speaking to me. Martha caught me sneaking back in when I knocked over a lamp.

Janine's talking enough for everyone, about our first stop, the Reina Sofia, one of two world-class museums in Madrid we're gonna be privileged to see. It's late spring and the sky's so blue and hot my eyeballs itch. I chugalug a bottle of water and might survive the day if I can dodge the daggers Martha stares through me when she's not taking notes.

Irregardless that the air conditioning in the Reina Sofia is for the benefit of the priceless artwork, not the tourists, I am appreciating it more than I'm appreciating the pictures the climate control's protecting. The basic problem is, much of the priceless artwork doesn't look like anything.

Janine's misty-eyed at the biggie, Picasso's *Guernica*. Pablo painted the picture after the Germans bombed the town of the same name during the Spanish Civil War. I'm sorry, but it looks to me like the aftermath of a boiler explosion in a meat market. Janine says *Guernica* never fails to move her. She's got Martha dabbing her eyes too. I ask how come there're guards swarming around it when in the other rooms there's only a single snotty bored guy or gal in uniform, who half the time is sitting down reading a book.

Martha's pointy-heads are named Bryce and Neil, which figures. They instantly have the answer.

Neil says, "*Guernica* is arguably the most powerful anti-fascist statement ever made, and there are those today, separatists and neo-Falangists, a resurgent and violent right wing in Europe who would love to deface *Guernica* to make a statement."

Bryce interrupts to be helpful, like he often does. Martha told me that him and his pal speak four or five languages. If you can do that, I guess you never have to shut up. Bryce rattles on about skinheads, about anti-immigration sentiment, about nationalistic resistance to the EU, about centuries-old regionalism, and so forth.

He's still yakking when we come to this picture that freezes me dead in my tenny runners. It's by this world-famous artist named Salvador Dalí and is the size of a supermarket tabloid. It's not Dali's usual weirdness I've been seeing of melted pocket watches and conglomerations of animals, vegetables and minerals and undressed ladies in midair, defying the laws of physics and common decency.

It's of a young gal and is titled *Muchacha en la Ventana*. She's standing at a window, looking out at a bay. A towel's laying on the windowsill. There's a sailboat on the water and dry land in the background. I say she's a young gal, even though I can't see her face, but not *too* young as she's nicely filled out in the derriere and leg departments. She's wearing a silky, two-piece dress with blue stripes. Her hair comes to the shoulder and is curly at the ends.

It's like my feet are stuck in hot asphalt. I haven't the foggiest why.

Martha's speaking to me again, having semi-forgiven me for last night. "Quit leering."

"I'm not leering. I'm art-appreciating."

Martha calls me a dirty old man and tugs my arm.

After we finish up this floor and another, Janine says since it's our first full day and we're suffering jet lag and our schedule will be hectic from tomorrow on, instead of surveying monuments we'll have us a leisurely rest-of-the-day grazing at *tapas* bars. No argument from me. I wasn't looking forward to checking out statues of dead generals on horseback, caked with pigeon guano.

The beer's cold and smooth wherever we go. A little hair of the pooch and I am vastly improved. *Tapa* is Spain's word for appetizer and appetizing they are, sausages and meatballs and olives and slivers of the whole hams the bars all got hanging up on hooks and omelet slices they call tortillas and prawns and other critters on toast wedges that are mighty tasty.

Buffalo chicken wings and deep-fried mozzarella are nowhere in sight. I am surprised that I don't care.

~ ~ ~

Next day. More Madrid, more culture.

The highlight's the Prado, the mother of all Spanish museums. The pictures are old and you can actually tell what they are. What many of them are is of Jesus and Biblical mayhem and violence, along that vein. There seems to be dogs in many of these masterpieces, even in a Last Supper picture, a hound laying in front of the table. In another, Rover's lifting its leg to irrigate a tree. In that regard, the Prado is, frankly, a one-trick pony.

Can't get my mind off *Girl at the Window*, the English name for *Muchacha Whatever* I doped out from Martha's little pocketsize Spanish dictionary. At this huge, dark Dutch picture from the sixteenth-century sport in a cape with a crinkly white collar, which looks like it oughta be on a cigar box, I inform her that I have a killer headache and am heading back to the room before I toss my cookies.

"But you'll miss the Royal Palace, lunch on the Gran Via, the Plaza Mayor, and the Cathedral," Martha says.

I say I'm disappointed too and boogie out of there lickety-split and catch a taxi to the Reina Sofia. I could walk to it in 15 minutes if I wasn't in such an all-fired hurry.

Maybe I'm sweating from the rush, maybe I'm spending too much time at *Girl*. In fact, I'm going nowhere else. On account of this, the guards who barely showed a pulse yesterday, they are paying me some serious attention. A *Guernica* Nazi moseys on over and gives me the stink eye. Him and another guard, they start whispering. I've worn out my welcome.

Downstairs at the gift shop, *Girl* is a popular girl. She's for sale on coffee mugs, posters, calendars, T-shirts, coasters and tote bags. Overkill, if you ask me. I grab me every *Girl* postcard in the rack.

My debit card bounces. This foreign bank computer they use, could be it's on the blink because it's on the metric system and our plastic isn't. No time to worry about it. The girl at the register's looking at me like it's *my* fault. I pay cash and scram.

~ ~ ~

Can't sleep a wink. Need to learn how come I can't get *Girl* out of my skull. It's like I know her from the deep, dark past, an old girl friend, or a girl I'd wished was a girl friend but wasn't.

When Martha's snoring loud enough to wake the dead, I ease myself out of bed and take her purse into the can. Martha has this tiny little computer gadget she never leaves home without. You can keep a thousand addresses on it despite us never having known in our entire lives a thousand people to keep track of. At least it's not one of those phones or tablets everybody stares at when they're supposed to be paying attention where they're walking.

We're not a computerphobic family unless you count me. Martha has a laptop, a tablet, and a cell phone (not one of those smarty-pants ones people are looking at when they oughta be paying attention to their driving), but they're at home since they don't speak European.

This gizmo, she says it's obsolete as a horse and buggy, but it's all she needs. It's all I need to find an address and phone number on it: my brother Stan in Idaho Falls, Idaho, where he's an auto body shop foreman.

I poke buttons till the gizmo glows in the dark.

This situation is bringing back the lousiest of memories.

Monday , October 4, 1971: the date that's always on my mind whenever I think of Stan.

That was when they found our mother in the Rosebud Motor Court on old Highway 99, south of Boeing Plant Two in Seattle, where they were at the time building the 727. A man not her husband and not my father had taken my mom's life with a .38 Smith and Wesson, and then his own, swallowing the barrel. His name was Brady Hardcastle. He was the used car manager at a Plymouth garage. They were found buck-ass-naked in bed, a bloody mess.

I was a year and a half older than Stan, in Army Basic Training at Fort Ord, California. I was sent home on emergency leave. Stan hadn't yet dropped out of high school to enlist like I had. Unlike me, who did my thinking with my fists instead of my gray matter, he hadn't quite got to that stage where he knew everything.

I barely remember Mom, other than she was thin and wore her graying hair short. I still can't see her tiptoeing off to motels. I didn't know Hardcastle at all. Nobody close to us knew him either or pinned down why he did what he did.

Stan took her death harder than me and a lot harder than Dad. He got remarried to a Boeing secretary coworker of his two months later, who he stayed married to for the rest of his life. Turned out Dad and his lady had the same action going as Mom and Brady Hardcastle did. The combination of trauma and hanky-panky, I firmly believe, had a lasting influence on Stan and contributed to his bad choices in wives.

I somehow make the address and phone number screen appear. I'm scribbling Stan's number on a piece of toilet paper and drop the damn thing. Batteries go a 'flying. I paw around and, *shit*, bang my damn head on the sink twice before I'm able to police them up and reload Martha's machine.

~ ~ ~

Last morning in Madrid. Got in another cathedral, then lunch. Six different *tapas* for me and a pitcher of sangria split with Martha, me hogging her half. Gonna have to poke another hole in my belt.

But I have got more immediate trouble.

Martha's hunting for a cousin's address to mail a postcard to on her tiny little computer and gets a blank screen, no matter how hard she pokes the buttons. She opens it up and sees the batteries are in backasswards and has a cow. Her "data" is gone. She's blaming the hotel maid for going through our stuff. Threatening to have her fired is what gives me the balls to kind of confess.

"Didn't want to wake you up," is my excuse.

"You wanted Stan's number? You rarely talk, except on Christmas Day."

"I'm homesick. Haven't ever been out of the States unless you count a year in Vietnam for Uncle."

"I knew you weren't sick yesterday," she says. "Homesick I don't know about either."

I got no answer. The great curse of our marriage is that I've never been able to competently lie to her.

~ ~ ~

Gotta keep moving, gotta keep on schedule.

We hop a bus for Toledo, a bumpy old town outside of Madrid they mispronounce over here as toe-lay-dough. It's got walls that in the olden days kept the bad guys out. Ed and Ted are sweating like racehorses. They're having difficulty keeping pace on the hills even with us geezers. Martha says that because of their dissipative habits, they're vertically challenged.

Martha also says that Janine is wonderful, don't I agree? "She imparts unique historical overviews."

Imparted overviews.

She's picked her new vocabulary up from her egghead professors of philosophy. Martha's been spouting a shitload of unMarthalike words lately.

We do the El Greco Museum. The guy was a Greek, by the way. He painted pictures mostly resembling himself, whoever they're supposed to be of. We do the cathedral too, naturally.

Tapas are top-notch. Chorizo. Artichoke hearts. Mushrooms cooked in garlic. Washed down with three beers. Yum.

Martha's made a discovery that's not cultural in any way, shape or form. You don't need a mall to shop till you drop. Toe-lay-doe's got stores coming out of its ears. Lots of tourist guys are moping outside them while their women are inside.

Martha's hauling me to and fro, exploiting bargains. We're getting presents for daughter Melanie (gold necklace); a silk tie for David, Melanie's fat cat gynecologist husband; and a wallet and purse (Spain is famous for their leather) for Jim and Ellen Hendrick, our best friends next door.

Martha's motto is you can't save money unless you spend money. By her reckoning, we've saved a fortune. She says shopping's a good release of the tension of the fast-paced international travel we've been experiencing. You probably can't notice too much tension release in me. Payback for my skulduggering could be part of the reason for the shopping expedition.

Martha's debit card's kaput too. The store's machine says it's maxed out. It ain't, can't be. Not even close. Martha says that this is an anomaly, a bank error, which we'll certainly check on and have corrected.

We switch to credit cards. No problem. By late

afternoon, our functioning plastic is warm to the touch.

The entire gang meets for dinner. We have what they're famous for in these parts: roast suckling pig, tail and snout and all. Janine's misty again over the sight on her plate and Martha says there probably are laws in our country about such a presentation, but I'll tell you what, everybody at the table's scarfing down every last morsel of crackly skin and meat.

~ ~ ~

I go out to mail postcards including one I made a production of writing to Stan. As I said, American cell phones don't work on account of incompatible satellites or whatever, so a pay phone it is. These phones got screens on them and are in Spanish. I punch "o" till I get an operator who speaks English. We finally get my brother dialed up.

"Lord almighty, who died?"

Oops, didn't compensate for the time difference. Stateside, it's oh-dark-thirty. I'm speaking to spouse number three, Miriam.

"Sorry, Miriam. Nobody died. It's me, Buddy."

"Buddy?"

"Buddy Whitacre. Your brother-in-law. Hoping to have an important word with my kid brother."

"Oh. Buddy. How are you guys?"

Miriam doesn't give a diddly-shit how we are. I tell her that we're in Spain and in the pink. She says that's good. I ask how she is and she says they're the same. I say that's good.

She goes and rousts Stan out of bed for me. Him and me, we were never much for small talk. I get right down to brass tacks and give him a blow-by-blow of my head scratcher.

He says, "How the hell should I know? I didn't meet each and every girl you had a stiff dick for."

"Please get on the Internet or go to the library and look up the picture. It's famous, it and the artist too."

"What if it's not on the Internet?"

"Everything's on the Internet."

"I don't like to surf. Miriam looks over my shoulder, thinking I'm looking at porn."

He was making excuses. "The library."

"Don't have a library card."

"Don't need a card. Don't have to check it out. Find one of those big coffee table art books on Dalí."

"Who again?"

"Salvador Dalí."

"Bali?"

"No. That's a country. This is an artist."

"Spell his name again."

"D-a-l-i. Look over the picture, Stan, tell me what you think, who she is, and I'll call you in a couple days. I'll owe you one."

~ ~ ~

Bus back to Madrid to catch the train to Granada.

There's a kazillion olive trees blurring by out the window. I ask Martha who grows the pimentos. Bryce pipes up and says they're for oil, that the Andalusia region is the world's leading grower, producing ten percent of the total annual output of olive oil.

Thank you, Mr. Wizard.

We're going to Granada for the Alhambra, a headquarters for the Moors when they ran the show in

Spain. Moors is what they used to call the A-rabs. We get in late and have dinner. I go for the kebobs. Everyone has gazpacho soup. It's cold, for crying out loud. Would it hurt to nuke it in the microwave for a minute? We wash the meal down with red wine and beer. Culture works up a hunger and a thirst in a person.

We're unpacking at the hotel. Martha finds the *Girl* postcards I slipped in a zippered pocket we never use.

She fans them out like a canasta hand. "I'm not snooping, but this stack is at least an inch thick."

I'm blushing like a teenager who got nabbed stashing a *Playboy* under his mattress. "Half inch, maybe."

"You were going to give them to your old shop buddies at Boeing?"

"You appreciate your art, I'll appreciate mine."

Martha's got a puzzled look on her face I recognize well. This ain't gonna go away. But her and me, we're too bushed to escalate into a full-blown beef. We watch TV that's in Spanish. She understands some of the words and tells me what she thinks they're saying and doing, and then we turn in early.

Thunder and lightning wake us up, sounding like war. The entire room shakes, rattles and rolls. The electricity goes out with a bang and an ozone smell.

Martha's as unreligious as me. She says God is expressing His annoyance at my behavior. She pinches me, so I know she's kidding. Sort of.

~ ~ ~

The Alhambra, it's got all kinds of arches and tile. It's up high on a hill and the view's terrific.

For lunch I have me meatballs, prawns, more of that

tortilla, four colors of olives, chorizo, two beers, churros for dessert, and I polish off Martha's sangria.

Me, a meat and potatoes guy.

~ ~ ~

To the airport in the AM. Last stop: Barcelona.

This Spanish airline of theirs flies A320's. Martha and me, we're a Boeing family with 48 years of service between the two of us. I make it clear to whoever will listen that I do not appreciate having to step onto a goddamn plane made by goddamn Airbus, a goddamn company that's nothing but a goddamn welfare program for goddamn Euro-trash aerospace loafers.

Martha is shushing me. I pay her no never mind. It's my turn to be cranky.

Ed and Ted come over and say that the airport cops that were giving *them* the stink eye, they're turning their attention in *my* direction. I clam up and get on board. Hate to admit it, but the flight's on time, smooth, and the stews are as sweet as pie.

~ ~ ~

Our hotel is a block off La Rambla, Barcelona's famous walking street. They got cafés and vendors and costumed mime acts and various and sundry hustlers of every flavor. La Rambla's a zoo. If you can get from one end to the other with your wallet intact, more power to you. Janine advises us to steer clear of it at night.

Ed and Ted are fidgety. They'd been looking forward to being on the sunny Mediterranean. They've seen the same postcards I have. High-rise hotels lined up like dominos and wall-to-wall sunbathers on the sand. Many of these vacationers are European, so the ladies don't bother wearing the upper half of their bikinis.

They heard there's a busload of German tourists parked by the waterfront. They head right down there before they unpack, rosy and lumpy in their Bermudas and tank tops, cold brews sweating in their grips.

I'd seen the Germans off our balcony and don't have the heart to set them straight. Number one, it isn't a beach, it's a port. Second, I didn't see any fräuleins in half a swimsuit. This is a bus full of geezers. They're so old I'm curious what they did during World War Two. Could be an antique Nazi or two there.

~ ~ ~

Nifty town, Barcelona is. Trees and funhouse buildings and wide boulevards. Gaudi, this architect of theirs, no criticism intended, he must not of known how to use a ruler or a T-square. His buildings are like the pictures in the nursery rhyme books we used to read to Melanie. All I can say is, wow, what was he smoking?

I check out this local specialty they have of white beans and sausage and give it a thumbs-up. Learned a Spanish custom on my own that if you ask for a mixed drink, the bartenders pour the whiskey till you say whoa.

More culture is narrated by Janine on Gaudi and the other far-out architects of the beginning of the last century. She's finally getting pissed at Martha's brainiacs knowing it all and interrupting her.

Florence, the gift shop lady, she's been accumulating purchases. They're not lightweight goodies like lace, but pottery and this cast-iron doorknocker for her nephew and a brass plate for cousin Maude. The bearings on one of her suitcase wheels seize up on account of the weight, so she skids it along. Florence tries to make eye contact with us menfolk. Chivalry may not be dead, but it sure as hell ain't worth a slipped disk.

~ ~ ~

Ed and Ted come on down to breakfast with shiners. They stay focused on their rolls and coffee. We're aware that the situation is not gonna be a topic of conversation. What I oughta do, I oughta take these boys aside and give the benefit of my experience from when I was in the service, stateside and overseas. I oughta clue 'em in that any cabby anywhere in the universe worth his salt can take them where they need to go in five minutes flat, if you catch my drift.

My only other idea is to nudge one or the other in Janine's direction. Ted slobbers like a lovesick puppy around her. But what to do about the odd man out? Janine doesn't seem the type for a ménage à threesome, even though she's probably been to France. Besides, they're big boys and Martha'd kill me.

~ ~ ~

We're having us a Gaudifest. We're touring houses he designed for rich folk who were smoking the same hemp he was. Lots of swoops and curves. Every color in the rainbow and some that aren't. This one building's chimneys are all dolled up in ceramics and one looks like a mushroom variety that may have been in Senor Gaudi's diet.

I'm loosening up, enjoying myself. Can go ten whole minutes without thinking about *Girl*.

Our merry band is mellowing out too.

The yuppie couple, Kevin and Kelli, located pastries and coffee that reminds them of Seattle. They've stopped bitching that you can't get a vanilla orange triple hazelnut decaf latte and that nobody takes American money. Florence lumbers to the hotel twice a day with purchases and loads them in her new luggage. The shutterbug, Dick, he had to buy another chip for his camera; if he still used film, he'd be spending a fortune. Ed and Ted are regulars at a La Rambla bar, but nobody's invited them home to meet their sisters.

While Martha's shopping, I slip away to consult with the Ed and Ted on *Girl*, to see what they think, which might explain to me what I'm thinking. I buy a round and show them a postcard for a reminder. They have got short attention spans where museums are concerned. I ask for an opinion, speaking hypothetical-like.

"Nice ass," Ed says.

"Yeah, I wouldn't kick her out of the sack," Ted says.

"Can't you boys ever get your minds out of the gutter?"

Their discolored eyes go big as saucers.

I stare at the foam in my glass and wonder to myself too why I'm in such an uproar.

~ ~ ~

We break for lunch near the art museum we visited and not far from the cathedral we're gonna visit next. I've having this chicken called *pollo catalunya*. It's got plums and pine nuts and peppers and olive oil in it. Good groceries.

I'm pondering seconds when Martha looks at me with that look of hers and says something's troubling her.

Uh oh. "Yeah, what?"

"You know what."

"Nope, I don't."

"I've been researching on your *Muchacha en la*

Ventana. The young woman is Salvador Dalí's sister, Ana Maria, eighteen years old when he, age twenty-one, painted her in *Muchacha*, in 1925."

"His sis?"

"Ana Maria Dalí was his chief model for years. Bryce and Neil pointed out what I'd completely forgotten, that adjacent your fixation is another study of Ana Maria from the rear, a shoulder bared."

"That's swell of Bryce and Neil."

"Furthermore, on the wall directly behind your obsession is his painted profile of Ana Maria."

"I thought it was a fixation."

Martha pulls a postcard out of a postcard book. "Would you like to know what she looks like?"

I shrug. For some goofy reason, I don't want to look, but Martha holds the postcard up in front of my face.

Girl is not what you'd consider overly pretty. Her eyes bulge a little and her chin is weak. She's homely in a classy classical sense, though much more attractive than most of the old gals in the pictures at the Prado across the street, with or without dogs underfoot. *Girl* looks like a very nice gal.

She resembles nobody I ever saw or knew. Certainly not Martha, who was and is taller and slimmer.

Then I gotta go and ask, "Why'd he go and paint pictures like that of his sis?"

"Like what?"

"You know, the picture at the window."

"I have to ask again, like what?"

I got no way of talking myself out of this corner. I spear a plum. "This chicken's first rate."

Martha sips her wine. "It's a harmless fetish, I suppose."

"I wouldn't go so far as fetish. I definitely wouldn't go that far."

"I would."

I shake my head. "You're out in left field, off the wall."

She smiles and squeezes my hand. "This is a young woman in a painting done nearly a century ago."

I keep shaking my head.

Still smiling, she says, "You're going to be sixty-four years old not too many days from now, Buddy."

"Martha , you gonna finish your veal?"

~ ~ ~

I got the hang of these telephones and the time zones now. I'm up with the chickens and catch Stan last evening. I think.

He's traced down the picture at the library and says it wasn't easy, all those art books they have, weighing like ten pounds apiece.

"I knew in a second who she reminds you of."

"Who?"

"Mom."

"C'mon."

"It's Mom. We have the picture in an album. I bet you got a copy too. She's standing at a window of the cabin we used to rent at Copalis Beach for a week every summer. She's young and looking out the window at the ocean. Remember?"

"I don't remember. Mom was built nothing like her."

"She was plumper in this picture and her hair's longer. We were in grade school. Dad took the picture. Remember?

This was before they started fighting."

"I don't remember nothing of the kind."

"You're older than me. You should."

"This can't possibly be."

"You go through your old pictures. You still got 'em?"

"In shoe boxes in the spare room."

"You go through 'em. You'll see. I'll mail this one to you if you don't."

"I'll let you know."

"You do that."

"Gonna tell me what this is about?"

"Would if I could."

I thank Stan, but he's already hung up.

~ ~ ~

In bed, I tell Martha I've figured everything out, although I gotta admit I'm reaching and I'm lying, both. I say that *Girl* is a young her.

She looks at me in the dark, slides my hand off her leg, and says, "Lose the twinkle in your eye, Mister. You'd have them closed, pretending I was her, whoever she is from your wild and woolly past."

I stare up at the ceiling, not blaming her. On the other hand, how the hell can I confess that *Girl* is every bit as likely my dead, murdered mom? Martha, she'd be contacting a headshrinker for me the minute we set foot on U.S. soil.

She's soon asleep. I get up for a drink of water. Warm night. Can't drop off for a lot of reasons. I step into shoes and trousers, and head down to the hotel bar for a nightcap, thinking Ed and Ted are closing the joint up. I need to apologize and explain my outburst without explaining too much. They been looking sideways at me ever since.

No sign of the rascals and the bar's dead as a doornail. Everybody's turned in from a hard day of Gaudiing.

I go outside for fresh air. I pat my shirt pocket for a smoke. Haven't done that in ages, not since Martha and me quit.

The wildlife on La Rambla is whooping and hollering. I head off in that direction, to see what's cooking.

Chapter 2

MARTHA

I am absolutely frantic.

I awoke out of a sound sleep to the morning sun glowing through the curtains, to no Buddy in bed with me or in the room. I threw on a robe and scrambled into the hallway, where I was met by Janine carrying a slip of paper.

"I was coming to see you," she had said.

I didn't like the gloomy look on her face. Janine is impressive. She is dedicated to her profession, a highly capable career woman. In my youth she'd be tagged a spinster, an old maid.

"About Buddy?"

"There was a commotion on La Rambla last night. Your husband was taken to the hospital."

"Oh my God."

Janine patted my arm. "Buddy's okay, Martha. He was treated for minor injuries and released. Two men brought in with him had more severe injuries."

"What two men?"

"I don't know."

In his youth, Buddy had a temper and was quick with his fists. He'd outgrown street fighting eons ago. Nevertheless, he does have a toilet mouth and doesn't hesitate to use it when his dander's up.

"Where's Buddy if he was released?"

"Unfortunately, Martha, he was released into the

custody of the police. They want to ask him some questions about the incident."

"Where have they taken him and what questions?"

Janine shook her head sadly. "My information is sketchy. I do have an idea how to get more answers. In the meantime, all we can do is wait."

~ ~ ~

So I wait.

And I think. I have gobs of time to think.

I have seen on the talk shows what can happen to older men who enter retirement without new interests or goals, without anything to strive for or to stimulate them. They enter a vacuum. They can go positively cuckoo.

Some become sex fiends. They do. Satyriasis is the scientific name. This is a theme the shows will devote the whole hour to, sometimes bringing on a pop psychologist with fancy interpretations why this occurs and what can be done. Not that I take these sensationalistic programs as gospel, although a fact is a fact.

Thank goodness, Buddy does not suffer that affliction. He developed a silly little fetish over a painting of a young lady, probably a reminder of an old flame in his adolescence. That's all. He should have opened up to me rather than playing games. But that is my Buddy, a male of the species.

However, Ana Maria's Dalí's curvaceous rear end does not explain why Buddy lost his wits, slipped out of our room, and wandered onto La Rambla at all hours. He knows better. Not that it's all his fault, not remotely. There are two sides to the coin and I should not have left things as they were in bed.

I carried him off kicking and screaming to Spain instead of Branson, Missouri, to expose him to enlightenment and the intellectual broadening of travel and personal growth while we still have the money and our faculties. I force-fed culture to a man whose idea of fine art is Elvis on velvet. That bug I put in his ear tickled loose *Muchacha en la Ventana* from unknown recesses in his consciousness and caused him to act like no Buddy I've known for thirty-nine years.

In the short interim since we retired, I've thrown myself into various activities with such abandon that I had Buddy's head spinning, not to mention my own. A big day to him was a doubleheader on TV and dinner at our favorite buffet. We are out of our workaday grind and have time to burn. Self improve or wither on the vine is my motto.

My formal academic education ended with my high school diploma, I do not consider myself an educated person. I am determined to change this. I am working on my vocabulary and diction and general knowledge, among other areas. Retirement is not for stagnation, rather the opposite. I plan in the fall to enroll in community college.

In retrospect, I should have slowed down. I should have altered my lifestyle less abruptly. I should have met Buddy halfway.

Janine has been such a sweetie. Why, she even cancelled a visit to the Sagrada Familia, Gaudi's cathedral, the highlight of the Barcelona leg of the trip, to personally escort me to the United States Consulate, to speak to somebody she knows there.

Ed and Ted, those lunkhead pals of Buddy's, bless their hearts, they've been so supportive also. They offered to stay behind with me. They offered to find out who put Buddy in the hospital and to "kick butt". Of course I declined. They'd lose their supermarket jobs and who knows what else could go wrong. I shall never forget their friendship.

They've gone home, on a flight out of Barcelona this morning, Janine and them and everyone, including Bryce and Neil, who, incidentally, dropped me like a hot potato. Those pseudointellectual phonies would not say hello again, let alone offer guidance and comfort.

I once asked Neil what philosophy is. He said philosophy is the synthesis of all learning. Well, he and Bryce gave me a philosophy lesson, all right. You are never too old to learn about people!

We're back in Madrid, Buddy and I. I flew in and they flew him in. These past two days have been a whirlwind. I'm at a hotel and Buddy is at a "police debriefing". I do not like the sound of that phrase.

My hotel has oodles of charm, closet-sized rooms, and ancient plumbing. I am not sure where it's located. I see a statue of Christopher Columbus from my window, surrounded by a fountain, bathed at night by powerful footlights. That doesn't narrow it down significantly. Janine informed us that there are scores of Columbus monuments in Spain. Bryce volunteered the exact number, which escapes me.

Buddy and I spoke on the phone. He says he's doing well and not to worry. All he could say on the phone about the situation was that he stepped in when some guys were bullying another guy. Buddy's twice as worried about me as he is about himself. That's my Buddy for you.

Mr. Timkins of our United States Embassy in the

Spanish capital comes to my room this evening. Janine, bless her heart, has influence. Her Barcelona acquaintance contacted Mr. Timkins and he has been kind enough to assist me. He is a serious young man whose glasses keep slipping down his nose. He's been frank regarding what our government and his office can do for us and what they can't. He's giving me an update on Buddy's status.

"You have seen him, Mr. Timkins?"

"An hour ago at a *Policía Nacional* facility, Mrs. Whitacre. He's holding up well and I think we're seeing light at the end of the tunnel."

"How does he look – physically?"

"He has some bumps and bruises and scrapes. Other than that, he seems unharmed."

Buddy is three inches taller than me. He and I have managed to stay what the personal ads term height-weight-proportional. Our BMI puts people half our age to shame. By any standards Buddy is in exceptional shape for a man his age. That is, except for that cute embryo of a pot gut. I was so proud of my meat-and-potatoes man at the restaurants and *tapas* bars, eating what was placed in front of him without question.

Depending on your eye, my Buddy is ruggedly handsome or bordering on disfigured. I definitely lean toward the former. My Buddy never backed away from a confrontation in his younger days.

He's told me more times than I cared to hear that a tavern free-for-all is not like in the movies. When you're hit over the head with a barstool, it doesn't bust up like kindling. And when you're thrown through a window you come out on the other side bleeding.

Mr. Timkins said they tried to reset Buddy's nose at the hospital until he protested. His nose has been that way for forty years.

Buddy ceased his ruffian behavior when Melanie was born. He'd gotten his midlife crisis out of the system in his twenties. Has he reverted? Is he going through delayed male menopause?

Police debriefing. The prospect of him in an interrogation room full of angry police officers with rubber hoses and a 1000-watt lamp over his head, Buddy exacerbating his dilemma with four-letter words, the delivery of which are four-letter words in any language – I have to stop this before the waterworks start again.

Mr. Timkins pulls a tissue from a table dispenser.

"I'll be fine, thank you," I say, taking it. "By light at the end of the tunnel, you mean what?"

"As I mentioned earlier, Mr. Whitacre is under investigation in several areas."

"Can you be more specific? I am thoroughly confused."

"There are vague allegations by the Spanish authorities that he was studying a museum layout and contemplating an art theft."

I laugh at the absurdity of this. "We're retired factory workers."

"Yes. You said. I don't recall what you did, you and Mr. Whitacre."

How clever of Mr. Timkins, double-checking for a consistent story, to see if we're really as harmless as we appear.

"After a variety of jobs and as a stay-at-home mom, I put in seventeen years in tool room administration. I'd trained right out of high school on keypunch, but those jobs have gone the way of the buggy whip. Office jobs weren't my cup of tea anyway. I prefer to be physically active, on my feet. Being on the plant floor, I had the opportunity to move around. I volunteered to fill in wherever needed when there were illnesses and vacations and turnover. I was in the 747, 767 and 777 programs, Boeing's wide bodies.

"Buddy went out with thirty-one years of service, all of it in Production. Counting breaks in service due to layoffs and strikes, his Boeing employment spanned nearly four decades. He was an assembly mechanic who had a hand in each and every model Boeing's manufactured in the jet age."

"You're obviously proud of your careers and justifiably so. Did your tour group have the opportunity to go to the *Museo Nacional Centro de Arte Reina Sofía*?"

He speaks the museum name with a Spanish accent. He must know we did. What's he driving at?

"Yes. It's fabulous."

"In the museum gift shop, Mr. bought every postcard they had of Salvador Dalí's *Muchacha en la Ventana*. He was described as 'furtive'."

"Buddy now and again gets a bee in his bonnet. He is not an art lover or collector or thief or art anything. He did develop a fascination for that particular painting, nothing more sinister than that."

Mr. Timkins smiles. "I'm sure his actions were innocuous, but some red flags were raised. Your husband tried to make his purchase with an invalid debit card. The receipt triggered an investigation."

"Buddy casing the *Reina Sofía*? That's the silliest thing

I've ever heard."

"In these turbulent times, museum security personnel can overreact," he says, nodding.

"Our retirement income is meticulously planned. We aren't rich, but we're as solid as the Rock of Gibraltar. As far as Buddy's debit card is concerned, we've had nothing but problems using our plastic since we've been in the country. Computer incompatibility or some such. I was going to call our bank, but with everything that's going on, I haven't had the time.

"Buddy being involved in something shady is ridiculous. The closest we have ever been to brushing shoulders with the criminal element is our three day-two night trips to Las Vegas. You know, in the Vegas casinos they stare down at you from one-way ceiling glass when you play to catch you cheating. It takes one to know one.

"Besides, I thought Buddy was being held because of the fight on La Rambla."

"Initially. That's a separate issue and Mr. Whitacre's name regarding it came up on the Barcelona police computers."

"Well, I'm glad somebody's computers work."

Mr. Timkins removes a sheet of paper from his briefcase. "I do have further details on that incident."

"Buddy coming to someone's aid is all I know."

The paper is an official-looking form. "Our Barcelona people faxed this police report to my office. Apparently a La Rambla shopkeeper of East Indian descent was attempting to close his establishment when he was accosted by a group of rowdies. There were five of them. They were identified as English soccer hooligans. Mr. Whitacre stood up for the shopkeeper."

"I've heard of soccer hooligans," I say. "The rampages, the riots."

He pauses. "It is a phenomenon that is difficult for an American to grasp. We Americans love our sports teams, yes, but our fervor pales in comparison."

"Buddy and I are dedicated fans of the Seahawks, Sounders and Mariners, regardless how often they break our hearts."

"European *fútbol* fans, by and large, behave themselves, if more exuberantly than we're accustomed to. This hooligan element is an entirely different subculture. You can't imagine. I won't pretend to comprehend the mentality. Are you familiar with the Champions League competition?"

"That's soccer?"

"Yes. The best club teams in Europe compete. The English team these men support played at home against FC Barcelona earlier in the week, losing four-nil. That is a humiliating margin. The loss eliminated their team from the tournament. Barça, as the local team is called, advances to the final."

"Is that like Europe's Super Bowl?"

"And then some. A quarter of a billion people will watch the match."

I reply, "So those lamebrains watched the game on TV and got liquored up and came to La Rambla even drunker and grouchier than usual?"

"Who can say? We do know they arrived here just two days ago, after the match was played, perhaps with mayhem in mind. The importance and outcome of the game may have been irrelevant. The altercation could have taken place if their team won. There is some indication that the confrontation with the merchant was racially motivated. Soccer hooligans keep their own agenda."

"Buddy prevented them from hurting the shopkeeper?"

"We believe so. Mr. Whitacre ordered them to lay off. They turned their anger to him."

"Oh my God. How many did you say?"

"Five husky lads. Your husband acquitted himself remarkably well. I suspect they underestimated him because of his age. One of the two hooligans taken to the hospital with him required emergency surgery. The three others remained out of the fracas and aren't talking."

I can only sigh. I can summon no other reaction. Heroic or not, it's high time Buddy learned to play the geezer card. Goodness, he could have yelled for reinforcements.

Mr. Timkins stands. "I presume the authorities are finally realizing that Mr. Whitacre is the victim of a bizarre array of circumstances and coincidences. Your ordeal should be over soon."

"How soon, Mr. Timkins? I can't even see him. I mean, where are we, North Korea?"

At the door, he says, "I wish I had a firm timetable. They said they would notify me momentarily."

"I'll be here. I'm not going anywhere."

"I have a good feeling. But."

Mr. Timkins is suddenly awkward. I sense that events are out of his control too and he doesn't like it either.

I take his hand. "I appreciate everything you've done. Buddy will too."

"Just in case," he says. "I can recommend reputable

32

bilingual attorneys."

Abogado is Spanish for lawyer. It is on my language tapes. I truly hope we are not in those dire straits. I am not ready to push the *abogado* panic button. When Mr. Timkins leaves, I stop procrastinating and dial the room phone.

"Melanie."

"Mother!"

"How are you, dear?"

"Mother, what's the matter? Am I still picking you up at the airport this afternoon?"

I take a deep breath, hoping to calm the stress she's hearing in my voice. "And David? How is your David?"

"He's fine too. Mother –"

"How is that wonderful new house coming along? You were having trouble with the drapery people."

"The drapes are up and they look great."

"Is David gone?"

"He just left."

"We can talk for a minute?"

"Mother."

"Don't be alarmed, dear. Your father and I have been delayed."

"Your tour has been delayed?"

I've lied to my daughter perhaps ten times in her life. You mothers out there might not approve, but it was always for Melanie's own good. I decide not to make it eleven fibs. I will not lie, I will evade.

"No, only your father and I are in the country. There's nothing to worry about. I didn't want you to go to the airport and us not be on the plane."

"Mother, what is the matter and where are you?"

Melanie is brighter than Buddy and I combined. She never misses a beat. She and David recently moved into a brand-new home on the Issaquah plateau, an affluent area east of Seattle. They bought one of those mock French Chateaus with the brick facing and the gables and the shake roofs. They have a three-car garage and I forget how many bathrooms. Do you really need 4000 square feet with no children, nor any prospect of children? But that's none of my beeswax. David has a highly successful gynecology practice, which Buddy has described with a few choice words.

"We're in Madrid."

"Not Barcelona? Your itinerary lists Barcelona as your last stop."

"Yes, well, your father is answering questions to the police regarding something he knows absolutely nothing about. It is a monstrous misunderstanding. I expect us to be on a plane by the middle of next week."

"It takes until next week to answer questions about something Father knows nothing about?"

"They have strange customs over here," I say lamely.

"Mother."

"Honestly, Melanie, it is nothing. I'm in the dark too. We'll explain after we're home."

She waits so long to reply that I worry that the line's gone dead. I can't blame her if it has. She's pushing 40 and I treat her like a child when there's the least crisis.

"I can pick up the mail and feed the cats."

"That's what I was going to ask. Thank you. Jim and Ellen are looking after the house through today. They're going to Portland, to stay with Jim Junior and Marcy and the grandkids."

"Mother, I was over a few days ago. I checked your answering machine. You have several messages from banks and a credit card company."

The daughter is sounding like the mother, an inevitability I am not prepared for.

"Oh, fiddle-faddle. These European bank computers messed up our account. We'll straighten it out when we get home. With everything that's been going on, I haven't had a chance to tend to it here."

"Mother, please be careful. Promise me."

I promise and we exchange "I love yous".

I get up slowly and go to the closet for my purse.

This has not been a peachy keen day. I cannot take my usual cheery view that things are going to get better before they get worse. If Mr. Timkins's optimism about a quick resolution to Buddy's situation is off the mark, I have to be prepared to do battle in his behalf. Have to, have to, have to.

I unzip my wallet and shuffle through the cards and scraps of paper. Buddy says women's purses are like black holes. Here it is, my Murganzer Stable Fund client services card.

I thank my lucky stars we have our retirement kitty safely invested and Murganzer Stable Fund working for us like a finely tuned machine. We sank every cent we had into MSF, the best move we ever made. Our monthly dividend checks have been like clockwork. Otherwise, we wouldn't have been able to take early retirement or gallivant off to Europe.

I go through the out-of-country telephone rigmarole and dial the MSF 1-800 number. We've never had to do this. From what they've said at the presentation and financial planning conferences and when we signed the papers, it's a breeze. An operator refers you to a representative, who processes your request.

You tell them how much you want to transfer from the fund to your checking account or to wherever else you stipulate. They discourage you from touching the principal unless you absolutely have to. That *is* a bad policy with any long-term investment, but it's available if you need it. After sensible security procedures, you should have your money within 48 hours. It's as simple as that.

I'm estimating that $5000 dollars to the nearest Madrid bank should suffice at the outset. Cash on the barrelhead in euros. No more of their unreliable ATM machines. I can return the excess to the fund if Mr. Timkins's optimism holds true.

I've misdialed. A recorded voice says the number has been disconnected.

I redial, slower.

The identical recording.

Pull yourself together, girl.

I try and try and try.

I don't stop until I break a nail punching numbers.

Chapter 3

BUDDY

The good news is I'm not pissing blood. The bad news is damn near everything else, physical and the rest.

Don't mind admitting that I'm all shook up and that I'm feeling my age.

This is how come. This is what landed me in the clink, stiff and sore and discombobulated.

See, I'm not two steps onto La Rambla, when I overhear this ruckus you'd have to be deaf not to. The La Rambla crowd at that hour was mostly young and spaced-out. Nobody's paying this situation no never mind, not that they'd want to get involved, how it is everywhere in this day and age.

These five scruffy guys are hovering around a souvenir shop. It's run by East Injuns, like our stateside cabbies. They sell the usual tourist crapola of clothes, postcards, trinkets, and knives and swords, which are big over here. I'd been in a couple times with Martha, browsing T-shirts and stuff. Nice folks.

One of them, just a kid, he's closing up for the day. These meatballs aren't letting him. They're in his face, screaming and cussing, calling him a bloody fucking wog.

I say to them, hey, excuse me, bug off, leave him alone. That's all I do or say. I was semi-polite and used no profanity. Not yet, anyhow.

This gets their attention. They come on over to me. I

stand my ground. Maybe it's cuz Martha about *Girl* or it's a conglomeration of factors. Whatever's going on between my ears, I am in no humor to take any shit from these losers.

They're skinheads or some Eurotrash like that. Two of them, they're so close, side-by-side, I about keel over from the halitosis. This one's got a belly like a medicine ball and beady little eyes. His partner's a string bean with an Adam's apple. The only hair on his pinhead is muttonchops sideburns. They got tattoos up and down their arms and are yelling at me in England English that's all Greek to me. Dotty old bloke. Blimey. Fucking this, fucking that. And so forth, et cetera.

I'm having me a flashback to my younger and wilder days before Melanie was born. I was an even bigger knucklehead than I am now. The beginning of Melanie was the end of my pub-crawling and fisticuffs. You think different when you become a daddy or you ought to. Martha'd had a belly full and was ready to kick me out.

According to my memory of the barroom brawling version of Marquis of Queensberry rules, when you're one against two, and there's little chance of a peaceful solution, you take out the tougher one quick, by any means possible. In my estimation, that would be Stringbean. I wouldn't like to go many rounds with that boy.

I lock my eyes on Fatso as a distraction till I turn and plant a swift kick to Stringbean's family jewels. I take him by total surprise. Otherwise I'd be dead as we speak. Stringbean lifts up on his toes, howls, and goes down like a pile of dirty laundry.

Good thing these boys are as drunk as skunks. They're looking at Stringbean, who's tucked hisself into the fetal position, crying and moaning. They're not believing their bloodshot eyes. Fatso then remembers what he's intending to do to me. He calls me a pooftah, their England word for faggot, and throws a punch as I drive one of my own into his blubber. His blow glances off the side of my head and hurts like a bitch. I connect dead-on at his belly button. He makes a whooshing noise, like an airlock in a sci-fi movie.

He starts grunting and flailing, landing stingers to my sides. I work inside on him. It's like kneading jelly. I do get in an uppercut to the bottom of his jaw that by the crunch it makes has cracked a bicuspid or three. But Fatso's twice my size and half my age. After thirty seconds, I'm sucking wind. I'm about through. He's doing no damage but is going strong. I knee him with all my might where I gut-punched him.

He lands flat on his butt and sits there whimpering. A mama's boy. The three others, they been cheerleading their pals, screeching like demented roosters. Now they're looking at each other and at me. Before they can come to any kind of conclusion and stomp me into a grease spot, the East Injun kid is at my side.

He's jabbering into a cell phone and holding one of those curved scimitar swords they sell in his shop, swinging it one-handed, swiping it close to them. The threesome remains calm, cool and collected till the *policía* and a meat wagon come for us.

While we're being loaded up, the kid tells me to come on back when I can. The scimitar, retail-priced at 280 euros, is mine. Free gratis. Too bad I can't take him up on it.

We may eventually be talking international incident

here. That is, if I ever get sprung. I've never had more than a ten-miles-over speeding ticket and haven't been arrested once in my entire life. I think they're finally beginning to realize that I am not a crook. I hope.

This Madrid jailhouse they shipped me off to has got a high metal gate and a higher wall. Looks like it's been in operation since El Cid. It is, I been told, some sort of federal facility, which they rattled off in Spanish. The interior stinks of piss and sweat and mold and shit and fright. It's got all the modern conveniences and ambiences of the Black Hole of Calcutta.

Martha, she's who I'm more worried about than me. They gave me five minutes on the phone with her, standing over me while we talked. She says she's in a Madrid hotel and holding up good, though for all I know they could of had her reading off a script. I worry about her nonstop when I see those guards outside this room they have got me in. They're a separate department altogether, wearing those triangular, patent leather caps that look like they're made of purses they stole out of a Salvation Army box.

Those goofy hats remind me of Martha because I was there when one of her pointy-heads told her they're called tricorns. I'm confident Janine'll do what she can for Martha. I'm sure her brainiacs, Breece and Niles, they pitched in too. They're very smart and if they stand up in her behalf, she's got valuable allies. Martha should be in good hands irregardless of what's in store for yours truly.

Then there's Mr. Thimblekins from our United States Embassy, who came and visited me. A good guy. He says I oughta be out soon and that Martha's holding up as good as can be expected. Hope he ain't blowing smoke at each of us just to make the other feel better.

Worst part of the situation besides the knots on and the confusion in my head is that I'm losing track of time. It's either two or three days since they glommed onto me. The best part of the cell they locked me up in last night is that I got no roommates. They say I can shower. I say no thanks. I've heard what happens when you drop your soap.

Matter of fact, I may have this jailhouse to myself. I don't hear prisoners sobbing themselves to sleep or anything else that goes on in prisons. That is a relief, but I'm not gonna take any chances with surprise company in the shower room and slippery soap. It's their problem if they don't like how I smell.

I think of Martha at night too. I'm remembering how when she was a girl, she looked kind of like an actress from the sixties named Carol Lynley, right down to that tiny little overbite. David, my gynecologist son-in-law, he says it's not too late to correct misalignment. He's got some ten-dollar word for the condition and says he has an orthodontist friend who'll give us a deal. Over my dead body, he will.

When I fall off to sleep, I dream of *Girl*. I dream of my mother's murder, the details I thought I'd forgot, like the motel maid who found them in the room, an older lady who had to go to the hospital for shock and almost died herself from it.

This theme, it's repeating itself on me like a bad *tapa*. I could pay a shrink a $100 an hour to lay on his couch and listen to him tell me what I am already aware of – that I blocked the murder/suicide out of my noggin so long that when it found an opening it came on like gangbusters.

Cops in this station house, they come and they go,

different teams of them in different uniforms and in plainclothes. Almost to a man they smoke. It's like an L.A. temperature inversion in here. There's a window they keep shut you can't see out of for the cigarette tar coating it. They have pictures on the wall of big shots, some old in their doorman uniforms and sourpuss faces. That dictator who ran this country for a long time, whatshisname, Franco as in Franco-American macaroni, he's not among them, but he'd fit in perfect with the décor.

There's a heavy screen and a door in it like the cage on cop shows, but this cage I'm in is roomier and not quite as ratty. The fluorescent lights built in the ceiling are a lot brighter than they've got to be for reading. Sometimes they flicker, which leads me to wonder if they get their jollies diddling them.

They ask me the same identical damn stupid questions, over and over and over again in broken English. What is my role in using bogus debit and credit cards? Why do you think you can steal priceless works of art from our museums? Do you have a history of criminal assault? They're like a broken record.

Nobody's in here with me now, not since Timkins was shown out. This is unusual. I got a hunch something's up and sure enough, in walks Ricky Ricardo, holding a notebook, wearing a jacket and tie and big smile.

Don't recall his actual name. He goes by three of them, Raul Gonzales Fernando Sanchez Gomez or some such. He's been in civvies ever since they busted me. I have got no idea what his department or rank is.

He's just plain Ricky to me, a dead ringer for Ricky Ricardo on *I Love Lucy* I remember watching with my folks when I was a tiny little squirt. It was their all-time favorite show.

Ricky's the only consistency I've had in this experience. The other cops, they play musical chairs. Ricky, he's constantly hovering, though not always directly participating in the third degree. Ricky flew with me from Barcelona on one of those goddamn Airbuses.

"Mr. Whitacre," he says, unlatching the cage to join me. "I trust our inconveniencing of you has not proved terribly unpleasant."

"Nah. I'm tickled pink. None of this was in our tour brochure. I won't be getting dinged for a surcharge for this extra fun, will I?"

He laughs and maintains that irritating smile that's plastered on his puss like a decal. "I admire your sense of humor under duress. You are being treated humanely, yes?"

He's a piece of work, Ricky is. A non-smoker, no less. Ricky's been doing good cop-bad cop on me all by hisself. That or he's schizo. He got this knack of making you feel at ease and at the same time the adrenaline's gushing through your system, on account of his other shoe's about to drop on top of your head. Ricky, he has a knack for keeping you off balance.

Weird thing is, I haven't been freaked-out scared. Should of keeled over from a coronary by now. Must be I'm still dazed and groggy and sore and punchy. But, no fooling, Ricky and me, we kind of hit it off. He's probably not a bad egg when he's off the clock.

"Thanks for asking. Your chow leaves something to be desired. Beans and rice and last week's fish."

"I can send out," he says sincerely.

"Yeah? For *tapas* and beer? This *tapas* custom of yours, your cafes do a topnotch job."

"No, I think not," he says, his smile switching off. "Perhaps later."

Ricky opens up his notebook. "If we can clear up a few discrepancies, you can board an airplane for your home with Mrs. Whitacre momentarily."

"How long's momentarily?"

"That's up to you, sir."

"How's Martha doing?"

Smiling again, he says, "Splendid. The same as the last five times you asked. A dutiful and devoted husband, that is admirable of you."

"That hotel you put her up at, how many stars? If you got her in a rat hole, upgrade her and I'll pay the difference."

"If you behave intelligently, you can board an airplane for your home, to eat your own American food, any quantity of *hamburguesas* and hot dogs you choose."

Insulting me and fine American cuisine in one breath. He's got his nerve. In a town where I've seen no less than 14 American fast food locations. I crank up a replacement smile and say not a single, solitary word cuz they'd be words I'd regret. I have informed him what I know, which is a big fat goose egg.

I'm holding out in only one unimportant area, *Girl*, and Stan saying it's Mom. They can go ahead and hook electrical wires to my gonads and that's gonna stay none of their damn business.

"I am still endeavoring to, how you say, to grab a handle on you, *Señor*."

"Lotsa luck."

"The postcards of a particular work, Salvador Dalí's *Muchacha en la Ventana*. The sales invoice copy we have indicate you purchased fifty-seven of them, the complete inventory in the display rack."

"I liked the picture. I'm giving them out as souvenirs to my friends."

"Your actions were puzzling."

"Martha's been saying that for years."

Ricky looks up from his notes. "How did you expect to succeed?"

"At what?"

"Passing a defunct debit card, in the manner of a hippie thief or an indigent."

"That's computer errors, is all it is. Their fault, not mine."

"What countries have you visited recently?"

"You got my passport. You can see the stamps. Till we came on this culture tour, I have been exactly nowhere aside from Vietnam fighting communism, unless you count Canada where we used to go camping and fishing up in British Columbia."

"What did you do in Vietnam?"

"I was a cook at Tan Son Nhut air base outside of Saigon."

"Why did you decide to become a cook?"

"I didn't. The Army said I was gonna be a cook and sent me to their cooking school."

"They trained you to be a chef?"

"They trained me to be an Army cook. Ever had S.O.S?"

"Not in my recollection."

"Shit on a shingle. The Army does S.O.S. better than

anybody.'

Madrid Ricky makes a face.

"Official name's creamed chipped beef on toast."

"That is unimportant. Did you kill anyone in Vietnam?"

"Not on purpose."

"¿Perdón?"

"My wife won't let me near the kitchen at home and that's okay by me."

"You are on a guided packaged tour of Spain, yes?"

"*Were* on a guided packaged tour of Spain."

"You gravitated from your scheduled touring activity to the second floor of *Museo Nacional Centro de Arte Reina Sofia*."

"Jesus H. Fucking Christ, I was art appreciating. Museums are for that, ain't they?"

He rolls his eyes like Ricky did when Lucy'd pull a bonehead stunt. "Please."

"Crime does not pay. That's my motto. Don't be trying to pin one on me that didn't ever even happen."

Ricky rolls his eyes again. At this part of the show, Fred and Ethel sashay into the room, and Ricky suspects Lucy and Ethel have hatched another squirrelly scheme. I've watched the shows when they have a *Lucy* festival.

"I am disappointed, *Señor*. I evaluated you to be a serious person."

I'm slouching in my chair, hands folded on my lap. Retirement is getting awful tiresome. Retirement is supposed to be for retiring. Not for running yourself ragged. Not for high adventure that lands you in the slammer 6000 miles from home.

"I have been informed that one of the hooligans had a

testicle surgically removed in the Barcelona hospital," Ricky goes on. "His friend has a rupture of the stomach lining. The individual you partially castrated is dismayed that he may never father children."

"What's wrong with that?"

Ricky laughs a genuine laugh. "I share your sentimentalities. We have our own *fútbol* hooligans. We call them *ultras*. The Englishman you gelded threatens to acquire a solicitor. Or is it barrister, their word for lawyer?"

"You gotta be kidding."

Ricky shrugs. "Yes, perhaps merely bluster. Who can say? We have escorted their *amigos* to a flight to London-Gatwick. If they return to Spain, they will be arrested. The pair in the hospital will depart at the earliest possible moment."

"Good riddance."

"I concur. I applaud your manliness, but remain unclear who initiated the confrontation."

"They were picking on a kid."

"The shopkeeper?"

"Yeah, five against one."

"You intervened."

"All I did, I said to bug off."

"Who struck the first blow? The English are insisting you attacked them."

"Okay, I admit it. I did what the Pentagon calls a preemptive strike. If I hadn't, they woulda made mincemeat out of me."

Ricky flutters a hand. "Of no consequence. You are a pensioner menaced by thugs. You reacted as your conscience urged you to. You were angered, yes?"

"Who the hell wouldn't be?"

"I have read that anger management education is a fashionable business in your violent country. Have you considered enrolling?"

"Why the hell should I take an anger management class? I already know how to get pissed off."

Ricky reaches inside his shirt and pulls out a gold chain and what looks like a religious medallion. It's crest-shaped, red and yellow and blue and white. There's a cross in one corner and then I see the soccer ball.

"F.C. Barcelona," he says. "Ninety-eight thousand people fill Camp Nou, our stadium, when *Barça* plays."

"Are you kidding? For a soccer game?"

"A *fútbol* match."

"Have it your way. There's football and there's soccer. I got kicked off my high school football team for playing hooky. That's how come I quit school and joined the Army. Football's the only reason I was staying in school."

Ricky's not listening. He's got this blissful look, like he was sprinkled with fairy dust. "We won a glorious Champions League victory against an English side on their pitch and you won a glorious victory on La Rambla against English barbarians. You deserve a decoration, *Señor*, a medal."

I shrug an ah-shucks shrug.

"Can you comprehend the importance of the match? How it must have inflamed your antagonists?"

I shrug again. "Nope, I honestly can't. It's only soccer, you know. Guys running around in their skivvies, with more advertising on them than a stock car and they can't even use their hands."

Big mistake. Ricky's fairy dust bliss washes right off his face. Knocking soccer to these people, you might as well draw a mustache on a picture of the Pope.

"In certain respects, I admire you. I do trust you will be forthcoming."

"I gave you what I have to give. You about done?"

"I ask the questions. Remember our roles."

"Our role pretty soon, it's gonna be international incident."

"I sometimes yearn for the old days of Franco. *El Caudillo* was before my time, but the stories are immortal. Flexible interrogation techniques under his rule did add velocity to the truth-finding process."

"Franco. That's the old boy's name. Like the macaroni and cheese that comes in cans. Pudgy little guy in a Nazi uniform, right?"

Now I've done it. Really gone too far this time. The stink eye he's giving me, it's lowering my body temperature 20 degrees. Ricky, he might be one of those closet fascists, like they have down in Argentina. He raises a hand. Somebody's been watching us. A tall, hefty boy in uniform marches in and makes a production of snapping on a latex glove.

Ricky, he can't miss seeing me gulp.

"We have no alternative than to complete our in-process procedure for long-term guests."

Ricky came down hard on the "long-term". I'm screwed. I got positively nothing to lose with a bluff.

I say, "Don't know what you're gonna be mining for, but I been irregular for a week."

I unbuckle my belt and throw up my arms. "Be my guest, gents. You'll be doing me a favor."

Ricky throws up his arms and spits out in Spanish you don't have to be a linguistical expert to catch the gist of.

Him and his finger-waving Buddy, they go out for a confab and, by God, it's like in a dream, the situation is moving so fast. They were the bluffers, I was the bluffee. Off we go, lickety-split, straight to the Madrid airport, not a word of conversation spoke in this big sedan, me squeezed in the middle in the back between Ricky and one of his no-neck gendarmes, two more in front.

I don't even have to go through Customs. At the gate to our plane, Martha, she's standing by Thimblekins He's on the tall, lanky side. Next to him, she looks small, shrunken.

We're hugging, not talking, squeezing so hard, I'm afraid I'm gonna crack her ribs. There are tears in her eyes and some in mine too.

I know my girl. A goodly percentage of those tears are tears of joy, but some aren't.

This mess, it ain't over by a long shot.

Chapter 4

MARTHA

Buddy says we were hornswoggled by a leapfrog Ponzi. Well, I suppose that's as good a way to put it as any, either one. Do you know what a Ponzi scheme is? Of course you do. But this is a new and creative wrinkle I'll try to explain a little later.

I take care of our bills. Buddy and I are in agreement that I'm the one with the head for numbers. That's what I'm doing at the dinette table now, sorting through what awaited us after Spain. I can see through our sheer curtains to Jim's and Ellen's. The Hendricks home is different than ours, not a mirror image, but our windows do line up. Her flowered curtains, my stripes.

The sun's in my eyes. I get up and drop the blinds. We haven't talked to Jim and Ellen, who are still in Oregon. We haven't talked to anyone except the kids, and we really haven't talked.

My head is spinning, it happened so fast.

I will not be registering this fall at community college. English and art were to be my courses, beginning with English 101, Freshman Composition, and Art 156, watercolor painting. I've been eyeing a corner of the second bedroom for an easel. It has wonderful north light.

My painterly urges will have to wait. We can no longer afford tuition, let alone art supplies.

I told Buddy before he went outside that the next time

the phone rings, I'm going to reach down and unplug it from the wall, and switch from a landline to a cell. I won't, but I feel like it. We've already had two solicitations from attorneys this morning and three yesterday. They're circling like vultures to sign us up for a class action lawsuit against Charles E. Murganzer d.b.a. Murganzer Stable Fund, LLC.

Oh sure, in five or ten or 20 years we *might* be awarded a nickel on the dollar, and the lawyers will rake off four cents.

Mr. Murganzer and his silver-tongued seminars. You've seen the newspaper advertisements and mailings on them. They're always at hotels near the airport. Attend and you are given a free lunch, your choice of chicken or fish.

He wasn't the Harvard MBA he claimed to be, a consultant to billionaires. He went no further in school than I. Mr. Murganzer and his duck-on-a-glassy-pond logo on his swanky Eastside office building. Him and his prospectus and brochures as slick as anything west of New York City. An evil, evil, evil man, even though he himself was also, in a sense, a victim. You shouldn't speak ill of the dead, but I can't help it. I've said it before and I'll say it again, you are never too old to learn about people.

We live not far from the Boeing-Everett plant where we retired, in an over-55 community. We hung on to the old house and its maintenance well after Melanie was out of school, much longer than need be. We downsized into Three Lakes Luxury Estates when we were deciding whether or not we could take early outs at Boeing or whether we had to hang on until we were older and grayer.

Three Lakes Luxury Estates has no lakes, nor is it particularly luxurious. There had been three ponds in the vicinity once upon a time, but they have dried up or have been drained. Buddy jokes that they were emptied because of mosquitoes and malaria.

Three Lakes Luxury Estates is *not* a trailer park. There is no metal skirting, there are no wheels. You will find no decaying major appliances on front porches, no junkers up on blocks on cracked driveways. Three Lakes Luxury Estates residents live in manufactured homes.

Anybody who has ever visited the factories comes away impressed. Sections and modules are constructed in jigs and fixtures, not unlike the aircraft assembly process. Tolerances are much finer than in a stick-built home, where you have yahoos climbing around on rafters, not paying attention to how many nails they pound, where drywall and framing and carpeting subcontractors are like whirling dervishes, they're in such a rush, quality be damned. No thank you. Modules are trucked out to the site and connected. The fit is precise. Windows and doors open and close without binding.

Our plots are compact and meticulously maintained. This time of the year we are a quilt of emerald grass and rainbow flowerbeds. We are for the most part proud, industrious, reliable people with time on our hands.

We have standards, we have regulations. Our homeowner association officers are bulldogs. Allow dandelions to bloom and you shall receive a letter. Do it again and you shall be fined. Before our lives were turned upside down and inside out, I contemplated running for the board.

We live on a cul-de-sac, the Hendricks on one side and the Nelsons, who are traveling in their fifth-wheel trailer, on the other. The fourth residence, on the opposite side of the Hendricks, is vacant, for sale. Addie and Bob Croller moved to Arizona, sick of the rain.

I am rambling.

A mental note: The peanut butter jar we keep on Buddy's dresser that's full of pocket change, take it to the supermarket. The machine that counts it out and gives us a voucher rakes off a percentage, but we can use the extra cash. Liquidity, as Mr. Murganzer would say.

The good news was that our equity from the old house got us in here free and clear. We pay only insurance, taxes, site rental and utilities. The bad news is that we refinanced to plunk an even larger sum into Murganzer Stable Fund. Our payment book is in the stack of bills.

The first payment on our brand-new 30-year mortgage is four days overdue.

Procrastinating, I set the bills beside the messages from our bank and the lawyers. How I'd love to say presto and make them all vanish.

MSF (NSF, the media jokesters are saying) was so seductive. I've frankly never had much sympathy for folks who lose their shirts in get-rich-quick scams like you see on the infomercials, neither Buddy nor I. Mr. Murganzer did not promise that he would turn a nickel into a million tomorrow. No goose laying golden eggs, nothing like that whatsoever.

He merely promised a solid income fund that outperformed the gigantic mutual funds by moving in and out of blue chip stocks and high yield bonds at the optimum instant. Timing is the bottom line, he preached. Timing is the key to cash flow. He compared the big funds to a supertanker that would be halfway through Puget Sound before it could turn around, whereas MSF was a hydroplane.

At his seminars, Mr. Murganzer had the statistics to back up his claims. Testimonials too from satisfied clients we were welcome to contact, and we did. Our first months with MSF were living proof, so it seemed. A steady-as-a-rock annual return of seven percent, indexed to inflation, paid monthly. No, we were not greedy, we were being conservative. So we thought. That was the genius of his pitch. We were intelligent, thoughtful investors maximizing our yields.

There I go again, talking myself back into the Charles Murganzer Fan Club. He was that good, the heartless creature! The seminars were like revival meetings. We were so foolishly eager to grasp at an opportunity to put us over the top into early retirement that we signed up at our second seminar. Icing on the cake was that MSF headquarters wasn't 20 miles from where I sit. That they were local somehow added to the sense of security and legitimacy.

Without further adieu, this is the big picture. It was all over the news while we were in Spain. A few years ago, Charles Murganzer received an inheritance from a loony, 90-year-old aunt. He was her only surviving kin. They hadn't seen each other in years, so the inheritance was a pleasant surprise.

The inheritance was in the low seven figures and the aunt was *truly* loony. When the neighbors began smelling bad odors from her decrepit old house, they called the authorities who found, besides her corpse and those of some of her twenty cats, money and more money. Some of the money was stuffed in her mattress. Really. Some money was stuffed in mason jars, in the refrigerator and freezer, in cupboards, under seat cushions, in the attic, you name it.

Any normal, decent person would be satisfied with such a windfall and live out his or her life in comfort on those millions. Oh no, not our Charles! He had a brainstorm named Murganzer Stable Fund, inspired by a *genuine* Ponzi, a multi-billion dollar hustle run by a New York swell.

Charles paid us our seven percent from *his* inheritance and sank *our* investment into the (unbeknownst to him) Ponzi that paid *him* a steady fifteen percent.

From what they suspect so far and they're not done digging, there are 2676 victims who Murganzer flimflammed out of between $14,500 and $766,000, for a grand total of $778,943,250. Fifteen percent of that per annum, at the end, calculated out to $116,841,488.50. At the start, of course, he made much less, but the best guess is that he cleared $70,000,000 gross.

That is, until the wheels came off the New York swell's Ponzi, taking Murganzer Stable Fund along with it, tumbling down like Jack and Jill.

I will not reveal how much we lost except to confess that it is in the midrange. They approximate that $40,000,000 went directly into Charles Murganzer's pocket and right back out into a Lake Washington mansion, nine cars, a yacht, an airplane and sky-high living. MSF's overhead and commissions paid to the scoundrels who sold for him accounted for the rest.

Cash flow, my foot. Our cash flowed into his pocket.

Mr. Murganzer had flings in Las Vegas, where he would

lose half a million on a weekend without batting an eye. He'd sit at the baccarat tables with those Asians, the ones they call whales the casinos fly in and comp to the nines. I can just picture what types of people he rubbed shoulders with in that town.

For you bargain hunters, there'll be a liquidation auction at an unspecified date. Much of the money is gone, frittered away. Sales commissions and lavish spending can burn through a fortune in a hurry.

One of his cars was an Aston Martin, that swoopy model James Bond drives. This automobile may not be available for auction as it remains in police impoundment. In the middle of the night, the car was found on the center span of the old Tacoma Narrows Bridge, the northwesterly one headed out of town. The driver's door was open. There was a note in his handwriting taped to the dashboard. It said: I LIVED THE GOOD LIFE, IF NOT A GOOD LIFE.

The man wrote his own smirking epitaph.

The death of Mr. Murganzer and Murganzer Stable Fund occurred while we were in Spain. We read the stories in the Seattle paper Buddy had Jim and Ellen save for the sports sections.

Following his suicide, there was a photo on the front page of Charles Murganzer and Lizabeth, his wife. They were standing together on their dock at their Medina estate. Their yacht behind them was so large that it filled the background of the picture.

Charles Murganzer looked younger in the photo and in person. His age was listed as 47, Lizabeth's at 31. He wore expensive slacks and a pastel green pullover. He had a keyboard of white teeth and hair blow-dried just so. Charles

Murganzer reminded me of a game show host.

Lizabeth Murganzer was in a form-fitting sundress. She had a hardened baby face and big hair. She's blonde, of course. Despite her tender age, there are a string of failed marriages in her past. Underneath all her pizzazz, I sense a basically nice, if insecure, person. They're satisfied that she didn't know what Charles was up to. There are not going to be charges filed against her.

I switch off the calculator and start water boiling for tea. Buddy's on the patio, sitting in a lawn chair, scratching Tangerine's belly. We have two big old orange cats, Orange and Tangerine. They're lazy congenial things, hound dogs trapped in feline bodies. People think they're twins, but they're unrelated, three years apart in age.

From the moment Buddy and I were reunited at the Madrid Airport, he has been disengaged, the word Melanie used (although she doesn't begin to know the full story). Buddy is dazed, listless and crotchety, as if his jet lag is a chronic disease.

It's like pulling teeth to get him out of the house to walk at the mall. Nothing interests him. He can't even get excited about the late innings of a seesaw Mariners game. I firmly believe that televised sports were invented so man and wife don't have to talk. Never has our silence been more deafening.

Buddy won't admit it, but that fight on La Rambla took its toll, psychologically and physically. Surrounded by soccer hooligans, he survived by fighting smart and dirty. Buddy, my two-fisted Good Samaritan. That Spanish jail experience must have traumatized him something fierce too, although Buddy, being Buddy, won't say so. Our financial plight was the knockout punch.

The Spanish police tried to make a mountain out of less than a molehill. The trouble with our plastic was not our doing. Add to that an ambitious Spanish detective making my Buddy out to be a dashing international art thief, like those characters Robert Wagner and Cary Grant used to play. Bosh! It's my opinion that detective has a political agenda. Angling for a promotion, no doubt. We continuously witnessed that behavior at Boeing, mediocrities clawing their way up the ladder, the Peter Principle in action.

If anything interests Buddy, it's his Charles Murganzer obsession. Buddy says he cheated us and he cheated justice even if he himself was cheated. Buddy says that 50 years in the can would be a proper punishment, 50 years locked up with perverted homicidal maniacs, 50 years in the shower room with them. That Murganzer's minions have been rounded up and some will do time is little solace. Buddy says since there is no recovered body, how do we know the bleepity-bleep is dead.

Buddy says we're damn near broke. That's how he puts it. Damn near broke. You don't have to do the bills to draw that conclusion.

There has been nary a peep out of him regarding Salvador Dalí's painting of his sister, Ana Maria, thank goodness for small favors. When I unpacked, I tied up that pile of postcards with a rubber band and left them in his suitcase, where they remain untouched.

However, since we have gotten home, Buddy has developed a bad habit. He's up at all hours watching TV. I hear him either talking at the television or in his sleep during catnaps. This is not normal behavior.

The teapot's whistling. As the bag steeps in my cup, I continue watching Buddy out there with the kitties. I'd ask Buddy if he'd like a cup, but he isn't partial to tea. Nothing tastes good to him, not even beer. It has become contagious. I spoon in twice my usual sugar and the tea's still bitter.

I sigh and switch on the calculator.

This is why we're in this pickle.

Investing our 401(k)'s and home refinancing proceeds into MSF (obviously). You take a pension hit when you retire early and me with only 17 years service, mine is a pittance. Buddy's is nothing to shout about either.

Charles Murganzer and MSF got their filthy paws on our checking account. At the eleventh hour, in a vain effort to stay afloat, Murganzer Stable Fund cleaned out everyone they had card numbers on. Our checking account and bank line of credit wasn't much more complicated for those bunco artists. Our monthly dividends were direct deposits to our checking account.

MSF found a way of opening the spigot and reversing the flow. Hacking, it's called. If you can't do it yourself, you can hire pimply kids or Russians to do it for you.

I am cautiously confident the credit card people will cover our losses. The bank I'm not so certain about. I'm going to lock horns with them when the smoke clears and we know exactly how much was looted. They can leave us alone in the meantime, thank you very much.

Our last "good" credit card is a problem in itself. At Madrid Airport, we had to book one-way passage home at the ticket counter, maxing it out.

It isn't as if we took early retirement like those software

youngsters who cash in the millions in stock options and live the life of Riley. We aren't those CEO crooks who ruin their companies and receive golden handshakes that would make King Midas blush.

We are not afraid of work. We worked hard all our lives. We have a snowball's chance in hell of getting back on at Boeing. Aerospace is in and out of the toilet. When we put in our retirement papers, management couldn't have been more delighted. We were *attrition*, two high-seniority jobs eliminated without pink slips.

Any other living-wage job for a high school grad (me) and a non-grad (Buddy) at our ages — forget it. I think of the places we pass on the road, fast food and retail, with their permanent NOW HIRING signs, and how sorry I felt for people who had to accept those jobs.

My 2003 Honda Accord sedan is paid for. Buddy's 1992 Ford F-150 pickup is too. The vehicles should last us indefinitely if Buddy will please quit tinkering under the hood of his rig. Aside from the furniture and appliances and electronics and the clothes on our backs, we essentially have no assets.

If we are careful, our savings will last six to eight weeks. By careful I mean no baseball tickets, no eating out, no movies, no emergencies. No leaving unneeded lights on, no tossing out leftovers, no waste whatsoever.

Yes, I know, the experts say that you should have X month's salary tucked away. We didn't and that's that.

Jim and Ellen Hendricks next door are amazing in their grasp of household finances. Jim was a furnace repairman who worked for various companies. Ellen cooked in nursing homes and schools, earning a shade above minimum wage.

Neither has a pension. They'd socked some money away, although not as much as they wished. They get by on Social Security and minimal savings. I'll subtly ask for budgeting tips.

I look out at Buddy. The lazybones pattern he got into after we clocked out at Boeing for the last time doesn't seem so bad in retrospect. That growing paunch of his is adorable.

Buddy and I were married 39 years ago next September. When Melanie was born six and a half months later, we'd joke that we were premature, not her. At seven pounds, two ounces, she was a tough sell as a preemie.

My pregnancy was no secret. Our parents are gone, but three of our four were alive then. They were very modern about the situation and threw us a lovely church wedding. While they were good sports, they confided privately that it wouldn't last. Shotgun weddings never do.

Ten years of serious effort did not produce a sibling for Melanie. We gave up. Nothing in particular was wrong with either one of us. It wasn't meant to be. I am an only child and Buddy's family is small too.

Oddly, Melanie was conceived all too easily. I have often thought, half in jest, of clueing in those fertility clinics that the magic potion might be a starry summer night in the back seat of a 1966 Chevrolet Impala parked off a dirt road. Moonlight and chirping crickets and cool Naugahyde.

I debate whether to take my tea outside. I decide not to. Buddy looks tranquil in his quiet time, staring off into space. Orange is on his lap, Tangerine curled up at his feet.

We have to talk and we have to talk soon. We have to work out our financial situation without Melanie and David finding out. We shall not accept a dime from them.

We are learning to cope. We are learning frugality. We are learning that technology is not necessarily what it's cracked up to be. Take the plastic toothpaste tube. You could tightly roll the old tin tubes and squeeze out every glob of paste. Try that now. We are also learning false economies. Buddy brought home a bag of house brand cat food. The kitties snarled at him and the bag went into the garbage.

The mourning period is over. We need to be proactive.

Worse than sudden poverty is the shame of being bamboozled, for being taken for suckers. We are uneducated working-class people and this is proof that we're stupid, that we're easy prey, that we're candidates for the soup kitchen.

We cannot bear the pity.

Chapter 5

BUDDY

"**A**re you positive you won't try a glass?"

I shake my head again.

"Half a glass, Dad? A taste?"

Sets me on edge when David calls me Dad. His own folks, they're retired down in Palm Springs, living it up, when they aren't traveling wherever they feel like going. His old man was a doctor too, the regular general practice kind.

"If you ask me, it's all sour grape juice, Dave."

Payback. A double zinger, on wine and his name. He's David (Please Don't Call Me Dave) and Dr. David to the ladies he tinkers on.

I take a swig of cold suds from the can. He delicately sips his glass of red. It was bottled in France the same year my pickup rolled off the line in Detroit. Martha and Melanie, they're inside fixing the salad and the spuds. Us menfolk are sitting out on the patio of this gigantic new house of theirs, getting ready to throw steaks on the barbecue.

Melanie and Martha, they're wishing that David and me are gonna do some male bonding. Dream on. Haven't managed to yet, in however many years they been married. We're polite and formal in each other's company.

Only topic we agree on is, of all things, art. We both like Norman Rockwell's stuff, me to look at, him to invest in. Not much common ground there.

David swirls his glass and holds it up to the sun by the skinny stem. He sniffs the rim.

"You don't know what you're missing. This vintage is silky smooth. It has a noseful of complex tannins and is brimming with cherries and a medley of fruit."

To the best of my knowledge, wine is made out of grapes. If there's any fruit brimming, I'm looking at him. We got no grandchildren and none are on the horizon.

I gotta wonder if him being a gynecologist is a factor. When Melanie first brought David home, I thought he had the world's spiffiest job. Then I got to thinking. You punch the time clock at nine and you punch out at five, and all you've been doing all day is looking at and fiddling with female private regions. You go home to the missus and then what? Even after years of marriage, there oughta be a little air of mystery. I once said something to that effect to Martha, and she spoke maybe ten words to me over the next three days.

"Should be vitamin packed," I say.

"We haven't had a chance to discuss your Spain trip. I love the tie. I'm waiting for the proper occasion. Mom must have related to you how ecstatic Melanie is over the necklace."

David's going plump and he wears clothes two sizes too small. That works on a gal if she's not too porky. On David, it's lost in the translation. He's only 40 and already has that fat that pooches out from under his belt. His top priority in life is money, money, money. Must be how come I'm so mean and skinny.

On the other side of the coin, I really oughta cut him a little slack. He's devoted to our Melanie, so on account of that alone, he ain't a terrible guy. Like Martha says, Melanie's almost as important to him as the almighty buck.

"The food's swell and the trip was an adventure."

I tick off the grub we had, from artichoke hearts to ham to sausage to jazzed-up zucchini and those omelets they call tortillas. "The chow's sometimes free if you order a drink, no huge sacrifice. What this country needs is a *tapas* bar on every corner."

David sips and frowns. He's not listening to me. "You had a harrowing experience we're unclear on."

"Us too," I answer, semi-truthful. "They thought I was mixed up in an international art theft ring."

"Mom was especially hazy on that aspect of your trouble too. I'm referring to the attack. I can't help but notice."

He's gesturing at the knot on the side of my skull Fatso gave me. I'm in better health than I deserve to be. I've had spots burned off my face and my prostrate's the size of a glazed doughnut, but that's about it in the medical malfunction department. The older you get, though, the longer it takes for bumps and aches and bruises and scrapes to heal up. I still feel like I went over Niagara Falls in a barrel.

I shrug my aw-shucks shrug. "They were picking on a young fella who was trying to close up his shop."

"Seven soccer hooligans confronted you? *Seven* of them?"

I flutter a hand. "Around seven. More or less. Thereabouts."

I give him a blow-by-blow, throwing fake punches, sloshing my beer, the whole bit. I'm finding to my surprise I don't mind telling my tale. I like it when David flinches at the boot to Stringbean's family jewels and the uppercut I gave Fatso.

He whistles under his breath. "You cracking his teeth. I'd love to see them. That was a remarkable feat considering."

He pauses, I finish.

"Considering my age?"

"Any age. I wouldn't have wanted to be in your spot."

"I used to be a hothead and idiot. Guess I still am."

"No, no. You did right. You deserved a commendation, not police harassment. I can't comprehend soccer hooliganism."

"Likewise. They have the nerve to call soccer football over in Europe."

"I can't comprehend soccer either."

I nod. David thinks golf is a sport.

"How was the police experience?"

"Coulda been worse. The cops rooted for me too, but it didn't get me sprung any quicker."

"The language barrier possibly played a role," David says.

"Martha taught herself some Spanish. I'll bet it cut days off how long they held me. Martha and the help we got from the U.S. Embassy."

"Her effort was commendable. I applaud people who continue the learning process, but there's no substitute for everyday fluency."

David's good at making up his mind. This is okay, as it looks like we're done on the subject.

His waistline chirps. He unholsters his cell phone I've never seen him without, excuses himself, and goes to a corner of this patio that's twice the size of our entire Three Lakes Luxury Estates lot.

Gotta be an emergency in a gal's luscious region. That's the only calls David takes on weekends. I wonder if he charges time-and-a-half.

Martha can get irritated at David too. She'll throw up her hands and say Melanie should of married that lawyer she was going with. I'd rooted for that boy my ownself. He's going great guns today, trolling for the whiplashed in a full-page Yellow Pages ad. In my humble opinion, when you got an overeducation sheepskin hanging up in your office, odds are it's a racket. Not that I'm casting aspersions at the shyster or David. Somebody's got to do those jobs or there wouldn't be anybody to build these humongous houses for.

There wasn't gonna be any dead-end factory worker in Melanie's life if Martha had anything to do about it. No ma'am. From when Melanie was a little girl, Martha told her that it was as easy to fall in love with a college-educated professional as a working stiff, me being the only exception in the whole wide world.

I'll give David credit. He's a helluva provider. He puts food on the table in spades. They moved out here on the Plateau from a four-bedroom split-level in a nice section of Bellevue, across Lake Washington and east of Seattle, they'd been in less than three years. Martha and me, we lived for twenty-plus years in a three bedroom, bath-and-a-half ranch house south of Everett and it didn't do us any harm.

This house of theirs is of the French Chateau persuasion according to Martha. To me that means plenty big and no shortage of bricks and shingles and dormers. They don't have it furnished too shabby neither. All they'd have to do to be in the Sunday magazine section is to phone up the newspaper and say, hey, come on out.

David's got two offices for his snatchecological business, one in Bellevue and the second in West Seattle. Traffic is gridlock on the lake's bridges unless you're tactical on your commute. David tweaked his schedule between those offices to "optimize" his patient visits. He also had privacy glass installed on his S-Class Mercedes, the darkest tint you can legally have. He can zip along alone in the carpool lane and nobody's the wiser.

David's got his back to me, staring out at the greenbelt, yakking away. Lord help me, but his standing position, one foot flat, the other heel up, his shape kind of reminding me of *Girl*. I hunted through every album and shoebox of photos we got. We keep the spare bedroom piled high with belongings we brought along when we downsized that we can't bear to throw out. Can't for the life of me locate that picture of Mom.

I phoned Stan and he agreed to mail his to me. If I had an ounce of sense I'd cap up that can of worms before they escape completely out of Pandora's box.

Charles Murganzer, the rancid son of a bitch, I can't get him out of my mind, how he cheated us on his Ponzi and got cheated hisself by a gen-u-ine Ponzi and cheated the law by taking a swan dive into the Tacoma Narrows.

Saw a TV show the other night on the life of Charles Ponzi, the father of the Ponzi. In the 1920s, this twerp bamboozled folks into buying notes promising he'd buy some bullshit called international postal coupons and sell them here for a big profit. He promised to double your money in ninety days.

There were no coupons and no money except for the early suckers who were paid by the later suckers. Word got out Ponzi was a crook and the swindle came crashing down.

Ponzi died of natural causes and Murganzer took the chickenshit way out. Two seconds in the air and splat. From that height, hitting water's like hitting concrete. If a man commits hairy carry, I firmly believe it shouldn't be so easy. When you're mostly hated, even by your loved ones, you oughta swallow the barrel of a gun like Brady Hardcastle did. There oughta be noise and blood and pain.

I got one problem about Murganzer's kamikaze into the drink. There has been no corpus delectable dredged up. What I'd like, I'd like to have conclusive proof that the fish had Murganzer for sushi. That he's not alive some place, having pulled off another flimflam. Even though he was never seen on the bridge – just his Aston Martin and his wiseass suicide note – they're convinced he's dead. There've been crackpot rumors, but no confirmed sign of him at airports or at faraway spots where he'd be retiring in style on our retirement money.

What I'd love to personally do is throw a net over him. Have him stand trial and get the book thrown at him. Fifty years in the pen, being cornholed in the shower room each and every time he drops his soap.

I squash my empty in my hands, pretending it's Murganzer's neck. It snaps, crackles and pops. David hears and turns, phone grafted to his ear. I grab me another cold one out of the ice chest, thinking how Jim Hendricks and me, on a nice summer day like this, we'll sit out on a deck, theirs or ours, and have a couple or six brews. If the

Mariners are on, we'd bring out a portable TV.

We'll be glad when him and Ellen get back from Portland. Won't be glad if they look at us and see something's haywire. Won't be glad lying, telling them it's their imagination.

The gals are coming outside with a platter of steaks, inch-thick, New York strips. Serious cow. Melanie's looking more and more like her mama, and this is good. She's filling out slightly in the hip area, losing some of her slenderness, and softening in the cheekbones. When the sun hits her honey-blonde hair, there's a strand or two of silver visible in the gold. She wears reading glasses now.

David flops the slabs of beef on his brand-spanking-new gas barbecue. A delicious sizzle shoots right on through my nostrils. This grill, a big wraparound job with shelves and side burners, it's the same model they cook with on the TV barbecuing shows.

The gals bring out the rest of the food and utensils. David and I dish up the steaks. We're small-talking, mostly regarding this house. David's in a pissing contest with some contractor regarding the marble countertops.

"They feel like sandpaper," he complains. "We didn't pay for granite out of a local quarry. Not at that price. We paid for *Italian* marble."

"Outrageous," I say.

Martha looks at me.

"Dinner is served," Melanie says.

The beef's so tender, you can cut it with a glance. Green salad's cool and crisp. The oven-fried potatoes are super tasty. I am in hog heaven.

Talking with mouths empty and full, we get around to

the David's practice, the Mariners, the weather, David's practice, weeds coming up in the sod the landscapers laid, the Seahawks, and David's practice.

Afterwards, the ladies bring out strawberry cheesecake Melanie made. We plow into it and when we're nearly done, David says out of the blue, "I count my blessings. We've been seeing on the news about that swindler who committed suicide, the one preyed on retired people with fixed incomes and was victimized himself by a Ponzi. This happened when you were in Spain. Did you hear?"

Martha lets me answer.

Eyeballs on my plate, I say, "Story kind of rings a bell."

"This character had a name like a bird or a duck. Murganzer. That's it. It must be horrible to be wiped out financially, virtually overnight, after a lifetime of scrimping and saving. I don't know how I'd handle it. I thank our lucky stars we're solvent and diversified."

We've never hinted at our financial specifics to them or anybody else. The cheesecake in my throat is turning to acid and I'm afraid I'm gonna urp it up.

Melanie glares at her spouse. He's on a fishing expedition.

"Lucky us," I say. "You can't be too careful."

Martha dabs her eyes.

"Mother?" Melanie asks.

"Smoke from the barby," Martha says.

I wash down the dessert with my beer. I play footsy with Martha, saying telepathic-like that it's okay. She looks at me, saying it's okay back.

"The watchdog agencies missed him by a mile. Nobody had an inkling until the wheels came off his scheme."

"David," Melanie says.

He looks up from his second helping, blinking. "Yes?"

"Eat your dessert."

That's code for him to put a lid on it and he does. Melanie's trained him like Martha trained me.

Her and me, we haven't sat down and really talked our situation out. I admit that's my fault. I'm dodging her like an all-pro halfback. My only contribution to our mess is when the bank calls getting snotty. Martha hands me the phone and I holler at them.

Martha's giving me time and we're running out of it. She says we'll be tapped out in less than eight weeks.

Scraping by is one thing, but I hate Martha having to give up her new activities and classes. My new activity is being unable to sleep at night. I watch the weirdness that is middle-of-the-night TV. Bad movies and talk shows and infomercials and cheesy car dealer commercials.

When I did doze off last night, I had me a dream where Orange and Tangerine hopped up on the counter by the can opener and this big pyramid stack of their cat food. They told me to start opening the cans, that we're on the same diet. Bone appétit.

Which was better than my usual dream. *I Love Lucy* is on, see. Ricky Ricardo's my Madrid Ricky and he's talking to me out of the TV, calling me *Señor* and asking me advice about Lucy, how to keep her from nagging him about appearing on his show at the Tropicana Club. Even goofier, I'm answering him back. Then I wake up and can't remember what I said to him, and *I Love Lucy* ain't even on. *Hawaii Five-o* or *Perry Mason* is on one of the oldie channels.

If this keeps up, I'll have to hire me a priest to exercise Ricky before I go totally bugshit cuckoo.

Don't know how yet, but Martha and me, we'll solve our own problems. We're each other's best friend. We lost touch with Boeing friends faster than we thought we would. It's like after you retire you've blasted off to a faraway planet. They gotta drag their butts out of the sack every morning and we don't. Martha says we're an island.

We're in unanimous agreement on one point. No way are the kids ever gonna learn we were wiped out and are damn near broke. No way will we accept a dime from them.

Me, I know I gotta get my act together pretty soon.

Chapter 6

MARTHA

Landing a fast food job is not the breeze one might presume it to be, not at my age, not in the summertime when so many kids are out of school, at loose ends, available for any shift. Employment is far from automatic.

But, gosh, you know, that's exactly what happened. Instantaneously! Luck was a factor, definitely, although three people not showing up for the morning shift is perhaps not so unusual, the work ethic being what it is in this day and age.

That Mr. Larionov, owner of this and six other franchises in the chain, was visiting when I asked to fill out an application, was an additional stroke of luck. The assistant manager in charge of this shift was among the missing.

Mr. Larionov is a bull of a man who drives an enormous black Hummer H2. He could be Melanie's age, he could be mine. It's difficult to tell because of the worry lines on his blockish face. His hands are enormous and rough. I later learn that he is an émigré from one of the former Soviet republics. I visualize him as having grown up on a collective farm, sharpening plowshares and changing tractor tires.

Mr. Larionov perused my application for all of 30 seconds and hired me on the spot, no exaggeration. Just like that, I am on the clock, on the job. Mr. Larionov plans for me to rotate assignments: the drive-through window, the kitchen, the front registers, and shift scheduling. He says that when I have an overview of the operation, the sky's the limit, relatively speaking. He likes employing people of a certain age, he told me. We're dependable. You can count on us.

I will not reveal where this restaurant is or even the corporate brand. I will only say that I'm a 20-minute drive from home and nosy neighbors, in the opposite direction of Melanie and David's, and that it is one of the prominent national chains.

I am not ashamed of honest toil, but obviously there are issues, particularly after David's unsubtle remarks. If Melanie discovers I'm working here, it would confirm what we suspect she and David suspect.

Is despair written on our faces?

They would insist on bailing us out. At the risk of sounding like a broken record, Buddy and I are of a mind that charity is intolerable. Buddy says he'd live in a cardboard box under a freeway overpass like a troll before he'd accept a nickel from Dr. David Moneybags. We are able-bodied adults who have to live with our mistakes. We got ourselves in this mess. We'll get ourselves out.

I shall be wearing a uniform. Although I can change in the ladies' room here, it does complicate secrecy. The biggest drawback of an over-55 community is that so many folks have nothing better to do than snoop. If I'm caught, and I eventually will be, well, I will simply explain that I cannot sit around the house in my rocking chair with the TV remote in one hand and a glass of prune juice in the other. I am not built that way. This is the whole truth, if not the entire story, as, frankly, fast food employment comes in a distant second to attending community college.

I must concentrate now. Mr. Larionov is gone and Felipe is breaking me in on the registers. Felipe is from El Salvador. He worked in the chain's California restaurants before moving north. He knows the ropes and I wonder if he has a green card.

The breakfast deluge is winding down and Felipe can take his time training me. When we're rushed and he's talking fast, Felipe lapses into Spanglish and my language study is of no benefit whatsoever. After we become acquainted, I plan to *practicar mi español* on him.

Things have dramatically changed since I worked at a root beer joint during high school. Back then, we had those clunky cash registers with the ornate scrolling on the sides. You pushed number buttons and the tabs popped up in the window. You *had* to know how to make change. As a matter of fact, you had to pass an arithmetic test to qualify for employment.

Here, you touch the menu item on the computer screen and record what the customer gives you. For example, this gentleman is having a large coffee and he's paying with a five. I input that data. A dollar-forty including tax pops up on the screen and three dollars and sixty cents is his change. It is so easy. To the degree our school system has declined, that's unfortunately for the best.

As I pour, Felipe cautions me to snap a lid on any hot drink whether it's for here or to go. He makes a knife across the throat gesture and says if you don't and Mr. Larionov finds out, you are *fin*. We've all heard what juries are awarding scalding victims in fast food establishments, even if it's their own fault. I do not need any more lawyers in my life.

My next customers are teenagers who order breakfast sandwiches (we sell six combinations) and hash browns. Three egg and sausage on a bun, two egg and bacon on a croissant for these youngsters. They're having soda pop too and I have to bite my tongue so I don't preach orange juice or milk for nutritional reasons. The customer is always right.

On to the touch-screen my orders go. They're relayed to another screen in the kitchen. Sandwiches are pre-made and warming. By the time the youngsters have paid, their food is coming up as if by magic.

The uniformity reminds me of Boeing. You follow procedures or else. You could go from here to this chain's restaurant in Madrid or Singapore or Dubuque or Jacksonville or Lima and you could expect to receive the same menu item, the same quality and promptness.

Mr. Larionov is starting me at ten dollars per hour. After six months he provides optional medical and dental coverage that is expensive and skimpy. Thank goodness we have ours through Buddy's Boeing retirement. I don't know what we would do if we lost that and fell ill. Medicare pays just so much. Fending off creditors will give us ulcers at the very least.

I realize I am not being paid a fortune. Figuring 40 hours a week, 50 weeks a year, my salary is $20,000 per annum. That is somewhat less than half what I earned at Boeing. Mr. Larionov could have offered me less. He could have offered minimum wage. Mr. Larionov is relying on my maturity, my dependability.

If Buddy can find a job paying similar money, we can

make it. We can squeak by until we can organize our obligations. Yes we can.

A young couple with an infant comes in. Do we have high chairs and youth chairs? I look around for Felipe. Where is he? I spot booster seats in a corner and point them out.

More customers are at the counter. I smile and say hello, may I help you. I'm on my own. I have butterflies, but I can handle the situation, yes I can. A positive attitude is the key.

Buddy is unaware of this turn of events. He was half-asleep when I said I was going job hunting and that I was determined to land one by day's end. To take the bull by the horns. I am hoping my success will make him proactive, will light a fire under him. Gainful employment may move him beyond his ennui (is that the correct word?) and his futile, poisonous obsession with Charles Murganzer. An example is worth 1000 words.

A person does what a person has to do.

I can do this. I can do anything.

Chapter 7

BUDDY

Martha, she has this knack for laying down the law without a lecture, without raising her voice. This morning, she's up with the chickens. She semi-awakens me by giving Orange and Tangerine pats on the head, and me a peck on the cheek.

Martha says she's going job hunting and don't be shocked if she's landed one by the end of the day. I think I'm dreaming but I smell this perfume she wears when she dresses up. And you know what, later on when the cats walk across my head to announce that breakfast hasn't been served, I pry my eyes open and look outside. Her Honda's gone.

Gotta do something and gotta do it soon, I notify myself for the umpteenth time as I'm making coffee. Martha says we have got to be proactive. We need to be working out an action plan. How much we need to live on and how we're gonna make what we need to make and whatnot. I've heard them say proactive on CNN too. You're proactive, the fickle finger of fate stops being a proctological digit.

That's gonna be me, Mr. Proactive.

Guess Martha's taking the first proactiveness plunge, her heading out into the job market. What kind of job's Martha looking for? She never said. Martha, she's in the same boat as me. Hell, she can't hardly type.

I assemble airplane parts is what I do. Even if I'd got

around to finishing high school in the service on a GED, what good would it do me? I'm sixty-plus years old and have got no skills to speak of. Outside of fastening aluminum skin, I'm experienced at puttering around at household chores and under the hood of my truck, which was built before they stuck computers in them. Strictly amateur status. My possibilities are mostly not possible.

It's dumb to wonder what-if and stew in your juices. Martha and me, we've never done that and don't intend to now. We're satisfied with our lives. We ride out the bumps in the road. This current one, despite being the mother of all potholes, we'll hang on and ride it out too.

I shower and shave and throw on clean slacks and shirt. First stop's the supermarket where I cash in our change jar in that machine they have and net $31.86 after their cut. Feels like mighty big bucks.

Next, I'm sitting in my pickup, drinking the dregs of the java I made, parked at our local 7-Eleven. It's six blocks south of Three Lakes Luxury Estates at a four-way stop, next to a dry cleaners, across from teriyaki, and kitty-corner from the Chevron station.

Except it's not a 7-Eleven. The owners are Orientals who bought the store out a couple of years back. They renamed it Spiffy-Jiffy Food Mart. I'm observing them do a land office business selling two or three items at a clip. They've had a customer a minute on the average, each carrying out doughnuts and coffee and cigarettes and/or filling up at the gas pumps. It adds up.

This is the store we stopped at when we needed a thing or two on the way home from Boeing. There were always different clerks whenever we went in. The NOW HIRING sign under the Budweiser banner I never noticed is yellowed from the sun. It's permanent, taped on the window. Come to think of it, when you'd buy gas, NOW HIRING APPLY INSIDE was printed on the credit card slip. Never had to pay attention to that stuff.

Oughta be heading on in to apply. Problem is, I can't make my butt Budge. What am I gonna do, work for peanuts, selling six-packs and gas till some carjacking dope fiends rob and shoot me? Spose I could wear a flak vest if they put me on nights. And I wouldn't have to stay if I didn't like the work. It's not like enlisting in the service. You can walk.

I quit waffling and go in. There's a customer nuking a sandwich in the microwave and another fishing a half-gallon of milk out the cooler. The young fella at the register, he may be the owner's son.

I think these folks are Korean. Don't remember seeing Caucasians since the store changed hands. They keep it in the family and there's nothing wrong with that. No point of me asking for work, sign or no sign. It's probably some equal opportunity hoop they gotta jump through.

Besides, everybody else at Three Lakes Luxury Estates comes in here and a man has his pride. I buy a six-pack, fill up the truck, and get a *Seattle Times*. To cut costs, we cancelled ours except for Sunday, me for the sports section and us for the sale coupons. For the hell of it, I invest a buck in a Lotto ticket.

Back home, I spread out the half page of want ads out on the dinette table. Martha says most advertising is online now and that's what's killing the newspapers. There's some, though. Tow truck driver, warehouse picker, administrative assistant, house painter (I did ours twice. It's a bitch even with a roller), restaurant line cook, auto parts clerk, phone book delivery (seasonal), apartment maintenance (you'd have to live there), retail sales (a bunch of these), meat cutter, baker, no candlestick maker, quality control, pizza delivery (my best shot) computer programmer (yeah, right), janitor (my next best shot), file clerk.

Apply in person, send résumés, contact Human Resources Department. Human Resources and HR, why did they have to go and change it from Personnel? Human Resources sounds like those commodities they trade, pork bellies and soybeans.

Me delivering pizza. The company thing on top of my truck, the little hat on my head. Running red lights to make it to the customer's house to beat the time limit where the pizza's free. Nah. Can't see me doing that. Can't. No way.

The mail truck comes and goes. We get ours early here, not what you'd consider a blessing. Our mailbox now is a time bomb. I bring in junk and bills. There's one with SECOND NOTICE written in red on the envelope. Rude bastards.

There's also a manila envelope from Brother Stan. It's stiff, like from cardboard protecting a picture. While I think about whether I really want to open it or not, I go to the fridge and reach for one of the cold brews I bought. I don't frankly believe that the earliness of the day that you enjoy a cold one is all that important so long as you're not getting behind the wheel again.

Irregardless, if I pop the top at this hour it'll be a first for me. I'm flexing that little ring, thinking. Sure enough, I do this and Martha'd pull into the driveway.

I do what I never do. I read my horoscope, which is a 7: *Changes over which you have little or no control require your full attention.*

I stick the brew back in the fridge and grab my car keys. There's something I've had an itch to do since we got home from Spain. I'm gonna go and scratch it.

~ ~ ~

I tool into this Eastside suburban business park, recollecting as a tiny little kid when it used to be trees and pastures, ponds and cows. Before they widened it to four lanes, the highway fronted berry farms and swayback barns. There'd been Burma Shave signs. This was when you drove from Seattle eastbound across Lake Washington, there was only one bridge and you were out in the sticks till you came to the next town.

Now everything's a blur of traffic and development. This complex is six or seven black glass cubes. The landscaping is summer flowers in ground bark and grass like golf greens.

Progress.

Head on a swivel, I scout for parking. The lot's jam-packed with SUVs and Audis and Jaguars and Volvos. I could cheat and take a handicapped space, but I wasn't brought up that way. At long last I spot a spot two buildings down from where I'm going. I get out, uncomfortable here. This business park is all about computers and money and pie in the sky.

Where I'm standing, it might be where Dad and Stan and me went fishing. There was a stream, a creek that's been paved over. You got to it off a gravel road. We'd bring home our limit in seven- and eight-inch rainbows. Mom would clean and cook them. This was in the good old days, long prior to Brady Hardcastle and the Rosebud Motor Court.

On the side of Charles Murganzer's black cube is MSF in neon in the shape of a duck, wavy neon lines underneath, like the MSF quacker's floating. The neon's turned off. There are FOR LEASE signs plastered on the windows.

I go on over and squint inside the doors. There's enough light coming from a skylight to see pretty good. A banana-shaped receptionist's desk. Sections of cubicles on either side. The center area behind the front desk is a great big tall room, an atrium like in hotels. A staircase winds up to what in the old movie theatres you knew as a mezzanine. There're offices on the upper level. Murganzer's would've been the largest and nicest. In a corner, naturally.

I'm picturing me chucking Murganzer out his window. It's not much of a drop compared to the Narrows Bridge, but right now I'd settle for giving him a broken leg or a ruptured spleen. A gesture on my part for Martha and me and the 2600-plus other suckers.

A rent-a-cop comes up to me. His gut spills over a belt that holds a ring of keys and a walkie-talkie.

"May I help you, sir?"

"Nope. Not really," I say, turning toward my truck. "Just wanted to see where my cash flowed to."

~ ~ ~

Medina is a town not too awful far from the belly-up Murganzer Stable Fund Headquarters. Medina's right on Lake Washington. Medina doesn't look like a town. There aren't many businesses on this main drag that doesn't look like a main drag. Medina is greenery and fancy houses. Bill

Gates lives in Medina. He's a neighbor of the late Charles Murganzer. Medina has got the gross national product of God.

I'm cruising the road closest to the water. This is where the swellest of the swells live. We saw overhead shots of the Murganzer mansion in the newspapers. I can ball park its general location. The lakefront side is trees and iron fences and hedges as long and tall and flat as aircraft carriers. These folks, they appreciate their privacy.

I cruise slower to check mailboxes. Many are just numbers, not names, sensible if you're that rich. I luck out and come to "-zer", a piece of a busted-off nameplate on a box. Gotta be him. I turn into a winding driveway that's blocked 50 yards down by a steel gate. There's a buzzer by a speaker to push and a people gate too.

I pull off the drive till the brush is fingernails on a blackboard on the side of my pickup. Doubt if anybody's around. If somebody is, they sure as hell ain't gonna buzz me in. The people gate is locked. I can rattle it, there's that much slop. I wiggle my worthless credit card in the crack. My plastic's useless for anything else. The bolt depresses and the gate opens. Some security.

I walk down this sloping flagstone driveway. Pruned trees crowd each side, neat and uniform, like spectators at a race. I come to a clearing. Sprinklers are arcing over the lawn, another golfing green. I see a rainbow.

Gardeners are busy trimming and weeding shrubs and flowerbeds. They pay me no never mind. Still heading downhill, I go around the house that from the front looks like a shoebox, nothing special. It finally levels off at a – I count the doors —nine-car garage. Looks like living space above too, a coach house for the hired flunkies. The garage doors are shut. There's one vehicle in the drive, a shiny black Cadillac Escalade with its rear hatch up and cardboard boxes in it.

I look out at the water and my jaw drops to my knees. Lake Washington is spread out, flat and glossy and dotted with boats, as it always is on a nice summer day. Across the Seattle side, you can see the tallest downtown skyscrapers spiking up behind the hills. A long wooden dock looks lonesome. That must be where that picture in the paper of Mr. and Mrs. Murganzer was taken, them and his yacht.

Swallows are diving at dragonflies above a fishpond on a grassy slope. Behind it is a brick patio the size of a basketball court. Built-in is a barbecue and a kidney-shaped swimming pool. The house, if you can call it that, on this side, is a pyramid, five levels of decks, enough view space for half the folks in Medina. This place makes David and Melanie's fake French Chateau look like a squatter's shack.

"Holy fucking cow!" is all I can spit out.

I'm not watching my step and stumble on one that leads up to the pool, and I damn near fall in, ass over teakettle. I scramble to my feet, clutching at a chaise lounge that splashes in instead. I pull it out and hold it up to drip dry.

"Are you with the gardeners the realtor sent? There's nothing that needs to be done in the back."

I let loose of the chaise lounge and focus on the lady addressing me from a doorway. She's a big-haired blue-eyed blonde with a drink in one hand and a cigarette in the other. She's in shorts and halter-top that are none too roomy. You can use your imagination.

She is Mrs. Murganzer, who I thought'd been booted

out of here by bankruptcy lawyers and asset liquidationer folk and law enforcement. She's even more of a babe up close and personal as in the pictures.

"Nope," I say.

"Well, who are you?"

"Nobody. I was curious where my money went. That's the honest truth."

Her eyes get bigger. "How'd you get on the property?"

"I parked and walked. You oughta get that gate up there fixed."

Sizing me up, she says, "One of Charles's clients, huh?"

"Afraid so."

"All the land lines have been disconnected, but I have a cell handy if I have to use it."

"I'm harmless."

"Have you seen what you came to see?"

I look around. "Guess so. Wherever you're going from here, it's gotta be a rung down from this."

"Tell me about it."

It dawns on me that I'm not being overly sensitive to her loss. The rancid son of a bitch was her husband. "Hey, listen, I'm sorry about what you been through. Must be tough."

She drops her cigarette and grinds it out with a heel. "Thanks."

She's gone as tense as a statue and her lips are quivering. I'm the sucker-victim, so how come I'm feeling like a jerk? "Sorry again. None of my business."

"Of all his cars, the '58 Corvette, the Ferrari, the Mercedes, the Escalade, any of them, the Aston Martin was his favorite. Overnight, Charles went from a master of the universe to also a victim."

I don't answer her.

"How much did Charles take you for?"

"Not a ton of money, but everything we had."

"I am so sorry."

It's getting awkward out here. "Yeah."

She lifts her glass. "Would you like a drink?"

"Little early for me."

"Vodka and grapefruit juice," she says. "You'd be doing me a favor. I'd drink the pitcher by myself. I made it extremely weak."

"In that case," I say. "We're talking serious vitamin C."

The widow Murganzer smiles and leads me into a kitchen that's befitting such a mansion. It's got marble islands (maybe Eye-talian, maybe not, but super smooth) and hanging copperware and stainless steel appliances. I cooked in smaller mess halls.

There're cardboard boxes on the countertops too.

She pours me one out of a pitcher, freshens hers, and clinks my glass. "To happier times."

"I'll drink to that," I say and do.

She extends a hand. "Lizabeth."

I shake a hand that's strong and dry for a lady's. "I'm Buddy. Buddy Whitacre."

"Some snotty columnist printed my full name. Lizabeth Chipperfield Hollis Doherty Carnahan Smithson Murganzer. He'd run out of ideas for Charles articles. I didn't steal anybody's money and didn't know Charles was, but I was guilty by association. That made me fair game, the prick."

"I think I saw the piece. Skimmed over it. I lose my

attention span after the sports section."

"They quickly lost interest too. I'm cute, but I'm broke and they're not going to prosecute me."

"Broke?"

"Long story."

She offers me a cigarette. I'm tempted. "No thanks."

She lights up and says, "I'm trespassing too, to tell you the truth. They gave me the bum's rush. I didn't have enough time to completely pack. The kitchen utensils are mine. Charles says —said I can't boil water. He was right. I collected my cookware for the look. It's lovely, don't you think, the copper and shiny metals? I may even take up cooking someday. The point is, it's mine, not the court's or the creditors'."

Cigarettes and booze are in her young voice, which doesn't make her any less sexy. "I agree. You're entitled."

"Buddy, how did Charles sink his fangs into you? Did you attend his seminars?"

I say, yeah, unfortunately we did, and tell our tale of early retirement and Spain. Somehow, my scuffle on La Rambla inserts itself prominent-like. We're sitting on stools across from each other, my elbows on the cold marble. I make fists as I give her a blow by blow. When I'm done, Lizabeth reaches over and runs a digit along my nose.

"That's how you got this?"

"Nah. My schnoz, what's left of it, that's ancient history. A misspent youth. The soccer hooligans tenderized everything else, though."

"There were eight of them?"

I shrug my ah-shucks shrug. "Roughly eight. Thereabouts."

"Awesome," she says.

I can feel myself blushing. "You do what you gotta do."

She looks past me, outside, and says, "The swallows are diving for bugs at the pond, zooming and swooping."

"I noticed."

"That would be a cool way to get your food. I like nature. I'd ask Charles why we couldn't spend some of our money to benefit nature, like saving the whales. He goes, okay, fine, let's save the whales. I'll collect the whole fucking set, quote-unquote, pardon my French."

"Sounds like he was a piece of work," I say. "If I'm disrespecting the dead too much, stop me."

She squeezes my hand. "No, no. After what he did to you and the others, he deserves no respect. Him being hustled too, he deserved it, but not with someone else's money. That cold, smug note he left on the bridge in the car? Charles did everything Charles's way to the bitter end."

She's puddling up. Over by the stove you could cook for an infantry company with there's a box of tissues. I hop up and bring it to her.

Following some sniffling and nose-blowing, she has got herself back together.

"Thank you, Buddy. Charles was a cutie and a charmer. He didn't look his age. He was pushing fifty and people thought he was my age. He had no blemishes, no scars. He had a crisp baritone voice and was so congenial. His hair gleamed. He had it swept back like the Gordon Gecko character in that 1980s greed movie I've seen on TV. He could be so dignified and formal. You'd never suspect he was dishonest. He hated being called Charlie, as he was before he struck it rich."

"I got a son-in law-like that."

"Charles showered twice a day."

"You're giving me more info than I need, Lizabeth."

"I've been married to slobs. Charles was a breath of fresh air, literally, but the longer I lived with him, the creepier his cleanliness was."

"Everyone's got their hang-ups. A headshrinker might say he was scrubbing the dirty money off."

"Not a bad analysis," Lizabeth says. "Have you been in therapy?"

"Not yet."

She lights a cigarette from the one she's smoking. "Don't bother. Trust me, psychiatry is overrated."

"Nice neighborhood," I say. "You got moneybags neighbors."

"Charles would get into a snit because they ignored him. Their intuition told them what he was. He complained that they were stuck up. I mean, what did he expect? That Melinda should bake cookies and drop on by and say howdy?"

"How'd you and Murganzer meet?"

"I'm a bartender by profession. I worked the dayshift at a restaurant near MSF. Charles would come in for lunch and hang around the lounge afterward nursing a cup of coffee. Charles wasn't a drinker or a smoker. He loved to lecture me on my vices. He loved to say that his body was a temple.

"He was mooning over me, bad habits and all. I served drinks to lots of guys who mooned over me. Guys have mooned over me since the tenth grade, when I got contact lenses and tits. My downfall.

"Well, they hired a new bar manager. He wanted to move me from weekdays to weekend nights and cut my hours because I wouldn't put out for him. By then, Charles was big-time smitten. I didn't tell him, but Charles had a way of detecting something was wrong and finding out what it was. He went ballistic.

"Most guys would get half a bag on and invite the manager outside. All that'd accomplish is me losing my job. Charles *bought* the restaurant. The same day. He fired the creep and gave him references that wouldn't win him a dishwashing job in Baghdad."

"Impressive."

"I *was* impressed. Dazzled. I fell in love with Charles then and there. What's the word? Panache. Until Charles did what he did, I'd only seen panache in the movies. Buddy, there's a hole in the bottom of your glass. Either that or your juice is evaporating."

"By golly, you're right."

Lizabeth tops off my tank and continues, "So I fell in love with Charles's panache. We were married two weeks later. Charles was a three-time loser himself, so I should have known better. I did have the good sense and bad luck to sign a prenup he had drawn up. I share the assets which no longer exist and the liabilities, which are mucho.

"See, Buddy, my problem is, I fall in love like other people catch colds. I do not as a rule fall in love with the all-American boy. My men have hang-ups, whether I recognize them at the outset or not. It's an instinct of mine, a curse. People get over colds and I get over love."

"You recovered from your Charles cold?"

"Months ago."

"You hung in there, though."

"You might say I married him for money retroactively. I can't swear on a stack of Bibles that money didn't play a teensy part in me tumbling for Charles. My other husbands were blue collar when they worked. Most didn't have a pot to piss in or a window to throw it out of."

"Martha, my wife, she'd lecture our daughter that it was just as easy to fall in love with a rich boy as a working stiff."

"Charles sold refrigerators to Eskimos."

I look at her.

"He was once the leading salesman at a Fairbanks appliance store. He was also mean as a snake. Not physically. Psychological. He was too smart to lay a hand on me. He'd call me a douche bag in one sentence and eye candy in the next."

"Think he's dead?"

She looks at me. "Do you?"

I don't reply.

"The courts are beginning the process of declaring him legally dead."

"No body," I remind her. "No corpus delectable."

"They say the evidence is overwhelmingly circumstantial. Why do you disagree?"

"I don't know. Wishful thinking maybe. If I had my druthers, I'd go upstairs and find him hiding under a bed and drag him out by an ear."

She laughs. "I'd take the other ear. Or a body part that'd be even more painful."

"Where're you staying, if I ain't being too nosy?"

"With my Daddy and his new young wife. Serial marriage seems to run in our family. I'm imposing on the honeymooners, so I'll be out of there as soon as I get a job and an apartment. You may have seen my Daddy on TV. Chick Chipperfield."

I snap my fingers. "The used car dealer commercials. When he isn't wearing a zoot suit, he dresses up in a devil's costume and smashes cars with his pitchfork, saying 'I've got a helluva deal for you'. He's famous!"

"That's my Daddy. He plays on nostalgia. Customers think he's poking fun at himself, pretending to be a crook. They find out soon that he actually is."

"He is?"

"Oh yes. Chick Chipperfield of Chipperfield's Preowned Automotive Elegance. says he's popular because he's a throwback to the 1950s, to Mad Man Muntz and Maniac Monahan and others like them before the consumer protection do-gooders, as he calls them, started interfering with free enterprise."

"I been watching his commercials lately on middle-of-the-night TV, on the old movies he sponsors. Those old TV series too, like *Hawaii Five-o*. He's got that big used car lot in the north end of Seattle on Highway 99."

"This week is the Troy Donahue Memorial Film Festival. I don't stay up late enough to watch."

I say, "Hey, you sort of look like Connie Stevens in those movies."

"I've never heard of her, but I'll take it as a compliment. Daddy told me he thought Charles was shady, saying that it takes one to know one. I didn't believe him."

"You or anybody else till it was too late. Used cars, they do not conjure fond memories for me."

"How so? Were you fleeced on one?"

"Haven't kicked a tire in years. I love my pickup truck. Bought it new. I'd get screwed if I traded it in. But that ain't it."

For crying out loud, I'm halfway through on Mom and *Girl* before I realize I am.

"That's horrible, Buddy. Can I tell you what I think?"

The big-eyed look on her face. I'm scared to ask. "Uh uh."

"You've got a thing for your mother and I've got a thing for my father."

"C'mon."

"Oh no, not *that* sort of thing. No. The girl in that painting gives you a yearning for your mother."

"Like I miss her again after all these years? Yeah. I guess I can accept that."

"We're yearning for what's gone or what never was. Just between you and me, you might not be seeing Daddy on TV much more."

Lizabeth's extremely weak drink is making me lightheaded. "How come? His commercials are sometimes better than the movie."

"Daddy is old school, with the gaudy, tacky clothes and the in-your-face style. His image doesn't fly any more. I talk to him until I'm blue in the face. Daddy can't or won't change."

"People get that way as they pack on the years. How'd he get along with your husband?"

"I never had a feel for that relationship. There was tension between them and backbiting, yet when we were together, they'd have long chats."

"Your dad wasn't an MSF investor, was he?"

"Absolutely not. Daddy once said he'd count the silverware after Charles was at his house. I didn't speak to him for a week. How wrong I was."

"You never know about somebody."

Lizabeth says, "Just between you and I, Daddy's in deep financial trouble. He's barely breaking even selling cars and selling off everything his wives didn't get in the divorces to keep his business afloat.

"He bought a lake lot between Tacoma and Bremerton when I was a child. I have many fond memories staying in the cabin in the summer. It's breaking my heart that Daddy has it on the market too."

We hear a heavy rig come down the drive. I turn and see a tow truck. It's maneuvering its rear to the rear of Lizabeth's Escalade.

She's on her feet. "Shit. This is my last car. They said they'd phone ahead. I'd've borrowed a ride from Daddy."

I follow Lizabeth outside and watch and listen to her plead her case to the driver. Can he come back for it tomorrow?

The driver's got coveralls on and a clipboard. He's flipping a remote control in his hand the bank or whoever gave him for the gate. He's listening and giving her some unsympathetic silence as he looks her up and down.

Then he jabs the remote at the rear of her Caddy and says, "You need to dump your boxes out, honey. This unit's coming with me."

I got this notion of repo men being bruisers. This one is a pencil neck with thin hair and a bloodshot nose. Looks hillbilly to me.

Lizabeth goes to do what she's told. I meanwhile slip

between the tow truck and her.

Pencilneck's driver's door's open. He's got one cowboy boot on the running board, writing on his clipboard. He looks up at me.

"You moving out of the way, Pops?"

It's the "Pops" that turns my feet to lead. "The lady made you a reasonable request."

He hops to the ground and slams his door hard. "The reasonable is that you shuffle your raggedy ass so I can do my job."

"Use your big mouth to make an appointment with the lady."

"Buddy, it's okay," Lizabeth says, hefting a box. "Let him have it. Please."

"Not okay," I say, holding eye contact with Pencilneck.

He's moved into range. He's bigger and younger than at a distance. He's rawboned and his neck veins stand out.

Seems like an hour passes by, but our staring contest lasts ten seconds max.

Pencilneck says, "I touch you, Pops, you go to the hospital and sue me."

I don't answer. He's saving face and I'd be a moron to not let him. In my youth, I'd've called him a pussy and it'd be Round One. Pencilneck gets in his truck muttering and lays rubber as he pulls out.

Lizabeth puffs up her cheeks and exhales. "Wow. I thought something was going to happen. I know when a barroom fight's going to erupt."

"Nah," I say, not all that certain at what I'm saying. "I'm likewise an authority on barroom situations and this wasn't gonna be one."

"You could've caused yourself a big problem helping me."

"I may be a dumb shit, but I ain't totally stupid. If I'm gonna be an idiot and a hothead, it might as well be for a good cause. C'mon. Let's finish loading you up."

She asks if I want another drink.

I shake my head. "If you don't mind me saying so, you ought not too yourself. We're both driving."

She does as I ask. When we're done, Lizabeth gives me a thank you and a hug that's slightly beyond friendly. A kiss on the cheek follows, then one on the mouth.

Since Martha and me started going steady, the only tongues in my mouth have been hers and my own. Till this moment.

Chapter 8

MARTHA

I pull into the driveway and gingerly swing my aching feet onto the ground. Even after the most frantic day on a Boeing shop floor, I do not remember wearing off so much shoe leather.

I go inside to Buddy at the dinette table, sipping a cup of coffee, doing nothing. This is peculiar. He is a sprawl-out-on-the-sofa man when he relaxes. And his beverage of choice comes from a brewery.

"How was your day, kiddo?" he asks.

Buddy's eyes say he's half crocked, but I do not smell beer. I sniff an aromatic combination I cannot quite put my finger on. A newspaper is open to the want ads, a positive step. The mail is in an unruly pile beside it.

I'm impatient to break my news and I do. I expect him to be flabbergasted. I expect him to be happy for me or down in the dumps or mortified or argumentative because I accepted such a position.

He simply says, "You told me this morning you were bound and determined. Good for you. Congratulations."

I did not expect a neutral reaction. I say, "Standing on my feet all day is the hardest part. Varicose veins will be blooming like spring bulbs."

"What's in the bag?"

"A surprise."

I go into the bedroom, take my uniform out, and slip it

on. Mr. Larionov went to another of his restaurants and found one that fit me. For a former commie, that man has certainly transformed himself into a can-do capitalist.

I wore it following the lunch rush and changed back into my civilian clothes when I clocked out. Our colors are light pastel blue tops and beige pants. I check myself out in the mirror. Both are a tad too snug for a lady my age.

I come out, twirling, modeling.

Buddy gives me a wolf whistle.

I lay the uniform company brochure and order form on the table, on the classified ads that have wrinkly coffee rings on them. "I'm sure I'll like the fit better on those I order. They're cut so anybody can wear them, not just the teeny size zeroes. You've seen some of those big ladies who work fast food.

"My first day on the job was an adventure. The intercom went on the fritz. We were shorthanded. Believe me, *that* is not unusual in this industry. I shuttled back and forth from the drive-up window to outside at the order board to manually take orders from customers in cars for a solid ninety minutes until Todd and Nicki came on shift and took turns relieving me. This is after duty at the inside counter. Whew!

"Those new touch-screen cash registers are a cinch once you're accustomed to them. I'd be twice as frazzled as I am tonight if not for, thank goodness, people being conditioned to bus their trays and toss their garbage, most people anyway. Teenagers are the laziest. It's like Boeing, Buddy, where everybody to an extent is a slave to rote and that isn't an entirely bad thing.

"Felipe is training me. He's been there for seven and a

half months and has more seniority than anyone except Shawn, the manager, and Mr. Larionov, the owner. Felipe once worked in the chain's Los Angeles restaurants and also in the kitchens of real restaurants. Felipe prefers fast food to sit-down because the cooks aren't temperamental, throwing tantrums over how someone prepared the duck stock or deglazed a saucepan.

"Fast food customers do not demand menu substitutions. Felipe likes that too and I can understand why. You order by number. Number Nine on the lunch menu, for instance, is the bacon cheeseburger, large fries, and medium soft drink. Five is the plain hamburger, regular fries, small soft drink. We're running a special on Eleven, the El Acapulco ChickenWich. The chicken isn't deep-fried and the guacamole is scrumptious. It is only three-ninety-five, good through Wednesday.

"So. How was your day?"

While I catch my breath and await his reply, Buddy goes to the stove for more coffee. He's wearing a loopy smile. It must be beer or whatever it was he consumed. Regardless, it was too many, too much. Buddy, the old fool, cannot guzzle a six-pack like he used to without becoming silly. If he thinks coffee will cure what's ailing him, he has another think coming. In his younger days, you wouldn't know he had touched a drop.

"Not nearly as interesting as yours," he says, sitting down and patting the want ads. "I'm kinda getting a lay of the land."

"Did anything jump off the page at you?"

"Not really. Except that I'm a square peg in a round hole."

"Well, you're starting. A job will materialize. I know it will."

"Uh huh."

"Tell me the truth, are you upset I'm working fast food?"

He takes a little too long to answer. "Nah. You're doing what you gotta do. It's kind of a shock, though, you in junk food."

His reaction has been too quiet. He hasn't even asked what I'm making per hour, the most basic of questions. The phone rings.

"Mother."

I hear background noise. Melanie's in the car.

"How are you, dear?"

"We're fine, Mother. We're on our way back from Arlington."

I know why. Arlington is north of Everett, where their countertops were made or polished, or this is the company that installed them. I can't keep it straight.

"How did it go?"

"We can give you the details in person."

"That would be wonderful. Where are you?"

"We got off the freeway at the mall and are on the highway."

Less than five minutes away. "You are close."

"I hope we're not barging in, Mother. Four-oh-five is gridlocked. David said you wouldn't mind if we killed some time with you until traffic cleared."

"Not a problem," I say. "You kids scoot right on over."

I hang up and tell Buddy. "It's short notice, but that's David for you. We're a convenience to him."

"Everyone's got marble countertops except us."

"Excuse me?"

He says quickly, "Who's handling the world's gynecologicing emergencies?"

"Be nice about David even if I can't."

"They're checking up on us."

"If they are, that means they love us. Please tidy up the table and stash those classifieds. Oh my God!"

"What?"

"Look at me," I say, looking down at me.

I hurry into the bedroom to change as heavy tires crunch our driveway gravel. They're in their Range Rover. I am reminded of Marlin Perkins in that old show, *Wild Kingdom*, bounding through the savanna, chasing gazelles. It's too late to change. The shirt is a pullover. I'd muss my hair and there's no time for a repair job.

I throw on my bathrobe. My pants are too long. I roll them up. I'll have to wash and iron my uniform for tomorrow anyway. Hopefully the robe will conceal the grease odor.

"Mother," Melanie says in the doorway. "Are you sick? It's a warm day."

"Sick? Oh, my robe and slippers. We had a stiff breeze a while ago. I felt a chill."

"We got funny wind patterns in this community. It can whip through," Buddy says, helping me. "Who can choke down a libation?"

"I'm driving, Dad," David says. "Do you have a Perrier or an Evian?"

"Not unless they're pumping it out of the tap, Dave."

I offer to make a pitcher of lemonade from a can of

frozen concentrate. Melanie and David take me up on it. I swear Buddy mumbles something that sounds like citrus overdose. He fills glasses with ice and out we go to the deck with our drinks. Our little yard and our stained wood deck that Buddy built with his own two hands are cozy. We have a man-high fence in the rear, so we're relatively secluded.

Of course David dominates the conversation.

"I had a light appointment schedule today. It was worth juggling the remainder to get this headache resolved. Sarah and Julie are tearing their hair out, making the rescheduling calls."

"Sarah and Julie are David's office managers," Melanie explains.

Buddy nods.

I thought it was Sue and Kathleen. Not important. Everybody has turnover, don't I know.

"I don't play hooky often and strictly for a good cause. Melanie and I had a meeting of the minds with the countertop people."

"Good," I say.

"It isn't just the kitchen," David says. "There are matching marble tops in the bathrooms and the rec room wet bar. The investment is significant."

"I can imagine," I say.

"They'll be out in the morning," Melanie says.

Buddy is stifling a yawn with a fist.

"They claim it isn't the quality of the stone," David goes on. "They claim it was quarried at Carrara. Did you know that Michelangelo insisted on white Carrara marble for his sculptures?"

"He did that gal with no arms?" Buddy asks.

"No, not *Venus de Milo*," David corrects. "*Venus* is Greek. As a sculptor, Michelangelo is best known for *David*."

Buddy opens his mouth, apparently to ask another question, but decides not to.

"They showed us the supporting papers from Carrara," Melanie says.

"They claim the polishing is done in Italy. It's quarried, cut to the contractor's specs, and shipped. They concede that they didn't check the work closely enough."

"I brought up the issue of dust blowing all over the house," Melanie says.

"The polishers employ a wet-sanding process," David says. "They claim they were trained in Italy."

"More lemonade?" I say, lifting the pitcher.

David raises a hand. "Not me. I'm already carrying enough processed liquid into uncertain traffic."

"Mother, are you sure you're all right?" Melanie asks. "You look hot in that robe. Hot and tired."

I am positively sweltering and cannot wait to change. I would dearly love to kick off my slippers too and air out my throbbing dogs. The bottoms of my feet must be as red as lobsters.

"I feel fine, dear. Perfect."

"How's it going with you guys?" David asks in an interviewing tone of voice.

"Life of leisure," Buddy says, smiling. "It's tough."

I smile in agreement.

"When are your neighbors returning home from Portland?" Melanie asks.

"Good question," I answer, looking at Buddy.

He shrugs. "I thought yesterday, today at the latest. The Hendricks are retired too. They got no timetable."

David leads us into small talk on monetary topics. The fluctuating price of gasoline. Their cars take super unleaded, ours regular, twenty cents a gallon difference. Inflation and the prime rate jumped a fraction last month, not cheery news for those on fixed incomes. I have to wonder if he's fishing again.

Buddy and I maintain our poker faces. The conversation runs dry and the kids go. I compliment Buddy on his restrained behavior toward David as I change. He asks if I want to go out to eat to celebrate. The buffet we like is nearby and has an $8.95 Senior Early Bird Dinner.

"The change jar loot burnt a hole in my pocket. Got thirty-one dollars and eighty-six cents."

"I'm bushed," I say.

"Me too, kinda sorta," he says, reaching into the freezer compartment for a stack of dinners. "Take your pick. I'll do the honors."

I select the honey-roasted pork. Nothing fried for me today, thank you very much. Buddy goes for the meatloaf and nukes them. I trust him in the kitchen no further than the microwave, provided he has read the package directions. The United States Army damaged my husband's culinary skills beyond repair.

Fast food is perhaps not outside his capabilities, however, though it might test his temperament. What I accomplished today might put a bug in his ear. Buddy and I together could earn $20 per hour to start, far less than either of us drew at Boeing.

Jim and Ellen probably get by on less too, if that's any

consolation. We'll organize a reasonable payment schedule for our debts and survive. If our creditors don't like it, they can lump it. You know what they say about blood from a turnip.

We try to watch TV. First the local news. An anchorwoman, just as cute as a button, says that Charles Murganzer was spotted in Honduras.

"Bosh," I say. "He's dead."

Buddy's wheels are turning. He finally says, "Besides, he couldn't put up with the filth they have in those poor, hot countries."

"Why do you say that?"

He shrugs. "Everyone knows he was a cleanliness freak."

Evidently everybody but me.

Later, they are rerunning shows we didn't much like the first time around. Orange and Tangerine and I are on the couch. Buddy dozes off in his recliner. I nudge him awake and aim him toward bed. This is a sign he might get a decent night's sleep for a change. He won't be in front of the boob tube, sound lowered so not to disturb me. I cannot conceive what dreck he tunes in at that hour.

As soon as my uniform is out of the dryer and I iron it, I'm ready to hit the sack too. I have the early shift. Our duties include straightening up the establishment prior to the 6 AM opening.

The dryer buzzes. Before my final chore of the day, I check the mail. I discard the junk. The bills can wait until tomorrow, especially the pieces with the red ink. Stridency will get you nowhere.

There is a manila envelope from Stanley Whitacre. How

odd. The two brothers never correspond. Not unless you count that bushwa in Madrid. To my knowledge, Buddy never did contact his brother and has not offered to explain what the sneakiness was all about.

Even odder, Buddy hasn't opened it.

What could it possibly be? I do hope Stan and the woman he's currently married to – I don't recall her name – aren't ill.

Buddy and I do not open each other's mail. It's an invasion of privacy and technically a federal offense. I replace the mysterious envelope where I find it. I pick up the Lotto ticket that's underneath.

Buddy paid a dollar for two tries at a fortune. He seldom buys lottery tickets. I have no idea what the jackpot is up to this week. My poor desperate man. I put the ticket by the phone.

I trudge to the utility room. It is an enclosed back porch. Our washer and dryer are there, along with ironing board and clothes hamper. The cats have a corner for litter box and food dishes.

Buddy had peeled off his shirt on the way to bed. It's half hanging out of the hamper. I sigh and pick it up. I smell what I smelled when I got home. I didn't recognize it because it was mingled with other odors.

I do now.

It is perfume and the perfume isn't mine.

Chapter 9

BUDDY

After a night of tossing and turning, Martha's up long before the chickens. Unlike yesterday, she's not taking any pains to pussyfoot around and avoid waking up the cats and me. Martha's slammed every drawer and cabinet in the house as she prepares to go off to work. Twice. Orange and Tangerine, they've vamoosed.

Out of self-preservation, I fake sleep, eyes clenched shut, covers pulled over my head. I try for the life of me to figure out how come I'm up so high on her shit list. Might be cuz her nose was twitching from the minute she walked in the door from her new job. It's an old wives' tale that you can't smell vodka on a person's breath, not when your drinks are as extremely weak as Lizabeth Murganzer makes them.

Add onto that a less than proactive job-hunting effort by yours truly. Having the help wanted section spread out on the table is one thing. Mainly for show, if a person's inclined to be sarcastic.

Then there's this possibility. Had me another Madrid Ricky dream while snoozing during my insomnia. Ricky confided to *Señor* that Lucy had gone frigid on him and what should he do? For crying out loud, I'm not Abigail Van Landers or somebody, but I tell him to try flowers and candy. If that doesn't do the trick, get her drunk. And in addition, Brady Hardcastle was at Ricky's side. He had on suspenders, a porkpie hat, and no face.

Could be I was advising Ricky in my sleep. Martha overheard and took it out of context.

Irregardless, if you think Martha's grouchy this morning, I'm lucky she didn't find out how I took on my vodka glow and who gave it to me. She'd have a cow. The racket she made, I'll accept it as a wake-up call. I'm gonna try to be positive about the situation.

I kick off my AM routine by shaking the cat food sack to entice the boys from under the couch, where they rode out Hurricane Martha. Normally they're at their bowl, screaming their orange heads off. I spruce up, fortify myself with strong black coffee, and flatten out yesterday's ads. The kinds of jobs I'm qualified for, it's a safe bet they'll still be open to qualified applicants.

I circle the JANITOR listings. I'm confident I can master the job duties quick, though Martha complains that I don't pick up after myself. There is a distinction between amateur and pro status.

I'll tell you what, I am brutally pissed that Martha had to go and jump into junk food. Her on her feet all day frying potatoes. I double up my fists wishing I could resurrect Charles Murganzer back to life and put him out of his misery my ownself.

There are four janitor openings. This one I'm calling pays $9.50 to $10.75 per hour DOE. I'm trying to remember what Martha said they're paying her. Don't recall that she ever did.

I look at yesterday's mail, neatly piled up, the fliers tossed out, Martha's touch. I look at Stan's envelope. I think about what Lizabeth said about yearnings. I think about her friendly kiss of appreciation. It's harder to get off my mind than Stan's envelope. How friendly and innocent a kiss is and how far past friendly it is, it's in your interpretation. Lizabeth, she's of a younger generation and she's been around. I have no delusionals about her and me, even if I was hot to cheat on Martha, which I ain't.

I'm in geezer territory. Having a half-naked young babe grinding up against me, you can excuse me if my reaction is to be on the verge of a dizzy spell. Right now I don't need to be stirring up my yearnings and whatever else when I got so much else on my mind. Lizabeth, she has *Girl* popping up in my thoughts left and right. I don't need that neither. I set Stan's envelope under the bills.

The mail truck pulls up. The mailman, a lady, comes to the door. I take mostly bills and fliers from her. The reason I'm getting this personal service is a registered letter I gotta sign for.

I tear off the postal sticker and see that it's from a law firm in New York City. I'm not any more thrilled about opening this envelope than Stan's, but I go ahead and do. When this is all said and done, we're gonna have lawyers coming out of our ears.

This New York City lawyer, his firm is the U.S. contact for a British solicitor in London, England. He's assisting in behalf of their client, Mr. Trevor Greenhenge. I know who Mr. Trevor Greenhenge is. Madrid Ricky told me. Trevor Greenhenge is Stringbean.

The equipment I crunched with my size 9 1/2 D is what this letter's pertaining to. As a result of my violent and unprovoked attack on their client, an innocent tourist visiting Barcelona, Spain, Mr. Greenhenge has suffered continuous pain and is disabled. Mr. Greenhenge is unable to resume his employment as a day laborer in the rendering industry. My "blatant culpability" in the assault has been verified by the appropriate Spanish law enforcement authorities. There is also a loss of consortium issue.

More gobblygook follows. What this lawyer's saying is that I oughta immediately contact them regarding a settlement in order to avoid litigation. He's wrote "immediately" in plump black letters in case I'm blind and miss his point.

Fuck this lawyer and the horse he rode in on.

This is the living end. I'm as steamed as I ever get.

I wanna throw something.

I reach for the phone to tell the lawyer what he can do with his blatant culpabilities. I'm wishing now Melanie had married the whiplash shyster. One thing's for sure, Madrid Ricky Ricardo is getting even cuz he couldn't pin anything on me and get a promotion. He's feeding these buzzards a crock of guano about me being the bad guy, encouraging them. Probably hasn't stopped pouting since we said our farewells.

I put the receiver back down, thinking that we're already so deep in the hole we can't see daylight. So what if they dig that hole deeper, all the way to China, be my guest. Also gotta question whether they actually can do this across international lines. I stick the letter under Stan's envelope. These two mailings, they're happening to me on account of we traipsed halfway around the world, culture and art appreciating. Life, it can be strange.

I reach for the phone again, to get the janitorial show on the road.

It rings first.

"Mr. Whitacre? Buddy?"

I'm braced for the growing bill collector invasion that's seeming like D-Day to the Nazis. I tell the lady, "Who the hell wants to know?"

The lady laughs. "Buddy, please don't yell. This is Lizabeth Chipperfield. I looked you up in the phone book."

"Who?"

"I was Lizabeth Murganzer when you rescued my car."

"Right, right."

"I woke up this morning and made a decision. I'm taking my maiden name back. I'm Lizabeth Chipperfield from here on. Should I remarry, highly unlikely, I'm Chipperfield till death do me part."

"Good policy."

"You need a job, don't you?"

"Afraid so."

"Daddy."

"Huh?"

"My Daddy, Chick Chipperfield. You could work for my father."

"Me in used cars? C'mon. I don't have a fast mouth."

"Chipperfield's Preowned Automotive Elegance is a large operation," Lizabeth says. "You wouldn't be selling. There are other jobs. Daddy is always searching for good people for support jobs."

"I don't know."

"Daddy says he'd like to interview you."

"You talked to him?"

"I took the liberty of laying the groundwork. I put in a good word. Daddy's doing a shoot today."

"A what?"

"The station's videotaping. Daddy's shooting a new commercial insert at the lot shortly. Heather and I are going to watch. Heather's my stepmommy, Mrs. Heather Chipperfield."

I hear giggling in the background.

"What are you doing in an hour?" Lizabeth goes on.

"I got a hunch you're gonna tell me."

~ ~ ~

Chick Chipperfield's car lot is half an hour south of Three Lakes Luxury Estates when traffic's not too god-awful. Prior to the freeways, Highway-99 was the main north-south route if you wanted to get from Vancouver to Tijuana and anywhere in between.

The commerce on this stretch of highway's a mixed bag. There are some motor courts that look like they came out of a 1925 time warp except for the gals standing out in front of them in purple go-go boots. There's gas stations and muffler shops and convenience stores and greasy spoons and strip malls and gun shops.

Old 99 provides you any number of ways to buy a car, new or used, and stores that'll sell you parts when they break down. Chipperfield's Preowned Automotive Elegance is easy to spot. It's in the remains of a belly-up new car dealer. I forget which one. They come and they go.

Chick Chipperfield's got a showroom and service bay combo of a building and plenty of lot space. The wood siding could use paint and the revolving neon sign on top has changed lettering too many times to count. Chipperfield's lot's full of his specialties, hot sporty cars and yupmobiles that look to me to be a tad past their prime. On

TV lately, he's been calling Chipperfield's Preowned Automotive Elegance a "superstore".

It's not opening time yet and the lot's roped off. There's activity by the showroom, some people and a camera on a tripod. I see Lizabeth off to a side at her Caddy SUV, arms folded. She waves me over. Lizabeth's wearing painted-on jeans and an I ♥ SEATTLE T-shirt.

"Glad you made it, Buddy. Heather's inside helping Daddy change into his costume. Tonight's movie is *Palm Springs Weekend*. Daddy wants to feature cars that appeal to younger buyers."

"Never been to a Hollywood function."

"You'll like Daddy. You'll like Heather too. I did as soon as I got past her being five years younger than me and the fact her favorite drink is a rum Shirley Temple. Would you believe, they're talking about having babies? I'll be going through menopause while my stepsiblings are in high school."

"How'd they meet, your daddy and his bride?"

"Heather was Daddy's hairdresser. She's a sweetie, but I wouldn't personally let her within ten feet of my tresses. Daddy says he fell in love with the job she did on his comb-over and how her sensitive fingers worked miracles for his scalp circulation. It went from there. You can regard her as a trophy wife, although I feel she genuinely loves him. Her own father went out for a pack of cigarettes when she was nine years old and that's the last she's seen of him. Don't tell anyone I said so, but Daddy fulfills more than one role."

Yearnings and hang-ups. I'm up to my eyeballs in 'em. Chick Chipperfield comes outside in his devil's costume. It's red plastic, made shiny by the sun. Has got to be as hot as you-know-where. He's a heavyset fella too. What he's wearing is stiff and tight. He's semi-waddling, using his pitchfork as a cane. Heather Chipperfield, I assume, trails behind, holds up his tail, like the whatchamacallit of a wedding dress, till Chick's in front of the camera.

Young Mrs. Chipperfield comes on over and Lizabeth introduces us. Heather's dimpled and blonde and freckled. She's bursting out of shorts and top that makes Lizabeth's outfits look like nunwear. Her hair's not big, it's huge. She's on the big-boned side and is already getting cottage cheese thighs. Heather Chipperfield will be plump at 40, to put it mildly. But nobody's worrying about that right now.

"How do," she says to me and then to Lizabeth, "Chickypoo's grumpy. He overdid margaritas last night, him and his salesmen at their weekly marketing meeting. I tell him, hon, what's you're doing encased in plastic is better than a sauna."

Chipperfield's taken his position at the fender of a jacked-up Camaro with a hood scoop. It's got a $3999 price on the windshield, next to a SUPER PERFORMANCE ON A BUDGET sign.

Lizabeth whispers, "He doesn't damage cars that are worth a ton of money. Like this beater Camaro, Bruno will arrange a slam-bang repair and they'll wholesale it out. If the car's really running bad, they'll haul it off to the junkyard to be put to sleep."

"Bruno?"

"Daddy's service manager. Shh."

They're rolling, however those TV and movie people say it. Chick's jabbing his pitchfork at the Camaro, saying, "You don't have to breathe anybody's exhaust fumes, not at the wheel of this rocket, not if you can afford one-thirty-nine per month, financed right here on the spot at Chipperfield's Preowned Automotive Elegance Superstore. Your past credit glitches are not, I repeat, are not a problem."

Then Chipperfield swings his pitchfork like he's chopping wood and mashes the Camaro's hood, creating a major dent. Now he's taking aim at a Honda Civic on the other side of him. It's got a spoiler and custom taillights and a big chrome tailpipe, the way kids these days soup up their cars.

He clobbers the spoiler, busting it clean in half. "Five bucks worth of baling wire and tape, guys, and this baby's still a chick magnet. Seventy-nine ninety-nine, *zee-row* down. Negative credit history doesn't exist once you step on these premises. Our financial wizards are here to serve you."

Chipperfield gives the spoiler another whack and yells, "I've got a helluva deal for you!"

The cameraman says, "Nice job, Chick."

Chipperfield peels off the headpiece and horns, and wipes sweat off his forehead. "Hey, they don't call me One Take Chipperfield for nothing."

One Take and Heather, long red tail in her hand, trudge back indoors.

Lizabeth tells me, "The regular spots have been taped. This is sale filler on Daddy's specials to be inserted tonight. He's a natural on camera, isn't he? He just lights up. He should be in show biz. "

"I thought he was," I say.

"Daddy'll see you after he's changed."

"I don't know, Lizabeth. Haven't interviewed for a job in thirty-some years."

Lizabeth's got me by the arm, steering me to the showroom. She shoves me through the doorway.

"It's like riding a bicycle, Buddy."

I wait in there with a Porsche and two Corvettes. I see some hairline fiberglass cracks on one of the 'Vettes. There's a piece of cardboard underneath the Porsche's engine compartment, to catch the drips. The superstore showroom smells of rubber and grease.

The Chipperfields return. Heather gives her Chickypoo a smack on the cheek and goes out to her stepdaughter. Chipperfield waves me into this sardine can of an office that's a desk, two chairs and a calculator. Reminds me of the Barcelona interrogation room where the *gendarmes* first took my statement. Must be where they wrap up deals with customers whether they're anxious to buy or not.

On the wall behind his desk are three framed pictures. Jesus is on the left, Richard Nixon in the middle. On the right is some wild-eyed character with a winking smirk and a hat that's a little like Napoleon's, who's standing against what looks like a tailfin of a 1957 De Soto.

He shakes my hand. "Heard you stuck up for my baby girl yesterday, Buddy."

Chick Chipperfield sports an all-season tan. He isn't a whole bunch younger than me. Chick's in green slacks, blue shirt, green-and-purple checked jacket, and radioactive purple tie. His patent leather shoes and belt are color-coordinated beige.

I shrug my aw-shucks shrug. "Did what anyone would do. That repo boy was nasty and unreasonable."

Chick nods. "Lizzie's going through rough times, no fault of her own. I told her Murganzer was a crook, but like they say, love is blind."

"Did you know Murganzer well?" I ask.

Chick rocks a hand. "Not well enough. You couldn't help but like him even when you know his paw's in your pocket."

"Did he seem like the suicidal type?"

"I thought this was a job interview and I was doing the interviewing."

"Sorry. Just curious."

"Anybody'd be suicidal if his back's up against the wall. He stiffed you too, huh?"

"Sure did."

"Took a bunch of good folks to the cleaners, the bastard. I'm not a religious man, but I have to hope Chaz is down there with the Stinko Prince, shoveling sulfur."

The Jesus portrait must be for show. "I'm with you."

"There are guys like Chaz in my profession, Buddy. They keep honest merchants like me constantly under the gun from consumer protection busybodies. Used cars. Two four-letter words as far as they're concerned."

"Ain't fair," I say to be polite.

"Lizzie's my only offspring I'm currently on speaking terms with, so her recommendation is gospel to me. What can you do?"

I stop and think. "I'm handy."

"Handy?"

"Yeah. I can maintain and repair stuff."

"What kind of stuff?"

"Mainly household chore stuff and our own vehicles,

what I can do to 'em in my driveway. My pickup has got a hundred and seventy thousand miles and runs like a charm."

"The fancy new computers and systems they have in cars these days, any experience there?"

"I'm kinda light in that area."

"Non-automotive, like plumbing and cleanup and general maintenance?"

"I can take the leak out of a faucet. Can putty a window."

"Ever been in trouble with the law?"

"Not in this country."

"Close enough. I need an associate maintenance superintendent. You'd be reporting to my service manager. Pays fifteen bucks an hour. Interested?"

"I am. Gotta discuss it with the missus."

"Not a problem. Let me know by tomorrow?"

"Can do."

"Any questions?"

"Just curious again. Ever run into a guy in the used car business named Brady Hardcastle?"

Chapter 10

MARTHA

On a day of roller coaster ups and downs, I end up on cloud nine.

And, no, I am not manic-depressive. That assistant manager who hadn't shown up for work when Mr. Larionov hired me? His name is Tim. He repeated his vanishing act today. We had a management crisis shortly after we opened and Tim was not on the clock. He later called in ill, yes, but that is no comfort when there's an executive decision to be made at 6:30 A.M.

A tractor-trailer appeared from the chain's regional commissary. Granted, this is unusually early. But as the driver explained, they not only didn't replace a driver who quit, they expanded his route by six restaurants. Isn't that par for the course in today's business world?

It was an ordinary frozen and refrigerated shipment: meat patties and eggs and individual pies and milkshake base and case upon case of French fries. Regardless, everything had to be unloaded and checked off and, most importantly, signed for by an employee holding the rank of assistant manager or higher. Jerry, the driver, wouldn't bend the rules. I didn't blame him. It was his job on the line.

The breakfast rush was in full bloom. It was all Felipe and Josie and Steve and Barb and Miranda and I could do to keep up, let alone get the supplies into the cooler and Jerry down the road. Well, I took the bull by the horns and located Shawn's home phone number in his chaotic, cluttered, little office. I awakened him out of a sound sleep and outlined our crisis.

I had met Shawn briefly. I'm impressed by him as a person and by his laid-back management style. Yesterday was his normal day off, yet he came in for a while in the afternoon. He wasn't due until around 10 today. He closes up most nights, so he puts in the hours. I felt terrible calling him. It also crossed my mind that my second day on the job would be my last.

Shawn did not lose his temper. He did not fire me. He sighed and mumbled unintelligibly until he was fully awake. He must be resigned to such disruptions. I don't know where he lives but he arrived 15 minutes later and supervised the delivery, with my volunteered assistance. I don't know how old Shawn is either. I have a hunch the acne makes him appear younger than he is.

After lunchtime, Mr. Larionov came by. I was invited to sit down with him and Shawn in Shawn's office, whereupon they promoted me to Early Shift Assistant Manager, Tim's job. A battlefield promotion, Mr. Larionov termed it. My initiative is a rare quality, he went on to say.

My increase in pay brings me to $11.50 an hour. No, not a dazzling jump, but not bad for two days on the job. My probationary review is in eight weeks. Another raise is not out of the question.

I'm on our street, nearly home. Perhaps it's the euphoria of the moment and the hubbub of the day, but I've simmered down about the perfume-drenched shirt. I simply had no time to fret. On my short, infrequent breaks, I kept my senses by practicing what I learned in brain aerobics class.

I did mental calisthenics by mentally reciting the alphabet backwards and the more challenging exercise of picking an arbitrary number and counting ahead in increased increments of one: 819 820 822 825 829 834 –. I was in the high eight hundreds before losing track. It's like doing crunches and pushups with your gray matter. You're supposed to regard the brain as a muscle. A side benefit of brain aerobics is distraction from your problems.

Such as, is Buddy in the early stages of satyriasis? If I am belaboring this worry, well, they say on the talk shows that it can strike hard and fast, like the swine flu. Buddy has been listless in a number of ways since Spain. This has not been a bone of contention as far as I am concerned, not until the perfume.

I am being silly. We have not cheated on each other in four decades of marriage. I know this to be a fact. My rival is Salvador Dalí's sister, Ana Maria. Should she be alive, she would be over 100, perhaps confined to a wheelchair in a Catalonian old folks' home. She is not flesh and blood competition.

I may be rationalizing, but I'm willing to write off the perfume as – as I don't know what. Is "aberration" the proper word? My Buddy could have been at the mall and passed too close to a department store fragrance counter. Those little girls are trigger-happy with their demonstration spritzers. Anything's possible.

The perfume has no logical explanation. An attempt to do so by my husband would have been considerate.

Oh well.

Buddy, bless his heart, has the tailgate down on his

truck. His toolbox is open, beer can beside it. He's sorting wrenches and screwdrivers, cleaning them with a rag. Could this mean gainful employment?

He looks warily at me as I pull into the driveway. I wonder if he's figured out why I was on the warpath this morning. If he hasn't, let him stew in his own juices. Two can play the male's non-communication game.

"You're industrious," I say cheerfully, getting out.

"Might be that I'm gonna be industrious, for real," he says, wiping a box wrench with a rag and tossing it into the box with a clunk. "That's how come I'm getting myself organized. I'll be responsible for my own tools."

"Please tell me."

"Got me a solid offer to be associate maintenance superintendent at a car dealership."

"That's fantastic. Which dealership?"

"Chipperfield's. He's up on the highway. Sells luxury used cars. Pre-owned. It's a superstore."

"Is he that character who dresses in a devil's costume and behaves like a maniac?"

"In person, Chick, he's a level-headed guy."

"Well, if you feel comfortable there, goodness, why not? How did you find the job? In the paper?"

"Uh, no, I kinda fell into it."

That's a mysterious answer if I ever heard one. Buddy has that expression on his face he had yesterday. He's not telling me everything and it really doesn't matter. I'll burst if I don't tell my news, so I do.

When I'm through, Buddy says that's great and gives me a kiss and a hug. I can name at least three neighbors who are certain to be peeking between their curtains and I don't give a damn. To my relief, I don't smell any perfume on him. I smell honest perspiration and afternoon beer.

"Chipperfield's starting me out at fifteen per."

"That puts us at twenty-six-fifty.

"How much per year?" Buddy asks.

I get out the pocket calculator. "If we work fifty weeks a year, fifty-three thousand."

We stand there for a minute leaning against Buddy's truck. I take a drink of his beer. We were earning double that at Boeing. We were drawing a healthy percentage of our working wages from Murganzer Stable Fund, exceeding what they say you need to retire without altering your lifestyle.

I savor our titles. Early Shift Assistant Manager. Associate Maintenance Superintendent. Yes, the titles and four dollars will buy you a latte. But they do massage the ego.

"We can make it," I finally say. "Our creditors will cooperate or we'll threaten bankruptcy."

"We wouldn't go bankrupt." Buddy is shaking his head so violently I'm afraid he'll give himself a concussion. "Never."

I squeeze his hand. "No, dear, I know we wouldn't, but they won't know that. We'll bluff them if they force us into a corner."

"They'll play ball, kiddo. Damn straight," Buddy says, raising a fist. "Or else."

"Yes they will. We'll have a smidgen left over if we're careful."

"Yeah?"

"I'll sharpen my pencil and do a budget on my day off."

"For your painting class and stuff," Buddy says. "Definitely. Hell, yes."

"And you."

"Whatever it is I wanna do in my spare time."

"You don't have to take the first thing that comes along to please me," I tell him. "If you're uncomfortable in that environment, working for that man."

"I know. I'm gonna sleep on it."

"I think Murganzer is alive," he says out of the blue.

"This is becoming unhealthy."

"Show me the body."

A horn blares behind us. I almost leap out of my shoes. A Cadillac sedan eases into the Hendrick's driveway. It's gold and a mile long and is so brand-spanking-new it doesn't have license plates yet.

Jim and Ellen open the doors and climb out. You can smell the leather from here. I stare, speechless.

"Welcome home," Buddy says. "What bank did you rob?"

The Hendricks are grinning from ear to ear.

Jim answers, "Better than that. One of their bigger lottery games down there."

Buddy shakes his head. "You're kidding."

Jim is a lean, leathery man without a hair on his head. I swear there's soot imbedded under his fingernails from all the furnaces he repaired throughout his working life.

"We're not kidding," he says, "Ellen deserves the credit. I deserve half the money."

Ellen and I hug. She's plump and silver-haired and comes up to my shoulder. Every dress in her closet is a flower print.

She's holding my arms, saying, "Martha, I still can't believe it. I have to pinch myself."

Buddy hustles inside and brings out beers all around. Jim opens his and says, "We were at this grocery store."

"Jim Junior's working nights at the warehouse this month, right outside of Portland. Marcy was holding down the fort with Jimmy the Trey and Angie."

"Angie had been coughing and had a fever," Ellen says. "Seven-year-olds scare the living daylights out of you. One second they're normal, bright-eyed and bushy-tailed. The next they're running a one-oh-two."

Jim says, "The pharmacy's in the supermarket where they shop. We been sponging off them so Ellen made up a list of things they were low on."

"There's no sales tax in Oregon, which is nice."

"Ellen picked the numbers."

"We were in a checkout line where they have the lottery cards in a rack."

"Above the *National Enquirers*."

"There's this little machine you can swipe your debit card in too."

"The machine picks your numbers if you want it to," Jim says. "Tell 'em what you did."

"No machine picks my numbers. I took a card out of the rack and marked in our date of births.. I did Junior's and Marcy's too. A dollar ticket. Two chances for a buck."

"Ours was the winner."

"We'd never played the Washington lottery, never once."

"Remember how I couldn't ever talk Ellen into going to Vegas with you guys?"

"I remember," I say.

"We did this on impulse. Don't ask me why."

"Have to pinch myself again," Ellen says, pinching herself on the wrist.

"The jackpot was ten-point-five million is what it was," Jim says. "We'll be able to keep up with you guys now, you jet-set world travelers."

Ellen says, "We chose to take the money as a lump sum. You can do that or you can spread the payments out over time. We don't have twenty years, not twenty good years."

Jim cringes. "The tax man took his cut off the top. Ouch."

Ellen says, "We're going to have to hire us a financial advisor or somebody like that. We'll invest the money smart so the kids and grandkids are cared for."

Jim's grin returns. "Invest wisely except for what we're driving."

They are Cadillac lovers. They worshipped them within their means. Their shoebox-shaped Sedan Deville, long ago paid for, was in mint condition. Jim washed it weekly, weather permitting.

"We drove by Cadillac on our way back from collecting our winnings and saw the new models," Ellen says.

"Lined up in a row, just for us. We went past, looked at each other, and went and turned around."

"The hardest part was picking out the color."

"You guys're in some hotshot investment deal that takes good care of your finances, didn't you say? You swore by it when you went out at Boeing," Jim says. "Maybe that's the deal for us too."

Buddy clears his throat. "There's proving to be pros and

cons in that situation. There's gonna be pros and cons in every situation. I'd go with your own financial experts, whatever they think you oughta do. Maybe get a second opinion before signing on the dotted line."

I see tiny Hendricks frowns forming and step in before they can give Buddy's morose statement further thought. "I agree. There are numerous options out there. What's right for us may not necessarily be right for you and vice versa. You guys come on in. Have you eaten? I can whip something up in a minute."

"I'll do the honors." Buddy thumps his chest. "King of the microwave."

The Hendricks decline. They're tired and have to unpack. They do want to hear all about Spain and what's new in our lives. We agree to make a dinner date toward the end of the week at our favorite buffet.

Jim does come over later. It's been a warm day and it isn't cooling off significantly. Buddy takes the portable TV out on the deck. They're watching the Mariners, at home versus Kansas City. Ellen has an open invitation to visit when the boys are watching their sports, but her vacuum is going. The walls in these homes are not as thick as they could be, although they are properly insulated. She is an immaculate housekeeper, bordering on fussy. It's my theory Ellen chased Jim out, said go next door to be polite.

I take this quiet time to go through today's mail. Buddy's envelope from brother Stan remains sealed. A new piece of correspondence on fancy stationery from New York has been opened. It's in the pile, envelope half torn off, fair game.

I grit my teeth after the second reading. As if we don't

have enough worries. How dare they, this Greenhenge hooligan animal and his shysters! My man was a *hero*, coming to the aid of that little Indian shopkeeper. I take the letter. Buddy will either ignore it or call somebody up and tell them to go to hell.

I shall handle this. I have an idea.

I'm at the dinette with lemonade. It feels so good to sit. I'm not as beat as yesterday, but my dogs are tingling.

Why is Ellen's vacuum cleaner annoying me? I can barely hear it.

Buddy and I completely forgot to give them their presents, the purse and wallet from Toledo. They'll come in handy after their bonanza.

It'll never be the same between us and the Hendricks. I would be naïve to believe otherwise. We're not just in different tax brackets, we're in different worlds. Our relationship already has changed. I can tell. I have those vibrations. I love Jim and Ellen to death and I am delighted for them. I'm also human and the human part of me is a green-eyed monster.

Earlier, when he came in for dinner, Buddy phoned that preposterous car dealer and said he'd take the job. He starts at Chipperfield's Preowned Automotive Elegance in the morning. I have my trepidations about him going to work for that man. I recall reading of consumer protection complaints. The Better Business Bureau probably has a thick dossier on Mr. Chick Chipperfield. On the same token, while Buddy tries to conceal his feelings, he is not thrilled about me being in fast food.

We do what we have to do.

I go to the edge of the deck. The Mariners are trailing

two-zero in the bottom of the sixth. They cannot get their bats going tonight. The customary amount of empty cans are on the table. What is unusual is that Jim and Buddy are watching the ballgame in silence.

At this stage of beer consumption in a disappointing game, with the M's producing goose eggs, they'd be kibitzing and bad-mouthing the Seattle players, how for the amount of money they make they sure as hell could get a base hit or throw a strike.

But the Hendricks' windfall exceeds many of the annual salaries on the field.

I return to my lemonade. When we began receiving our annuities from MSF, Buddy and I pitied the working stiffs out there in today's dog-eat-dog society. He joked that we should set the alarm, so we could listen to the traffic reports in bed. Listen to tales of gridlock as icy rain pelts our warm, snug home, then go back to sleep. We never did and I'm glad we didn't.

My restaurant is opposite the traffic flow. I zip along. Between here and his new employer, Buddy can get stuck in a jam-up with all the stoplights, depending on when he leaves. It won't be like before, however, contending with the freeways and those hellacious Boeing parking lots.

My cup is half full, even if my lemonade glass isn't.

I am going to bed.

I notice that Buddy's lotto ticket is where I put it, by the telephone. Below the six numbers is the drawing date and time. Two minutes from now. I turn on our living room TV to the station that has nightly live coverage of the Washington State Lottery's various games.

I'm getting a little bit excited. Wouldn't a winner be

something? A coincidence to beat all coincidences.

A young lady, a State employee – they rotate personnel so everybody gets to be on TV – is drawing for the various games. That three-number game is first. It's like the numbers tickets the Mafia sells on the street Back East, in New York City, like you see in the gangster movies. Then comes keno and other silly games. They are all sucker bets. Only the format and the odds vary.

The girl does Lotto and Mega Millions last. They are the biggies. This Lotto jackpot is six million, which Jim and Ellen and their $10.5 million would dismiss as peanuts. Chicken feed.

The Mega Millions, however, at $127 million, makes their bundle look like chump change. Ping-Pong balls shoot up a tube lickety-split and come to rest in a row. It takes mere seconds to transform the life of a lucky ticket holder. I compare the winners to those on Buddy's ticket.

Not a single number matches. Nary a one.

Why am I not surprised?

Chapter 11

BUDDY

Got me a decent night's sleep last night. Madrid Ricky didn't pester me, not once. Maybe he's working on Lucy's frigids, testing out what I told him to do.

I use one paper towel instead of two to wipe up breakfast coffee I spilt. That's the kind of thing we been doing. Nothing comes in this house that's not house brand or on sale. Hope Martha's pencil's sharpened sharp when she said we can get by with what we make on these jobs.

While I'm turning every inch of that towel brown, I'm thinking of Jim and Ellen. Wow! Ten-point-five mil. Makes my $15 per hour look like less than a drop in their bucket. I whip out the pocket calculator and calculatorate how long you'd have to work at $15 per to earn $10.5 million. Comes to 357 years. Add in Martha $11.50 per and we could shave off a lifetime or two.

Couldn't of happened to nicer, more deserving folk than Jim and Ellen, though I wouldn't of minded if it'd been us instead. Can't find that Lotto ticket I bought. Not that it'd matter.

That's when I see this guy coming onto the property and go around to the side by our driveway. I'm thinking he's gonna repo my pickup truck and remember it's free and clear, one thing Murganzer Stable Funds didn't get their grubby paws on. If he's looking to serve papers, you'd think he'd come to the door. The phone calls have tapered off, so they're probably gearing up for the next stage of financial badgering. I go around to the living room and peek out. Can hear him but can't see him.

What the hell, I take a deep breath and go on out.

He's a meter reader reading our water meter, who says, "Meter reader."

"I can see that," I say, heart clobbering the inside of my chest.

~ ~ ~

I report for duty to Bruno, Chick Chipperfield's service manager. Chick said on the phone last night that Bruno'll be my line supervisor. He's the only employee on the premises so far. Bruno's in the service bays, steam-cleaning the engine of a metallic red 5-series BMW.

I stick out my hand to introduce myself and all he does is say, "Whadduya think of this here unit?"

"Nice looking car," I say, speaking up to be heard over the sprayer. "Worth some bucks."

Bruno's got the lowest hairline I've ever seen outside of a zoo and his eyebrows are like a parking strip. He's in coveralls and has got a cigarette dangling out of his mouth as he talks and steam-cleans. There's a rattlesnake tattoo curling out from under his collar.

"This unit was owned by some tight-assed rich-bitch housewife who was too wrapped up in her creative writing classes and tennis luncheons to get around to adding oil when it got low. I put some additives in the crankcase, so it has a few thousand miles before the clanging and smoke-belching starts up again."

Bruno might be 35, might be 40, might be 50. Him and this BMW, they've both had some hard miles.

I ask, "Then why're they're selling it here?"

"The Beemer dealer stuck their noses in the air. They took this rat in trade and wholesaled it out to us. I sent it down the street to Bondo Boris to have the dents halfassedly knocked out. He's a miracle worker. This society lady had a habit of backing into things. We detailed the interior too. Got rid of the dog hair. She was one of them who drive with their poodle on their lap while she's on the phone. When I'm done, we'll put it out on the lot, priced to sell."

"Some history for such a swell-looking car."

"That's what we tell 'em when they ask why it's on sale."

"You do? The whole, entire history?"

"Nah. Bits and pieces. Don't want to bore them."

"Huh?"

"Don't go there. That's all you need to know."

"We'll make money?"

"Oh hell yeah. Chick ain't in the charity business. He thinks the world of you, by the way."

Meaning Lizabeth Chipperfield does. "Yeah?"

"He didn't say why," Bruno says, snooping, looking sideways at me.

I don't bite. "Unlike his dead son-in-law?"

His sideways look turns to head-on.

"This car, will it have a warranty?"

"Five minutes or five miles, whichever comes first."

Bruno's not laughing, so I don't know if that's a joke or not. When he has the forlorn engine clean enough to eat off, he leads me to what he calls the Hey Asshole Room. There's pegboard on a wall, with tagged car keys on hooks. There's compressed gas tanks leaning in a corner and a table piled with balloons and rolls of string.

Bruno waits for me to ask why it's the Hey Asshole Room. I can't resist.

"That's Chick's sense of humor for you," he says, whipping a yellow-toothed smile on me. "We doll up the lot so you're driving by, you can't help but look. The lot's saying 'Hey asshole, come on in'."

Bruno's laughing. I force a smile. He briefs me on my assignment. The tanks hold helium. I blow up enough balloons for the mother of all birthday bashes. After I attach the strings and take them out and tie them up on whatever I can find to tie them up on – Bruno didn't say where – I go in for the keys. The system on the keys is that there's no system. I finally sort 'em out and unlock the cars. Some of the doors creak big-time. I raise the hoods and turn on the emergency flashers of every other car. Gotta question how the batteries of some of this merchandise will hold up.

Bruno comes out and nods his approval. "You got a gift for exterior decoration."

I'm gonna ask Bruno what he wants me to do next, but he gives me a pat on the shoulder that almost dislocates it and walks off. Can't just stand around with my thumb up my butt. Couldn't at Boeing neither. I was looked at as an oddball for that reason. At the Lazy B, there was an art to looking busy and doing nothing. I never did get the hang of it.

There's litter on and by the lot. This's a busy highway. People toss their garbage out the window going by. Pedestrians contribute their share. I go into the shop and scrounge me a plastic garbage bag and a pair of gloves. I'm not too proud. I'm getting paid a wage and I'll give the man a return on his dollar.

Chick Chipperfield makes the scene in a Jaguar of unknown vintage with dealer plates. There's mud on the tires and lower body. Don't think a Jag is a vehicle you take off-road, but he's the boss.

Chick doesn't see me. He goes inside yawning. It was dumb to ask if he knew Brady Hardcastle. The question just popped out of my mouth. How could he of known the killer of my mother? They were of two separate generations. Must have been that picture in Chick's office of the guy leaning on the De Soto tailfin and the fact that Hardcastle sold for a Plymouth garage, which may've been a Desoto-Plymouth agency till they stopped making DeSotos. Must've lit a light bulb in my subconsciousness.

Since Spain and *Girl*, Brady Hardcastle and what he did has been on my mind. It's like Mom was murdered yesterday.

Soon as I asked him, Chick answered me a flat no. But what if had known Hardcastle? Haven't the foggiest how I'd handle the situation.

I keep on policing up trash. I've figured out that as Associate Maintenance Superintendent, I'm a glorified lot boy. Haven't even needed to take my toolbox out of the truck.

Got me severe doubts regarding this job and this outfit in general. Like how many other cars they're peddling are as decrepit as that Beemer? If I stay on the payroll here, I'll be a sleazeball by association. I decide to finish out the day and give Chick my resignation. He doesn't need two weeks notice. Any fool can lift hoods and inflate balloons.

Martha won't be too upset. She wasn't crazy about me taking this job. Those janitor openings pay only a little less and you don't have to be party to cheating the public.

My thoughts drift as I work. Jim and Ellen and their jackpot. Jim and me watching the ball game last night, we should of had a bunch of catching up to do, yakking nonstop. Where we'd been and what we'd done. We didn't. I didn't say ten words on Spain and none of them included La Rambla and Stringbean. I got a lump and a couple of bruises that're not quite gone. If they caught Jim's eye, he didn't say.

It was like we were scared to open our mouths. Him afraid he'd sound like he was lording it over me. Me on account of the mess we're in slipping into the conversation.

"What are they asking for this?"

A guy's on the sidewalk. Didn't hear him come up behind me till he spoke. He's young and has short hair, and is wearing a jacket and tie.

"Which one?"

"That red BMW there."

He's pointing at the very same turdmobile Bruno steam-cleaned. Salesmen are arriving. I should refer him, but they're standing outside, smoking cigarettes, nursing hangovers, paying us no never mind.

"Don't know."

"I'm kicking tires," he says. "I like to early, before the salesmen are swarming. They won't leave you alone."

"Good policy," I say.

"I see a car that strikes my fancy, I go on the Internet and comparison shop."

"Uh huh."

"I'm not casting aspersions against you, but I'd never buy here."

"How come?"

"Ever seen his commercials? Chipperfield's got a rep as the biggest crook in town."

I keep my yap zippered and stoop to pick up a pop can.

"Don't know what they're asking?"

"Nope."

"I'm looking to move up. I'm driving a Jetta. Good car, but a Volkswagen's not a BMW."

"Nope, I guess not."

"Looks like it's in good shape. That's a great shade of red. I love the metallic reds when the sun hits them."

I don't reply.

"Isn't it?"

"Isn't it in good shape or isn't it a great shade of red?"

"Good shape."

This is none of my business, but what the hell. "Beauty's only skin deep."

"What do you mean? The car has mechanical issues?"

I am not lying to this fella, period, let alone to save a job I don't want. "Under the hood, it's a piece a shit. The crankcase oil's been doctored up and there were dents that were dinged out on the cheap."

He's looking at me funny. "A piece of shit you say?"

"Yep."

"You work here?"

"Yep."

"Really?"

"Scout's honor."

"And you're telling me it's a piece of shit?"

"Yep."

"Come on. What's really wrong with it? What's the

skinny?"

"What isn't wrong with it?"

"You don't have your eye on it yourself, do you? You know, to buy at an employee discount."

I laugh. "You picture me driving a car like this? My old F-150's not as pretty, but it'll outlast this BMW."

"What do you think they'd take?"

He's got that shiny stuff in his hair Martha calls gel. He's yuppie scum and he's getting on my nerves. "Don't know."

"Chick Chipperfield," he says, laughing. "Is he a nut job or is it all an act?"

"In person, Chick, he's a level-headed guy."

"We'll see about level-headed. Armed with the knowledge you've given me, I have some leverage. Thanks."

"No problem."

He quicksteps by the salesmen like he's returning a punt and disappears into the showroom. You know what they say about a little knowledge being dangerous. What that boy's armed with could explode in his face like a gag cigar.

Bruno yells at me. I go to him and he unrolls a long banner made out of white vinyl. It says FUN FAIR in bright red.

"Chick had this made up to catch the eye of kiddy car customers, the ones he's going for in the commercials he ran last night on his movie. He's going for the amusement park look. Draws the little shits like flies to honey. To get 'em to buy is another thing. Business ain't been for diddly."

Bruno and me, we're up on ladders, attaching the banner above the front doors. I see the red BMW pull out, but can't see who's in it. Then Bruno has me move the featured cars up front, backing them in fan-shaped-like, which is tricky if you never tried it.

The jacked-up Camaro and the Honda Civic from the shoot are amongst them. The dent and the busted spoiler look as good as new. Bondo Boris's magic? I thought it'd take longer than this just for the paint to dry, but what do I know? I move a black Subaru with chrome wheels alongside the Camaro. It makes a noise when you put it in gear. Completing the fan shape is a silver Toyota Celica that's been lowered so low, you run over a pebble, it'll bottom out, reminding me of the Princess and the Pea, a story we'd read to Melanie when she was a tyke.

Bruno says Chick likes to Reddi Whip prices on the windshield like they used to in the good old days. Reddi Whip's out today. It's warm and it might curdle. We tape cardboard dollar signs and numerals and exclamation marks on the windshields. They come in radioactive pink and nuclear green.

"Bring on the assholes," Bruno hollers, raising his fists.

It's lunchtime. The day's flying by. I eat by myself across the highway at fast food, a different chain than Martha's. I have the double bacon cheeseburger gutbomb and fries, wishing it was t*apas*.

Lizabeth telling me that her daddy's an old school dinosaur and that his business is not going super duper, well, after witnessing the operation, I gotta agree. I have a view of the lot as I eat and see nobody except slicky boy salesmen smoking cigarettes. This pizzazz of Chick's and the perception he's a crook, it seems to me that what I've observed with my own two eyes and ears in half a day's employment, his daughter's right. He *is* a crook.

And I'll tell you what, I got my doubts about Lizabeth too now that my hormones have simmered down some. How she knew zilch about Murganzer's Ponzi and unPonzi. How she didn't set some money aside instead of ending up broke. Dirtiest thought of all I have about her is how she must of felt when they broke the news about Murganzer's swan dive.

It's ironical how things are full circling. Me in used cars, a racket. Me in Brady Hardcastle's racket. Me in a racket thanks to the widow of the rancid son of a bitch responsible for the biggest racket to hit Seattle in many a year. Martha and me, the astronomers who write the hororscopes, they'd say our planets are misaligning throughout the universe, caroming like pinballs.

I finish my lunch. Chick shuffles out to see me before I've set both feet onto Chipperfield's Preowned Automotive Elegance.

"That guy you asked me about, Brady Hardcastle, the name sounds familiar. Did he sell cars?"

"Long time ago."

"In Seattle."

"Yeah."

"Still alive?"

"Nope."

"What's he to you?"

"Sort of a friend of the family way back when."

"See those pictures hanging up on my wall, Buddy?"

"Couldn't miss 'em."

"Hey, I'm not political and I'm not religious, but that trio in my estimation are the three greatest people who ever lived. Jesus Christ, Richard Milhous Nixon and Maniac Monahan."

"You lost me on the third, Chick."

"I broke into the profession in the car sales Mecca, Los Angeles, California. I broke in, under the Maniac. He was one of the first car dealers to embrace television and take marketing to the next level."

"Reddi Whip?"

"Not five minutes after the product came on the market in late-1950s, the Maniac was Reddi-Whipping low-low-low prices on windshields. He was a visionary. I had kinescopes of some of his early commercials on tape. They got lost in the shuffle during one of my property settlements with the little woman of the moment."

Chick's eyes are getting glassy.

"Quite a guy, huh?"

"Maniac Monahan was a pioneer, an innovator. He'd do his TV spots in a straight jacket. He was my guiding light. I know some people in town who also dated to the Maniac. I'll ask around about your boy Hardcastle."

"Don't go to any bother, Chick."

Then he gets to the point. "Buddy. What did you say to our good amigo, Randy?"

"Randy?"

"The gink you jawboned on the red 535i," Chick says. "What the hell'd you say to him?"

Chick's so close to me I can smell his breakfast, which might've been a banana daiquiri. I'm not gonna soft-soap. He blows his stack and fires me, so be it. Saves me the trouble of quitting.

"I told him the car was a piece of shit."

Chick's frowning in deep thought, scratching his chins. "What else?"

"That was pretty much it. Oh yeah, he asked what you'd take. I said that was between him and you."

"Nothing else?"

"Let's see. Oh yeah. Beauty is skin deep. I said beauty's only skin deep."

Chick makes a face. "That's the last thing you ever say to a prospect."

I shrug.

"He bought the car."

"He bought the car?"

Chick shakes my hand. "Reserve psychology, man. Whatever you said, it worked like a charm. He came bopping in like the cat who swallowed the canary and the canary was me. We went for a test drive and he said he was ready to wheel and deal. Know what? Randy and me wheeled and dealed."

I take my hand back. "I wasn't psychologizing him. I was telling him the truth. You didn't tell him the engine was shot?"

"Why should I? You did."

"You didn't know that I did."

"You're splitting hairs, Buddy. We're in a gray area. The bottom line is Randy thought he was getting over on me. Hey, that boy sashayed into my office, looking at me like I'd dropped my drawers, bent down, and grabbed my ankles. After we went for our spin, he named a figure. I countered. He lowballed me and I counter-countered. Randy bought himself a luxury automobile at a competitive price. In the pre-owned automotive arena, you're in your basic caveat emptor mode. Both parties are happy."

I say, "I don't like it. Didn't much like the guy, Randy, but liked less teaming up on a swindle whether I knew I was or not."

"You were honest to that boy, Buddy, like you're being to me. What's not to like if honesty sells cars?"

"I'm through. I quit effective right now and immediately," I say. "Had enough flimflam to last me a long while. Don't need a second helping whether it's me getting skinned or not."

He looks at me open-mouthed, like I ran him through with a spear. "It's not fair that you tar me and Chaz Murganzer with the same brush. That's what you're doing. I'm giving something for something, not taking everything and giving nothing like Chaz does."

"Now who's splitting hairs?"

He glances at his watch. "Four hours in the car business and you're an expert. Okay fine. You want another sad story, you talk to my accountant. The marketplace is vicious. A superstore's overhead is vicious. Randy boy is our first paying customer in two days."

"Cheating's cheating. It ain't just about cars."

He smiles a sad little smile and stares at me like I belong in a rubber room.

"Tell you what I'll do," he says.

Chick takes a roll out of his pocket that's as thick as a soup bone. He peels off a hundred and gives it to me. "A severance bonus. The C-note's your share of the commission. You'll be mailed a check for your wages. I got to further analyze that reverse psychological technique of yours, man, the bluntness of it."

"Don't have any technique. Answer me something. What if my honesty cost you a sale instead of making you a sale?"

He's walking away and turns his head. "Then I'd've had to can your ass."

I wad up the hundred. My impulse is to yell at him. When he turns around, I'll slam-dunk it on the ground and walk off into the sunset.

I don't do any of that. I pocket the bill and go to my truck. As soon as I verify none of my tools've been stolen, I head for home.

Chapter 12

MARTHA

Let me tell you true, early shift assistant management is no bowl of cherries. My shift is supposed to end at 2:30, but Talia, a late-shift worker, called in sick. Then Teri, late shift assistant manager, had car trouble. Shawn was gone too for an orthodontia appointment. Shawn's getting braces today. Anyhow, I juggled three tasks at once until Teri arrived. I was delayed further escaping that madhouse, listening to the circumstances of her fan belt failure.

The overtime will come in handy. Our house payment sinks deeper and deeper into arrears and there will be a late charge. The payment will be made on my payday.

I have that outrageous lawyer letter in the glove box. I go to the library and get on one of their computers. Ours is a relic so old it has a three-and-a-half-inch floppy drive and my tablet's Internet-useless because I didn't make the payment to the provider. I'd counted on them having a scanner, but they don't, so I set up a file and rewrite the letter verbatim and attach it to an e-mail to Mr. Timkins.

I ask for his advice and assistance, and tell him I think that it is greedy, mean-spirited malarkey instigated by the Falangist storm trooper in charge of interrogating Buddy. I add that this is not a blanket indictment of lawyers, and if he does has a law degree, I certainly am not tarring him with that brush.

I play online for a while. A surprising number of

websites and chat rooms devoted to Charles Murganzer have sprung up. They are a combination of support groups and forums for venting. Surprising too is the number of Murganzer sightings. They're like flying saucers. With due respect to my husband's obsession, you will have to prove to me that Murganzer is alive.

If I'm not mistaken, on the way home I am being followed by a dented, older gray sedan. The car has been in my mirrors since shortly after I got off the freeway. It's driving erratically, changing lanes without signals. There are two beefy men in the front seat and they're either drunk or lost. I'm not overly worried until they tailgate me into the complex.

They could be carjackers, although I can't comprehend their motivation, as they already have a car that isn't worth a great deal of money. Why would they want another? They could be something else altogether, perhaps connected to Buddy's Spain-related problems, private eyes who flunked surveillance class. Or they could be bill collectors, one of their strong-arm tactics to soften us up before the harassment begins in earnest.

I am not stepping out of my car until I understand their intentions. If Buddy's not home from work and Jim and Ellen aren't home either, I'll drive around the complex until I see someone I know. If push comes to shove, I'll park in the middle of the street. One hand wrapped around my pepper spray, I'll lay on the horn.

Oh Good Lord, there's a FOR SALE sign staked in Jim and Ellen's front yard! They don't let the grass grow under their feet, do they? Fat chance we will follow through on our tentative dinner date at the buffet. The Hendricks and their massive Cadillac are not at home. Buddy is home and that's a welcome surprise. He expected to be on the job until five and it's only 4:30.

My pursuers pull in behind me, the rear of that old car sticking half out in the street. Buddy on the porch waving to them. Evidently they're not too terribly dangerous.

They pile out of their wreck, wearing Cheshire cat grins. Why, it's those two likable lummoxes from our Spain trip, the grocery checkers who think with a part of their anatomy other than their brains. Each is bearing a six-pack with a bottle uncapped.

"*Buenos nachos, señor and señorita,*" says either Ed or Ted. I get them mixed up.

My Buddy is beaming too, an unusual sight of late. "You boys come on in before you die of thirst."

"Not to worry," says Ed or Ted, raising an open bottle.

"Martha," he says, opening my door for me. "You remember Ed and Ted."

My opinion of those boys altered dramatically after they stood by me in Barcelona. "I certainly do. It's absolutely wonderful to see you again."

"Ma'am," they say in turn, offering tentative handshakes.

"Stop the ma'am. You age me ten years. I'm Martha."

Buddy says, "They got our number from Janine and were curious how we were doing. I said c'mon over."

Ted (I think) says, "We were worried they still had you locked up."

"Martha sprung me. Brought a cake to the slammer with a hacksaw baked inside it."

And to me, Buddy said, "The boys weren't too far, so I

thought I'd fire up the barbecue. Just got back from the store."

Ed (I think) says, "We brung our appetites. The beer is a hostess gift."

Ted says, "We were thinking flowers, but you can't drink flowers."

I should be annoyed that Janine gave out our personal information, but I'm not. I have an upbeat Buddy and the two sons I'm thankful we never had. We go though the house and out to the deck, Buddy taking a handful of beers from the fridge en route, microbrews no less.

It is Weasel's Breath, an amber ale produced in a small Idaho town. Buddy is the beer consultant in our household. He claims the more disgusting the name, the tastier the micro. This brew must be pricey. Buddy says spending seven bucks for a six-pack is against his religion, superior taste or no superior taste. Not when Bud and Miller by the case is often on sale.

Thank goodness I'm not in uniform. I fought fatigue and impatience and took the time to change at the restaurant. Ed and Ted are not particularly observant. They weren't in Spain, not as far as historical significance was concerned. But my MARTHA nametag and ensemble would be difficult to miss. It would take some explaining.

Buddy lights the charcoal. He throws on gigantic T-bones when the coals go gray. He also bought a big bag of salad and a baguette the size of a baseball bat. I dump the salad into a bowl and slather real butter on the bread. I add garlic salt and put it under the broiler. Oh, the extravagance, never mind our arteries.

But this is a special occasion. We're both working and

there will be o.t. on my paycheck. I enjoy a Weasel's Breath while I work. It is dark and chocolaty and rich and delicious.

As usual, Buddy's steaks are done to perfection. During dinner, we small talk about the Mariners and the Seahawks's prospects and the nice weather. We talk about Buddy's ordeal on La Rambla and what came later.

Buddy demonstrates his "preemptive strike" against the *nine* soccer hooligans, shuffling his feet and jabbing his fists. He looks silly and cute. Our guests show their approval with high-fives and yelling "awesome!"

Ed and Ted have been best friends since high school. They started working in the same supermarket during their junior years and never left. The store changed hands a few times, acquired by a large retail chain that was acquired by a larger chain. Ed and Ted are the two constants.

"Too dull and lazy to move on," Ed says.

"And proud of it," Ted says.

"Who else would hire us?" Ed says.

I wonder if that line of work might be for me if I burn out as an assistant fast food executive. Buddy in used cars, who can guess how long he'll be happy there. He is extremely uncomfortable around smooth-talking people. Slicky boys, he calls them. That Buddy didn't as much as fidget during Charles Murganzer's seminars was a testament to the man's deceptive skills, to his evil genius.

Several beers later, in the twilight, Ed announces that Ted and Janine are an item. They're inseparable when she's in town.

"Ted took her to some foreign film festival she wanted to go to. They were art movies. Nothing was in English and the subtitles made no sense. He didn't even care."

Ted turns eight shades of red. He is so sweet. I recall that his tongue was hanging out any time he was near Janine. I also recall that she began paying attention to him when he and Ed came to our aid in Barcelona. I do believe he's in love. They would be an odd couple. Serious, urbane Janine and, well, Ted. Far be it from me to say it can't work. Love blurs the lines and erases the labels.

The subject of Janine has dredged up future cultural aspirations. There will be no more international travel for us. I will be fortunate to ever afford watercolor class and the supplies. If I someday can, I will settle for painting the Coliseum from a photograph. I shall never ever see it in person. Janine's agency does tours to Italy and France too. For next year, I'd been contemplating a Rome-Tuscany-Umbria-Venice loop. I'd planned to sell Buddy on Italy soon after we returned from Spain. I blow my nose and blame pollen.

"That's how we got your number," Ted says. "Normally Janine doesn't hand them out. She apologizes if it's not okay."

"It's okay," Buddy and I chime.

The beer has taken charge of the conversation as Ed pauses and whispers in Buddy's ear, "Ted thinks Janine may be a virgin."

Ted belches softly and nods solemnly. "I really respect her for it."

I pretend not to hear. It is a common misconception that when a person attains a certain age, their hearing is automatically defective.

Buddy yawns. I yawn. The suds and hard labor have gotten the best of us. His work and mine have not inadvertently entered the dialogue, however. We remain a carefree senior couple with time and money to burn.

Our yawns remind Ed and Ted that they have to get up in the morning. They go on their way, promises made all around to stay in touch.

Ed embarrasses Ted at the door by saying we'll get wedding invitations. Ed's jealous whether he realizes it or not. If Ted and Janine tie the knot, Ed is on the outside looking in.

I am dying to hear how Buddy's first day at work went. You would think he would be talking up a storm, but he doesn't say a word, even after I relate the trials and tribulations of my extended shift. This is too peculiar. I go against every instinct and refrain from pressing him. He has a confession of some sort to make, and Buddy's confessions come forth at his own speed.

Buddy turns on the television. We remember the Mariners aren't on. This is a travel day, the first of a grueling road trip. We sit at the dinette table, me with a bottle of water, having arrived at my beer limit and then some. Buddy has a fresh Weasel's Breath. Orange and Tangerine come out of hiding, rub against us, and curl up on the couch. I notice out loud that Buddy has a glow on. He says it's the result of extra vitamins and minerals in micro brews.

Ellen and Jim are still gone. They're early to bed, early to rise people. Money changes a person, though. I take the opportunity in our quiet time to move the New York lawyer's letter to the center of the table. The envelope from Brother Stan is unopened.

"I was gonna talk to you about it," Buddy says. "Keeps slipping my mind."

"What were you going to do about it?"

He drinks and shrugs. "Haven't decided yet. It's a crock."

I tell him about what I did at the library with the attorney letter. I omit my Charles Murganzer surfing. Buddy's notion that the man is alive needs no encouragement. "This is a railroad job, pure and simple."

Buddy gives me a thumbs-up. "Good plan. Thimblekins might be the key. Great, kiddo."

I cannot stand it any longer. I can't. "Well, how'd your first day on the job go?"

Buddy hesitates. He reaches into his pocket and plunks a wad of bills and change on the table.

"Dirty money," he says. "The last of it."

I wait.

He exhales loudly and starts talking. The laconic Buddy treats me to a record-length monologue. It is an outlandish sequence of events that takes us from yesterday morning to the empty shell that is MSF headquarters to trespassing on the impounded estate of Charles Murganzer. He clears his throat at the part where he meets Lizabeth Murganzer, the widow. I visualize the newspaper photograph, her and her big-hair brittleness.

This explains the fragrance on his shirt. Women like that apply perfume with a heavy hand. It would cling to anything in a 20-foot radius. At least I hope he wasn't closer to her than that. He discusses their encounter in detail, how she's left with the clothes on her back and her cookware and maybe her Escalade, dependent on the generosity of her father, a newlywed. His voice lowers as he speaks of a confrontation with a tow truck driver, testosterone kicking in as he does.

I about fall out of my chair when Buddy tells me who Lizabeth's father is. Then comes the story of his demeaning tasks at the car lot and the swindling of a man who bought a BMW on its last legs and his abrupt resignation.

"The rest of the hundred went for dinner and –," he says, hoisting his Weasel's Breath. "I look at it as found money, found dirty money. Randy, the sucker, to me he's almost as guilty cuz he was looking to screw Chick. You gotta knock off style points for stupidity."

"My, you've had a busy two days," I say, largely speechless. Weasel's Breath is a highly effective tongue-loosening elixir. "I'm proud of you for quitting that awful man."

"I was looking at janitor jobs in the paper when this came along. I'll make some calls tomorrow."

"I've been thinking. If we could save a little money, if we found promising fields that strike our fancy, we could enroll in courses at the community college. You take one thing, I could take another."

"You mean like flower arranging?"

"Vocational classes. Some of the programs don't last long and the college has a placement service. We're old, but we're not ancient. We have to work, so we might as well make the most of it."

"Yeah, we could do that. Sure."

He's saying that to be agreeable. The phone rings and a woman asks for Buddy. She has a young yet husky and sultry voice.

Buddy takes the receiver and I listen to a one-sided conversation.

"Hello."

"Uh huh."

"No."

"How come?"

"Yeah?"

"I don't know."

"It's not your fault."

"I know he's your daddy."

"Water under the bridge."

"Oh yeah. When?"

"I guess. What the hell, I'll give it a whirl."

This goes on for a couple of minutes. It's like listening to a teenager.

He hangs up and I ask, "Lizabeth Murganzer?"

"She's gonna be Lizabeth Chipperfield. She's taking back her maiden name."

"The lesser of two evils."

"Chick told her I was a prude."

"We can take that as a compliment. Give what a whirl?"

"Restaurant work."

I am speechless.

"Better pick your jaw off the floor before you trip on it," he says, smiling. "I can fry eggs to order in my sleep."

"Goodness, she does know your life story."

He shrugs. "Might've mentioned my Army service as a cook when I rattled off the fleecing we took by her husband. Lizabeth has to get back in the workplace herself and that's her line of work. She has got contacts in the food and beverage industry. Now that I'm thinking about, it'll be like riding a bicycle."

"Is that the sort of work that interests you?"

"Haven't really thought about it. I know one thing. It's something I done before and I can't say that for too many other areas. Lizabeth feels guilty getting me mixed up with her old man."

"She means well," I say, hopeful that she did. Attraction to mature men by insecure young women is not an unknown phenomenon.

"Lizabeth wants to meet for breakfast and we'll map out our strategy."

"Breakfast," I say.

"Is that okay?"

"Of course. You don't need my permission and this sounds like an opportunity."

"There's something else, Martha. Chick was referring to Murganzer in the, you know, like it's right now."

"Present tense."

"There you go."

"You have Murganzer on the brain. You're entitled to. Please don't get carried away. If he is alive, he's some place exotic, a million miles from us."

Buddy nods. He's tired.

We sit there for a moment. I am frazzled too. My back is sore, my knees ache, and my feet tingle.

He's looking at me. There's a twinkle in his eye. I snag his twinkle with my twinkle.

I feel refreshed. I yawn theatrically, stretch and get up.

When I go into the bedroom, he is very close behind.

Chapter 13

BUDDY

If I had dirty thoughts about Lizabeth Chipperfield throbbing inside my subconscious skull, Martha, my sweetie, she sure as hell got 'em out of my system last night. Furthermore, Ricky had the decency to mind his own business and not be a peeping Tom.

Enough said.

Girl hasn't budged from my noggin neither, but her and that painting, they've been eliminated from the dirty thought department.

Laying in bed this morning before I got up, I remembered Mom's funeral. Closed casket. Dad sat between Stan and me in the front row. He didn't cry. Dads weren't supposed to then. I remember him crossing and uncrossing his legs a lot. He had one blue sock on, one brown. Figured he couldn't think straight out of grief. But maybe he was just careless, not caring all that much, his girl friend in his thoughts more than my mom, his late wife.

As for *Girl* being Mom, I gotta get proactive with Stan's envelope pretty soon. Martha, she'll be steaming it open.

She's up at oh-dark-thirty and long gone to work before I head out the door for my breakfast with Lizabeth Chipperfield. For crying out loud, there's a second new Sedan Deville at the Hendricks, blue in color, parked by the FOR SALE sign. Maybe Jim and Ellen, they're gonna buy a Caddy for every day of the week.

They're plumb out of driveway space. I'll bet where they move, which is wherever they want to, they'll have the mother of all driveways. I've seen these new houses out on big wooded lots in the burbs past Melanie's. They have got a three-car garage and a fourth for the RV. That'd be right up Jim's alley. He's always hankered after a Winnebago.

The restaurant Lizabeth and me are meeting at is a couple of miles down the road from Chipperfield's Preowned Automotive Elegance. It's a hash house, catering to working stiffs, the kind of establishment I'd break into the profession in. Breakfast is served 24 hours.

I go on in there and wait by the cashier. Don't think punctuality is Lizabeth's long suit. By the time she shows 20 minutes late, I've had me a brainstorm and an itch as fierce as the one I scratched by going out to MSF Headquarters and the Charles Murganzer estate.

"How 'bout rolls and coffee to go?" I say before Lizabeth can say hello.

"Go where?"

"Where's this lake lot your daddy's trying to sell?"

"Lake Chester in Kitsap County, off the highway to Bremerton. Why?"

"Then you get there from here and back by taking the Tacoma Narrows Bridges?"

"Yes."

"That's the clincheroo. I got another idea for breakfast. Let's go."

~ ~ ~

We're in my pickup, with our coffee and blueberry muffins I bought us at one of the kazillion espresso stands between the restaurant and Lake Chester. As another concession to be getting my way instead of her, I let Lizabeth smoke if she cracks her window. It's only right we should burn my gas too. I tell her my brainstorm, including, "You said yourself that your daddy and Murganzer had long chitchats."

"Swapping lies. Buddy. If Charles was alive and in cahoots with Daddy, don't you think I'd at least suspect?"

"You don't? Not at all?"

"Well, Charles was Charles and Daddy is Daddy. Other than that, no."

"Your daddy referred to Murganzer as Chaz, in the present tense, like he's amongst the living."

"You know as well as anybody that you take anything that comes out of my father's mouth with a grain of salt."

"This lake lot, have you got to go through the mud to get to it?"

"Well, there's a potholed dirt road to it from the main road."

I tell her about the muddy Jaguar Chipperfield drove onto his lot. "Does he take his luxury elegance pre-owned used cars stump-jumping?"

"It hasn't rained in days," she says. "There are tree overhangs above the road going in, so it doesn't get much sun and rarely dries out. Daddy was probably just checking on the cabin. If he was there."

We're on one of the Narrows Bridges, the one headed out of Tacoma. Lizabeth points to the right. "That's where they found Charles's Aston Martin."

I don't answer.

"Is it your theory that Charles got out of the car and walked to another car he had stashed on the other side without the toll taker seeing him and drove to the lake lot?"

"It occurred to me." I say. "The toll taker collects before you get on the other bridge headed into town and was busy."

"You have your reasons for wanting him alive."

"Don't you, Lizabeth?"

She sighs and mulls it over. "Job hunting can wait another day, I guess. I don't need anything confusing my widowhood status."

~ ~ ~

The access road to the Lake Chester cabin is rough and sloppy and dark from the overhangs. I doubt if it ever sees sun.

"Buddy, you don't have a gun on you, do you?"

"Martha won't let me keep a gun in the house."

"That's not my question."

"Nah. Am I acting crazy to you?"

I can see her eyes out of the corner of mine. "A little."

Lake Chester isn't big, but you can barely see cabins on the other side on account of the lots are as shaggy as this one. There's a bunch of privacy. The cabin's an A-frame and no spring chicken. The shingles on the north side are fuzzy with moss and mold. A short dock into the water is swayback. This property's in the same shape as Chipperfield's used cars. There's an alarm company sign on the door, but nothing from realtors. No FOR SALE sign, no nothing.

"I don't recall an alarm," she says. "Let me try."

Lizabeth turns her key in the lock and open sesame. No sirens go off.

"Daddy must have but it up to discourage burglars and vandals. Oh look!"

She picks up a salt and pepper set off a table. They're glass, old-timey, and the peppershaker's got a chip out of the base.

"I remember dropping it when I was a little girl. The rest of the furnishings aren't much, but this, it's like stepping out of a time machine."

"Anything used lately?"

"People have been here recently, maybe sales prospects, but there's no indication it's been lived in."

The place smells musty, the bathroom even more so. The cabin could use window washing and dusting. I nose around and go up the ladder to the loft. The beds have bare mattresses that smell damp. If Murganzer was the hygiene freak Lizabeth said he was, he wouldn't put up with this state of affairs.

"Satisfied?" she asks after I climb down.

"I reckon."

She looks at me. "What do you want worse, your money back or your pound of flesh?"

I don't reply. I can't. I truly don't know.

And/or is probably the correct answer.

~ ~ ~

I been gone six hours for breakfast and burned ten bucks of gas on a wild Murganzer chase to a deserted cabin with Lizabeth Chipperfield and there's no prospect of a job. Martha, she'll have a cow. I'd best get my ass in gear.

I drop Lizabeth at the restaurant and her SUV. We say we'll get together and do this again, real actual job hunting, but my field trip may of taken the wind out of her sails as far as her introducing me to the food and beverage profession.

It's not easy to find a pay phone. The goddamn cells everybody's got grafted to their ear is putting the phone booth in the category of the dodo bird. I finally locate one outside a convenience store and call on that janitor job. It's been filled. I buy a morning paper, open it to the want ads, and MAIL ROOM jumps off the page at me. Self-starter wanted. Immediate opening. Contact a human resources guy named bjrussell at blah blah blah dot-com. Yeah, right.

There's a street address too and it's in our neck of the woods. The company is Unity P&C. I don't know what the hell Unity P&C is, but it won't cost me anything to drop on by.

~ ~ ~

Betcha I drove by this dump 1000 times. It's a block off the old highway, a two-story office building that's been around forever. It's a box with those green shiny panels and the aluminum trim, how they used to build them when I was a pup. It's got UNITY BUILDING lettered over the entrance, individual letters that look like they'd fall down on top of your head if you slam a door.

The main floor is not offices, not any longer. It's been split up into shops that are from left to right – dry cleaners, vacant, tattoo parlor, two glass entry doors to the offices upstairs, vacant, adult toys, vacant, teriyaki.

Painted on the glass doors is:

Unity Property and Casualty Insurance Company. Regional Headquarters.

That explains the P&C. Being an insurance company, this doesn't excite me a whole helluva lot. As far as I'm concerned, insurance is a racket. They're crooks who break the law legally. On the other side of the coin, you have to take into consideration the bean counters and stock insiders and CEO's in the news, their hanky-panky could teach the Mafia a trick or two, not to mention my last employer.

Seems like I can't avoid rackets. Guess it's impossible any more to punch anybody's clock who doesn't have their hand in some cookie jar or another.

I go up steps that smell like soy sauce and into a reception area that has a table and chairs so rickety looking, I'll stand as long as it takes. I introduce myself to the young switchboard gal and ask to see Mr. B.J. Russell regarding the mailroom opening. She's hefty and it sounds like firecrackers going off when she pops her gum.

"Do you have an appointment?"

"Nope. Didn't say so in the ad."

She works her eyebrows like she doesn't believe me, gets on the phone, and says, "Bobbi Jo, there's a Mr. Whitley for Ian's job. He doesn't have an appointment."

"It's Whitacre." I hate it when they mispronounce your name.

The girl makes a face at the receiver and hangs up. She's been set straight and corrected, and doesn't like it.

"Have a seat."

I go over and stand by a chair. Reading material on the table is strictly insurance industry. I pick up a magazine that's got a cover story on toxic mold. The one under it headlines asbestos claims. The one under it, hurricane damage. Cheerful line of work they're in.

A chunky gal comes out and gives me the firmest handshake I've ever got from a female of the species.

"Bobbi Jo Russell. You're here for the mail clerk

opening, Mr. Whitson?"

Bobbi Jo is a cheerleader's sort of name, but I don't think she ever was. She's fortyish and it's not like she's naturally homely. She just tries hard to be, with her baggy slacks and blouse and short hair and no makeup and skin tone of a vampire.

"Buddy. Buddy Whitacre. Yes, I am."

She gives me a once-over, like she's USDA and I'm a side of beef. "Your maturity is refreshing. Let's go on back."

After I sign in and clip on a visitor's badge, Bobbi Jo leads me through a conglomeration of cubicles and offices. I catch a whiff of cleaning solvents from below. The carpet's bare to the underlayment in spots and they've made liberal use of duct tape to hold the cubicle partitions upright. People are in some of the cubes, on the phone and staring at computer screens. Some have manuals and files stacked waist high on the floor.

We go on past the office of B. J. Russell, Human Resources Manager, to a rear corner and the mailroom. It's got a cabinet with mail cubbyholes, a sorting table, a postage meter and shelves of supplies. There are boxes and binders and miscellaneous stuff piled helter-skelter.

Bobbi Jo says, "This is the lucky applicant's empire. Buddy, is it?"

"It is."

"Please summarize your background," she says, arms folded.

"Thirty-one years at Boeing building airplanes. I'm retired out of there. As far as mail room expertise goes, I'm a little light in that field."

"Computers?"

I cock a thumb, stalling. "Like them out there?"

"They're three generations obsolete. New technology isn't in our budget."

"Yeah?"

"We knock on wood every morning when we boot up."

"My computer skills, they're likewise semi-rusty.

"Not a problem," she says. "If a machine dies, you may be asked to unplug it and store the components in here. Good luck finding space. Ingenuity and organizational ability is a plus in this job. The routine is basic and simple. Cyndi, the clerical supervisor, will break you in. It shouldn't take more than a few days. You'll deliver and pick up mail at everyone's in- and out-boxes twice a day. If somebody tries to bully you into overnighting a document, you refer them to Cyndi or to their supervisor, who has to okay the expense. There's too much money wasted needlessly in this office. You'd also be in charge of inventorying and maintaining office supplies. I'll alert you when someone gives notice. There's a tendency to stockpile stationery that ends up in their homes. You can use the pool car for trips to the post office. Be careful of the brakes. They're metal on metal. Home Office won't approve repairs until our loss ratio improves. Think ahead when you need to stop."

"You saying 'you', are you offering me the job?"

"I'm getting ahead of myself. Does the job appeal to you?"

"I think it might."

"Let's go to my office."

Bobbi Jo closes her door behind us, which shuts part of the noise out, the keyboard clunking, cabinet drawers slamming, people talking, sometimes yelling.

Soundproofing and acoustics leave something to be desired.

"What do you know about Unity P and C?"

"You're an insurance company."

"We're the western regional office for a property and casualty carrier that has been around for a century and a half and has written bizarre and notorious risks. There's a joke that we wrote group life on the Seventh Cavalry and hull coverage on the *Titanic*."

She ain't smiling.

"Did you?"

"Yes and no. Years ago, when we wrote life insurance, we had coverage on several members of the Seventh Cav."

"On Custer?"

"Not him. We did have a piece of the *Titanic* too, through Lloyd's. That loss almost put us under, pardon the pun. Today, our book of business remains in the high-risk category. Do you think anybody would be stupid enough to write a policy on a lumberyard that's next door to a fireworks warehouse?"

"Sure don't."

"Then you haven't met our underwriters. We had auto and life coverage on a serial killer who drove around trolling for victims. We write in niche markets too, truly weird specialty lines."

"You've hung in there," I say. "This company hasn't gone belly-up."

Bobbi Jo makes claws. "By our fingernails. We're financially creative. What we make leasing the main floor out pays our office overhead. We watch our budget. Low salaries, for instance. This job starts at twelve dollars per hour. Does the position still appeal to you?"

I'd be taking a three-dollar pay hit on the job I quit yesterday. This'll throw a monkey wrench into Martha's calculations, speaking of budgets.

I'm realistic about my options, though. I better do what I gotta do. A bird in the hand's got extra value if there ain't any left in the bush and there's no bush neither. I'm not exactly a ballplayer hitting .365 who's negotiating a zillion buck no-cut contract.

"I'm willing to tackle new situations and I don't figure I'll be starting out at the top."

"There is no top at Unity P and C," she says, maybe another unsmiling joke I don't get. She gives me an application. I go out to an empty desk to complete it.

I go back to her office. Bobbi Jo Russell takes a minute, no more, to scan the form and says, "I meant it when I said your maturity is refreshing. I'm tired of the kids we get in the mail room who think this is a day job until their rock band scores a recording contract. Their headphones go full blast when they aren't napping."

"Ian?"

"Oh yes. Ian. Ever heard of Plutonium Gecko?"

"Nope."

"Ian's their lead noisemaker."

I'm picturing a dope-fiend kid dressed in solid black with earrings all over his face. "Don't think I'm familiar with his tunes."

"Count yourself fortunate," she adds. "I'm making you a formal offer."

"I'm accepting."

We get to our feet and shake again. Bobbi Jo says I can start in the morning and gives me income tax forms to mark and sign, which, come to think of it, Chick Chipperfield never did.

She looks over the papers and says, "This is personal, Buddy. You don't have to answer. Are you doing this for pin money?"

"You guessed it."

"Gravy over and above your regular retirement income?"

"There you are."

"Bored because of an excess of leisure time?"

"Yep."

"It's my experience that seniors are motivated self-starters."

"That's me, yours truly."

"Does your wife work too, if I may ask?"

"She's an executive in food service management."

"Excellent. Welcome to Mother Unity. I hope your time with us is rewarding and enjoyable."

I thank Bobbi Jo and as she walks me to the door, a guy leaves ahead of us. He's in a shiny brown suit, wearing an old-timey hat nobody wears any more. He's got a bowling ball gut and a ratty leather briefcase. He could of busted out of a sci-fi time warp.

"Who's that?"

"Frank Rambaugh," Bobbi Jo says. "World's oldest claims adjuster. We're working on having this confirmed by the Guinness people."

She is smiling, but by the looks of this Rambaugh, it may not be a joke.

"Frank was with the company in 1972 when Unity had this place built and moved from downtown Seattle. He comes to work every day and does his job. You have to run him out the door with pepper spray to make him take vacation. He won't retire and nobody's had the nerve to downsize him."

Frank Rambaugh is out the door, gimping down the steps, a man on a mission. By the time I'm outside, he's gone. Maybe this job will be okay. Can't be all bad, even if they're an insurance company. This outfit's kind to their geezers.

I go out of my way to take a shortcut by Chipperfield's Preowned Automotive Elegance Superstore, cruising so slow that horns are honking behind me. There are no prospects on the lot. I see steam billowing inside the service department, Bruno at the controls of the engine-cleaning machine.

Don't know why I took this detour. Maybe I'm expecting Charles Murganzer to sashay out of the Hey Asshole Room. It'd sure be fitting.

Chapter 14

MARTHA

Last night was magical.

I shall leave it at that, with a song in my heart. I do not kiss and tell.

Conversely, my day at work has been hideous. Absolute hell. The gods are compensating, balancing the ledger.

From the start of the shift, Felipe has been sulking and grumbling under his breath that I was promoted to assistant manager instead of him. Based on his experience and my lack thereof, this is a legitimate grievance. Felipe broke me in. Felipe is my fast food mentor. He holds his resentment fairly close to the vest until Shawn arrives. Thankfully it is our mid-morning lull.

Felipe confronts Shawn (an ambush, really) the instant he walks into his office. There is a brief, heated discussion in English and Spanish and Spanglish. Felipe is compact and has an angular nose. I can visualize his ancestors battling Hernán Cortés's *conquistadores* tooth and nail.

Felipe's side of the conversation is explosive. My *español* is good enough to recognize vulgarities. *Mierda* is often shouted. Shawn has his new braces on and spits and lisps when he loses his cool too, rightfully blaming Mr. Larionov.

Felipe storms out of the office and flings his apron. I don't think he blames me. Upper management, whoever is handy, is the goat. However, he does not say goodbye and I cannot help but feel indirectly guilty. He kicks a door open and departs.

Customer reaction to the brouhaha is a non-reaction, their mouths bulging with cholesterol and empty calories.

Shawn asks me in and says not to worry. He's self-conscious about his speech irregularities more than anything else and apologizes for sounding like Daffy Duck. I assure him that Melanie became accustomed to her braces in only a few weeks and enunciated perfectly thereafter.

Shawn chats with me on the obviously transient nature of fast food, the continual turnover. He cannot remember the names of everybody who has come and gone in the five years he has been at it, beginning his junior year in high school. He says Felipe had been waiting for an excuse to blow his top and it's not my fault. That is scant consolation. There is also the issue of me being short my most seasoned employee.

Well, that's nothing compared to what happens when Mr. Larionov comes by and drops his bombshell. He releases it on Shawn and I privately, and gives us the leeway to inform our people in any manner we see fit.

Mr. Larionov is putting his restaurants on the market, all seven of them.

In the confines of Shawn's office, the worry lines on Mr. Larionov's square face is a roadmap. I smell alcohol, doubtlessly vodka, despite him sucking on a mint. The man must have a band of monkeys on his back.

Mr. Larionov speaks quietly and bitterly. He says that there is no money in traditional fast food any more. Eating habits are changing. The country is on a health kick. The American hamburger is under assault. The witch-hunt against fried foods is never-ending, the fats and sodium regarded as cyanide.

The trend is toward vegetable wraps and salads and subs, and those chains are sprouting like crabgrass. This particular chain hasn't kept up, treating bean sprouts and arugula and the like as a fad. Supermarket delis and a greater variety of microwave meals are cutting deeply into his revenue too.

He's barely clinging to his operation. In the last year he lost more money than he made in the previous two. Corporate Headquarters throws fuel on the fire by offering ridiculous specials. Our highly popular El Acapulco ChickenWich, Number Eleven on the board and the registers, is a prime example. Corporate forces him to price the El Acapulco on sale for $3.95 when it costs him $4.15 to make. Even when it goes back to the regular $4.39, they'll throw another loss leader at him.

Mr. Larionov has prospective buyers, investors from Vancouver, British Columbia. They are Hong Kong Chinese who emigrated when the Reds took over in 1997. They have deep pockets and have assured him that if the purchase goes through, our jobs are secure. Nevertheless, there will be a hiring freeze until the future is clearer.

I am not prejudiced, but I do have to question what Asians know about double bacon cheeseburgers. I refuse to worry. I won't, I won't, I won't. I was searching for a job when I found this one.

Buddy is home. I'm dying to hear about his breakfast with Lizabeth Chipperfield and the subsequent restaurant job. He tells the oddest tale. I maintain my composure as he relates his insistence to her that they check out a

Chipperfield family lake cabin to surprise an alive and hiding Charles Murganzer, as if he's Saddam Hussein in his rat hole before he was captured and hung. Afterward, he didn't accept a job slinging hash. He didn't even apply. Goodness, he has joined the insurance industry!

Buddy is almost bubbly as he describes his new job. While his salary isn't thrilling, insurance companies are stable employers. This Unity outfit, of which I am unfamiliar, strikes me as marginal. But who knows whom or what is solvent until you read about a corporate meltdown on the front page, a former blue chip now a financial basket case?

Or when you hear it from your boss this very afternoon.

Buddy as a mail boy. Could you have guessed it scant weeks ago? Not me. I remind myself that these are new beginnings, his and mine, baby steps.

I congratulate Buddy and relate my stressful day.

Buddy shakes his head and says, "They must've sold five billion of their burgers and that doesn't count with cheese. How the hell can you be upside down when you got a license to print money?"

Speaking of bubbly, Buddy stopped on his way home to buy a bottle of champagne for the occasion. Not Champagne, but a refreshing sparkling wine from California at a fraction of the price. Buddy pops the plastic cork and we drink a toast in our good crystal.

"To us, kiddo," he says.

I touch his glass, making a musical note. "To us, licking the situation one day at a time."

I prepare a tuna casserole for dinner, how Buddy likes it with crushed potato chips on top. The blue Cadillac is next door. It's a robin's egg blue, Ellen's favorite color. The gold car is gone and so are Jim and Ellen, the gadabouts. They used to be such homebodies. I do wish that they keep the money and their new life in perspective.

Buddy has treated himself to extra helpings of the fizzy wine. He says it'll go flat and spoil if we don't polish it off. We're watching the Mariners at Minnesota. There have been six errors so far between the teams. You'd think for the amount major leaguers are paid, they could hang on to the baseball.

Buddy is snoring now, craggily angelic. I mute the ball game. Buddy says he doesn't snore. He says I do snore. I'll have to tape him sometime to prove that he has it backward. He is out like a light, but he is *back*. I have my old Buddy, full of sass and vinegar. I've never been more certain that we shall get through this.

I scramble to pick up the phone on the second ring.
"Mother."
Melanie sounds frantic. "What's the matter, dear?"
"Mother, do you have the TV on?"
"Yes, the Mariners."
"Turn on the six-thirty news. Hurry!"
"Which station?"
"Any of them. They're all covering the story."
"What story?"
"Mother!"
She's been so emotional lately. I wonder if it's she has a hormone imbalance. "For heaven's sake, Melanie," I say, as I obey and surf the local news channels.

I freeze at one of the reporters. She has raccoon eyes from the makeup, blonde hair that wouldn't flutter in a typhoon, and a shrill voice. She's standing above an instant live eyewitness whatever caption, announcing her name into a microphone.

In the background is a gaudy CHIPPERFIELD'S PREOWNED AUTOMOTIVE ELEGANCE SUPERSTORE banner. Seconds later, the anchors bid us good evening.

This is too much of a coincidence.

I play dumb. "What's on that's so all-fired important?"

"*Hawaii Five-O*. You know, the old cop show."

"Melanie, you are making no sense."

"Father!"

"Your father is on *Hawaii Five-O*? Melanie, what have you been drinking? Are you inhaling Carrara marble dust?"

"Mother, Chick Chipperfield, that sleazy used car salesman who dresses up like the devil and bashes cars with a pitchfork. You've seen him. He sponsors *Hawaii Five-O*, other old TV series, and night owl movies on Channel eighty-one."

"Yes, I do recall seeing him, vaguely," I say, suddenly queasy.

I quickly switch to Channel 81. There's Wo Fat, Steve McGarrett's Red Chinese nemesis. He's speaking to a pockmarked man in an aloha shirt. You don't need sound to know that they're up to no good.

"Original *Hawaii Five-O* reruns are David's secret vice," Melanie says. "He tapes them. He won't admit it but he has a hang-up about McGarrett's hair and overacting. He's always making a crack about it being bulletproof. I think he's envious because Steve is a stud."

Steve. It sounds as if my daughter is the one with the hang-up. "Melanie, will you please get to the point."

"Chick Chipperfield was raided today for breaking consumer protection laws. Father was on a surveillance tape. It looked like he was on a ladder. Him and another man who looked like an escaped convict were hanging a banner that said FUN FAIR. He wasn't arrested or accused of being mixed up in anything, but why was he on that ladder, on that tape, *there*?"

"Oh bosh. Dear, you're seeing things."

"It was Father, Mother. I know what my father looks like."

"Dear, everyone in this world has a double unbeknownst to them."

"In the same city?"

"Please calm down, Melanie. I'll stay tuned in. I'll let you know. Please don't fret. There is a logical explanation."

I hang up and continue watching with the sound on slightly as Wo Fat and his goons attempt to undermine our national security. This episode involves a counterfeiting plot to destroy our economy. McGarrett naturally thwarts Wo Fat in the end and chases him away in his communist submarine. I remember the series from the 1970s. It was one of our favorites too. Bald and husky, Wo Fat made a deliciously evil serial villain. The closing credits roll as do commercials for cheap carpeting and windshield repair.

I glance at my husband. His snoring is interrupted by a slurp and a snort, before resuming. I cannot bear to wake him and break the news. It is just one thing after another. He was in the wrong place at the wrong time when the authorities were laying their trap for Chipperfield.

If Melanie will settle down, perhaps our latest family crisis will blow over. If there is a proper moment for lying to your child and burying your head in the sand, this is it. You protect your loved ones.

I switch back to the baseball game. A ground ball skips over a multimillionaire shortstop's glove. I am not the only person having a bad evening.

My world is topsy-turvy.

Life is dumfounding me.

At least tomorrow is payday.

I hope.

Chapter 15

BUDDY

This dream's too goddamn weird.

I'm back at the *Reina Sofia*. Madrid. Ricky's inside of *Girl,* which has become 3-D. For once Ricky's not giving me a ration of shit. That's cuz he's looking inside at the left-hand side of Ana Maria, stretching his neck and head in, so he can leer at her ass.

If he makes a move to touch her, I'm gonna put my fist right through the picture. But he doesn't. He just stands there drooling.

In addition, that nice bay Ana Maria's gazing out at? It ain't a bay. It's Chick Chipperfield's Preowned Automotive Elegance lot. Instead of a sailboat, there's an Audi convertible with flames licking out from under the hood.

Bruno's next to the car yelling. I think he must be yelling for the fire department or a bucket of water, but I listen again and he's yelling "Hey asshole".

While Martha's putting on her makeup, I'm convincing myself I oughta be climbing out of the sack. My T-shirt's still damp from where it was drenched with sweat after I woke up. She gives me a smooch on the forehead, pats the cats, and then the bald spot on my noggin, and she's out the door for work.

Martha, she's acting goofy. I been half asleep since she got up. I can see her eyeballing me through my eyelids. It's one of those telepathological deals. It's not that she's pissed at me, scaring the hell out of Orange and Tangerine in the process, nothing like that at all. Just acting goofy. Like she's got something to get off her chest, but as hard as she rummages through her thoughts, she can't find the words. Like she dented a fender or clogged up the garbage disposal.

Except this situation has to do with me, not her.

What did I do now? Martha, she'll eventually clue me in.

Both Caddies are parked next door. I wonder what color the third and fourth and tenth will be. There's a meter reader four units down. This one's in uniform. There's been a lot of meter reading going on in the neighborhood, if you ask me, not that I'm paranoid.

I got a little time to kill and go in the spare room and prowl the shoeboxes we keep photos in. Most are pictures of Martha and Melanie and me through the years. Me running alongside Melanie first time she rode her bike without training wheels. Fourth of July, Martha holding out a sparkler. Aftermath of a blizzard when everything shut down and the three of us went sledding down a hill a block from the old house.

There's pictures of family get-togethers. Stan and me at a picnic, wrist wrestling. He's with whatshername, his second wife. There's a cousin of Martha's from Oregon, Hazel or Adele, one or the other, next to somebody's Christmas tree. We got three times as many pictures of cats as shirttail relatives. The three of us, we like cats. Melanie can't have one now. Dr. David's allergic, so he says.

The memory I finally locate in this one box is not near as pleasant. Stan and me split up some of Mom's personal effects. I got the death certificate. Cause of death: multiple gunshot trauma.

Besides that, the box contains a necklace made of red beads and rings that're silver and hold colored jewels too big to be real. No wedding or engagement rings. Can't remember if they buried her with them on. Don't think Dad hocked them or gave them to the new wife. Sure hope he didn't.

I'm out of the house and report for duty at Unity Property and Casualty Insurance Company. On the drive there, I make myself a promise. It involves keeping my trap shut and doing what I'm told. My mouth ended my employment mucho pronto at Chipperfield's Preowned Automotive Guano. Not a bad thing, but it happened. At Boeing and I fired from the hip more than once. It queered promotions to foreman, which I never wanted to be anyways.

The gum-chomping gal on the front desk is actually sweet to me. Her name's Lori. She wishes me luck, saying we're in the same boat. Bobbi Jo Russell comes out for me so quick, I don't have time to ask what Lori means. From what I've seen, I can make a wild guess.

We're going by a cube where two guys are arguing whether TGIF is an abbreviation or an acronym. The nameplate says one of them is Holcomb. Bobbi Jo picks 'em up and puts 'em down. She's in a hurry and she's uptight. I'm not exactly sure what an acronym is, but I know TGIF. It dawns on me that today's Friday. When you're not gainfully employed, Friday is a day no niftier than any other.

We fill out more papers in Bobbi Jo's office, for payroll deductions and beneficiary elections and so forth. I take notice of her personal effects. There's plaques and certificates on the walls from human resource and insurance courses and for belonging to various organizations. She has these little ceramic cats on her desk and a framed photo of a skinny shorthaired lady.

Bobbi Jo brings Cyndi in, introduces us, and hands me off to her. Cyndi's the clerical supervisor, my boss. Cyndi moves even quicker than Bobbi Jo. She's a human dynamo who comes up to my shoulder. Her hair's half brown, half gray, like she's worrying herself into old age.

By the time we've gotten to the mailroom and covered what Bobbi Jo covered with me, I get to hear Cyndi's life history. She started here as a file clerk right out of high school fourteen years ago. Her hubby's at Boeing, lucky dog, a tooling mechanic on the 777 line. They like fly-fishing and bowling. They got four kids, all in sports. Cyndi's one of those soccer moms when she's off-duty at Unity.

"You should catch on easily, Buddy," she says. "Ian and some of the others."

She pauses to sigh.

I tap my temple. "Not too quick on the uptake?"

"I could never figure them out. They were always keeping time to music I couldn't hear. Bobbi Jo says you're bored with retirement and doing this to make some mad money."

"That's me."

Cyndi says, "Steve and I are looking forward to retirement in eleven years, when the last of the kids are out of school. Is retirement what it's cracked up to be?"

"Every day's a new adventure."

We make a mail run together to the offices and cubes.

Cyndi's explaining what rates first class and what should be bulk mail as I push a shopping cart along. We stop at an empty corner office, the biggest on the floor. It's dark and there's nothing on the desk and the shelves. The nameplate's been peeled off the door, lifting some paint with it.

"We call it the Tomb of The Unknown Regional Manager," Cyndi says. "He was transferred here from Southern Region when they closed that office. He wasn't here a month when he was downsized. We barely knew him."

"Not gonna replace him?"

"No. They're experimenting with managing us at Western Region directly out of Home Office. It's a pilot program. We report to five different people who usually contradict each other. It's crazy."

"Where is the home office?"

"The company was founded in Hartford. Headquarters moved westward to St. Louis, then Topeka, keeping one step ahead of union activity and rising overhead. Presently, Turpentine Springs, Arkansas. That's why the powers that be felt they could consolidate and eliminate Southern Region."

"Bobbi Jo says Unity writes weird specialty insurance."

"If it hasn't fallen apart or burned up yet, we'll write it. We have boutique risks nobody else will touch. Did you know Unity is the major insurer of tattoo parlors?"

"Like the one downstairs?"

"Who else could be so lucky? Home Office is finding out that there are interesting diseases transmitted by contaminated needles. Uh oh! Now I know why Bobbi Jo's been on edge today. The Angel of Death."

Bobbi Jo Russell's standing in the doorway of her office talking to this guy. Her arms are folded so tight I'm afraid she'll crack a rib. He's in his forties, slim and natty in a tweed jacket. He's got anchorman's hair and the grayest eyes I ever saw on a human being.

"The Angel of Death?"

"Bobbi Jo's boss, out of Home Office H.R. He phoned from a hotel this morning. When he drops by on that short of notice, there's trouble."

"Downsizing?"

"Unity's payroll has shrunk ten percent in the past year and he's the hatchet man," she whispers. "I can't say he enjoys what he does, but I don't think he hates it either."

I know a thing or three about downsizing, on account of aerospace being boom and bust. I was personally familiar with Boeing-style downsizing before they invented the word. You're laid off. You come back after they get more orders from the airlines than they can handle. Then they force overtime on you.

Everybody on our route has one eye on Bobbi Jo and her boss. They've gone inside her office.

I'm taking mail out of an out-box belonging to a guy in marketing named Ridberg. He's got shiny skin and cologne strong enough to degrease auto parts.

He asks Cyndi, "Who's going bye-bye?"

"Nobody's been called in yet."

"New hire?" he asks me.

"First day on the job."

Ridberg laughs a salesman's horselaugh. "How much of a gold-plated handshake would that be? Lemme see. Eight hours seniority. That should rate forty-five seconds severance pay. A buck ninety-eight. Good luck, pal."

Cyndi moves the cart and me forward. I don't have a chance to answer this turdbird punk, which is what I promised myself I won't do, me and my hot-tempered mouth.

"Jerk," Cyndi mutters out the side of her mouth. "Sales and marketing scum. They think they're indispensable."

"Slicky boys. Are they?"

"In their feeble minds."

"They're still here."

"So far. The day's young."

Cyndi shows me the ropes on the postage meter. I'm humping a basket of mail out for my first post office run. One of the guys who was in Holcomb's cubicle walks out in front of me, headed for Bobbi Jo's office. I'm assuming he's Holcomb, as there's nobody left in the cube.

Holcomb's jabbing his thumb against his chest as he goes, saying plenty loud for anybody who cares to hear, "TGIF. This Guy Is Fucked."

I'm out the door opening up the pool car, a Ford Tempo, a model the Ford Motor Company's not manufactured in this century. Bobbi Jo's not kidding about the brakes. They sound like fingernails on the blackboard. I wanna stick my foot out the door to slow down. What nobody told me is that the steering's got a mind of its own. It favors left turns irregardless of the driver's choice of direction.

I make it back in one piece and dump new mail out of the bag. The geezer, Frank Rambaugh, wanders into the mailroom. I'd seen him earlier on my rounds. Once him and the Angel of Death crossed paths. The Angel wouldn't make eye contact with him. I was impressed.

Rambaugh's wearing that same brown suit and has that same hat tucked inside the arm that's holding his ancient briefcase. We make our introductions. He asks if I'm done with the car.

"You're welcome to it."

"Did it make any peculiar noises?"

"A few."

"Did it smoke excessively?"

"Only out the exhaust pipe."

"Good."

"You do your share of field work, huh?" I ask.

"There is no substitute for investigation," he says. "The professional claims man forgets this in the day of the telephone and computer and allied technologies. Electronic devices are overrated crutches."

I'm warming to this old boy. In my book, he rates high in the common sense department. "I agree. Where're you off to?"

"To interview a claimant submitting a second claim against Mother Unity."

"You can do that?"

"He was waiting to give me a statement on an automobile accident when a chair in our lobby collapsed. He is allegedly in too much pain to leave his home."

Rambaugh talks like he's afraid to make a grammar mistake. He's been looking at me funny.

"Guy's faking his injuries?"

"I earn my living listening to people lie to me," is Rambaugh's answer.

"That must get old fast."

He shrugs his free shoulder. "It is an integral and unavoidable cost of doing our business, like rodents in a grain silo. An insurance claim is often not an open-and-shut morality play. It is not television and the movies with defined conflicts between good and evil, and a pat resolution at the end."

Rambaugh is sounding and looking like an ugly old Gary Cooper or Duke Wayne. "No happy endings?"

He raises eyebrows as white as Santa Claus's. Rambaugh wears horn-rims. They're down over his nose. "Too few."

I didn't even think when I left the house what I was gonna do about lunch. The clock hits high noon. Nobody's said when my lunch hour is, so I mosey on over toward the employee lunchroom, hoping they got vending machines.

Holcomb's cube is cleaned out. Ridberg's too. I go by Bobbi Jo's office. Her and the Angel of Death are gone. So's her plaques and diplomas and cat figurines and the picture of the skinny shorthaired lady.

Chapter 16

MARTHA

On my morning break, I run across the street to a telephone store and splurge on a new cellular telephone. It's not a smart one, it flips up like the Kirk-to-Enterprise thingy William Shatner had when he was on some strange planet, and they have a special deal on the monthly minutes.

I shall buy now, sell Buddy later. They cost far less than they used to, a relative pittance. I will stick to fundamental usage; a phone is to make and receive calls. With my overtime pay, we can afford this and it's more of a necessity than a luxury. I mean, what if I have car trouble?

Next step is a upgrade to a state-of-the-art PC with CD burner and the latest operating system. When we are solvent, of course. I shall save my nickels and dimes, and one fine day simply come home with one and transport us into the 21st Century.

My day is nice and smooth. The workflow is steady. We are shorthanded, of course, but Shawn is in earlier than usual, and he's juggled the shifts so we overlap when need be. We're running like a finely oiled watch.

Then the paychecks don't arrive.

They come on Fridays, sent by the payroll company Mr. Larionov uses. Given fast-food turnover, most employees don't opt for direct deposit. The regular deliveryman has come and gone. He brought a case of napkins we desperately need, but no checks. Shawn cannot reach Mr. Larionov and he gets the runaround from the payroll firm.

Shawn looks genuinely frightened. He apologizes to us and requests our patience. He'll resolve the problem. I do have my doubts. However, I am not deserting this ship and Captain Shawn today, regardless how much water we take on. Everyone else but Emily stays on too. Emily was hired the day after I was. Her paycheck will be piddling, but she says loudly, not three feet from a table of senior citizen regulars who while away two hours over breakfast and coffee, that she, and I quote, "doesn't need this shit", and storms out.

The minute hand on my watch is made of lead. It's depressing to be depressed that a fast food paycheck is late. I drew almost as much working a Saturday at Boeing than I do in a week here, eight hours at time and a half. Late is hopefully all the checks are.

I leave at the end of my shift exhausted, albeit feeling optimistic. Shawn has been in his office for the past hour on the phone. I wish him luck for the entire crew and myself. Apparently, Mr. Larionov, a former Soviet Communist, is not grasping free enterprise.

Tomorrow is my day off. Coincidentally, on a rotating basis, it is Saturday. There are no weekends in the restaurant industry. Customers always have to eat. It didn't occur to me that I would be working Sundays, but my name is on the schedule. I'll go in, but the paycheck situation needs to be resolved before I do anything further. Loyalty, while a virtue, is a two-way street.

David's Mercedes is in our driveway. There is a travel trailer in Jim and Ellen's, hooked to the gold Cadillac. They have hankered for an RV as long as we've known them, but I didn't know you could install trailer hitches on those limousines. The rear end of the trailer protrudes out into the street. It's so wide that the blue Cadillac is parked at the curb. What this exhibition is about, I cannot fathom. I don't care how much money you have, such congestion is a violation of homeowner association rules. I have half a mind to write a letter.

I go inside to face the music.

Melanie is up off the sofa like a jack in the box. "Mother, I was worried sick when you didn't get back to me."

David gives me a nod and a quick wave. He's in Buddy's recliner, footrest up and his shoes on. My hubby would not like that one tiny little bit. David is watching the stock market ticker on CNBC, a folded newspaper on his lap.

I say to my daughter, "There is absolutely nothing to worry about."

David noisily unfolds his paper. He is not happy. I know Melanie dragged him along.

Melanie is eyeing me strangely. "Mother, please come clean with us."

David thrusts the paper at Melanie and says, "This monkey business with that car dealer could be serious."

Melanie's holds up a section, displaying an ARREST IN OPERATION TO SELL SHODDILY REBUILT VEHICLES AS UNDAMAGED headline and a photograph of Chick Chipperfield, hands behind his back, being led away from his car lot by a police officer. There is a smaller photo under it, a fuzzy shot like from a bank camera, of Mr. Chipperfield and a man standing by a BMW sedan as my Buddy and a man on ladders hang a FUN FAIR banner.

David and Melanie brought this newspaper with them. I sit on the edge of the couch and read that Chipperfield's Preowned Automotive Elegance was the center of a ring of scam artists who sloppily restored smashed and salvaged vehicles, laundered their titles out of state, and received clean titles in Washington.

The State of Washington requires vehicles wrecked and considered total losses by their insurers to be issued titles declaring them as salvage. But the title laundering circumvented that process. A salvaged vehicle can be worth less than half as much as an undamaged one, but Chipperfield sold them at normal prices.

"The work is shoddy too. These cars are dangerous. It's theft, it's fraud," says Randall Avery, 33, the undercover agent who made a sting buy of a BMW.

Avery was present when detectives slapped cuffs on J. R. (Chick) Chipperfield, 58, and led him away, the article continues. He was booked on first-degree theft, document altering, and criminal profiteering.

Chipperfield's only comment was, "This is (bleep) Nazi Gestapo tactics. I thought this was the (bleep) United States of America. I thought I had due process."

I'm numb, although not shocked. Would anybody be, knowing what we know about this man? I set the paper aside without reading to the end.

"Mother, please come clean with us."

"Well, yes, yes it does look like your father. Apparently I was mistaken. It is a long story."

"What *is* the story?"

You know, that is an excellent question. I have formulated no persuasive answers for the kids. The truth is too painful. "Your father and that man had a chance encounter. We may take legal action."

"A lawsuit?"

"If it comes to your father's good name being wiped through the mud."

Melanie laughs. "Father hiring a lawyer? That'll be the day. He says they should all be herded into the ovens."

"He may rethink that position when I break this news to him."

"Father didn't know? Doesn't know? What was he doing working at a used car lot?

"It is very complicated and the complete facts aren't in."

Melanie doesn't reply. She continues looking oddly at me. David has turned his attention from his investments and is looking at me too. I look down at myself and, oh Lordy, I am in beige and pastel blue, as if my MARTHA nametag isn't conspicuous enough. Of all the days to forget to change. I was more distracted by our paycheck woes than I thought.

"Mother, I smell cooking oil on you too. How long have you been working – there?"

I try to erase the horror on her face with a smile that does not come easily. "Buddy and I can't sit in rocking chairs, dear. We're not that kind of people. I'm already the early shift assistant manager."

"Mother, please be honest with us. We've suspected since Spain that you're somehow in financial trouble."

My attempt at a laugh unfortunately comes out as a snort. "Us? Nonsense."

I take my new phone out of my purse and flip it open. "Look. Would I have bought this if we were destitute?"

"Mother, they're dirt-cheap these days. Even the smart phones are."

"Not if you can't afford one. There are monthly and per-minute charges if you're not careful. The first four hundred minutes are free and they're gone before you know it. In that respect, these phones are beyond the budget of a pauper, wouldn't you agree?"

My Melanie can be a bulldog. "You had those messages from banks when you were gone. Now you taking a job at a hamburger joint. We'd be happy to see you through any crisis."

"No, dear, really, no. I do appreciate the offer, though."

"Wouldn't we, David?"

"Loan you whatever you need. At the prime rate –," David pipes up.

"David."

" – plus a point, which currently –"

"David," Melanie says to him in a level voice I do not often hear.

David imperceptibly flinches. He's pinking.

Then to me, she says, "David got a carpool lane ticket this morning. He's grumpy."

David shakes his head and says, "A hundred and five bucks. I had a waiting room full of patients."

Melanie says, "Mother, I'm not comprehending Father's role in that man's business."

"He has no role. I'm surprised you would think he has, dear."

"I'm not accusing Father of anything. By the way, where is he?"

I check my watch. I don't remember if Buddy said what

his hours are at the Unity Property and Casualty Insurance Company. Our lives are moving too fast to keep up on the fine details.

I say, "Your father was antsy too. He's accepted a position at a major property and casualty insurance carrier. Busy, busy, busy. That's us."

"Doing what?" Melanie asks skeptically. "He doesn't have an insurance background."

I cannot merely say Buddy is their mail boy. "Information and communications. It's quite complex. He just started. You can ask him when he gets home."

A gigantic black and chrome SUV pulls in behind the kids' Mercedes. So much for my complaints about the Hendricks's vulgar excesses. A striking, big-haired blonde emerges, taking the last puff on a cigarette. She has been crying and her makeup is smeared. I immediately know who she is.

Stomach aflutter, I go to the door.

"Mrs. Whitacre?"

Her voice is the same as on the phone: alcohol and tobacco and overripe sexuality. I decide to be as cool as a cucumber and let her have the floor, to allow her state her intentions.

"Yes, I am."

"Is Buddy in? I need to apologize to him and a phone call isn't enough. I'm sorry to drop in unannounced. You're listed in the book. I have a terrible confession to make," she says as she dissolves into sobs.

An introduction and the reason for the visit gush forth.

Who her late husband was, if my husband hadn't already informed me. Who her father is. The arrest.

"I'm Martha. My husband isn't here, but you can come in and wait. He shouldn't be long."

"You may not want me in your home, Martha."

What's wrong with me? Why can't I hate this girl?

"My daughter and son-in-law are here. They informed me of your father's predicament and Buddy's picture in the paper."

Lizabeth Chipperfield Murganzer says, sniffling. "I love my Daddy, but I know him too. He's a pathological liar. He can't help himself. He was born with a liar gene."

She's coming to pieces again. I hug her. Is she bewitching me too? A worldly woman, she is surprisingly soft and fragile. I smell liquor on her. I repeat my invitation and whisper, "Please mention nothing about your late husband and his leapfrog Ponzi fund, as Buddy terms it."

"Did Buddy tell you? I'm Lizabeth Chipperfield till death do me part. If I don't hear the Murganzer name again it won't be soon enough."

I introduce Lizabeth to David and Melanie as Chick Chipperfield's daughter, adding, perhaps inappropriately, "People don't get to choose her parents."

"I need to apologize to Buddy for Daddy," Lizabeth says.

We take seats. David has turned off the TV and lowered the footrest. Forced smiles ensue. This is a rather awkward klatch.

Lizabeth breaks the silence. "Daddy's no angel, but when I visited him in jail, he said he didn't know those cars were wrecked until he was arrested. It was Bruno's doing."

"Bruno," I say. Buddy mentioned Bruno.

"Bruno was Daddy's service manager. He's on the lam. They have a warrant out on him. When he was in the pen he met some Russians who ran chop shops and did fraudulent car repairs. Bruno was connected to the Brighton Beach bunch and organized by the time he got out."

"Russian mobsters?" Melanie says, wide-eyed.

I say, "I've had my fill of former Soviets for the day."

David smirks and says, "And they claim you can't learn a trade in prison."

"Gangsters, goons, I don't know. They definitely weren't choir boys," Lizabeth says with a demure shrug.

She is addressing my daughter and son-in-law. David has a habit of staring at female midsections when he makes a woman's acquaintance, a component of his profession, I think. He has been taking in Lizabeth Chipperfield from top to bottom. She's in a matching pants and top outfit, brushed cotton, lingerie pink in color. Nothing fits skintight, but perfect curvatures show at crucial spots. Men passing her in the street would walk into walls and lampposts.

David wets his lips and says, "I've seen his commercials. They are creative."

Melanie rolls her eyes at me.

"Heather's gone down there to the jail to bail him out," Lizabeth says.

Then to me, "Heather's Daddy's new wife. She's younger than I am."

What was the name of the girl in that old novel? Lolita? "Yes, I believe Buddy may have mentioned her too."

Speaking of the devil, in walks Buddy. He freezes in his tracks. He has the silliest expression on his face and who can blame him.

He clears his throat and says, "Well, well, the gang's all here."

Chapter 17

BUDDY

"Holy fucking cow" is damn near what flies out my mouth instead of the thing that did. This is one goofy and disorientationing scene I'm coming home to.

Dr. David's in my recliner. That's his big Benz hogging the driveway. Melanie's with him. And Martha, oh shit, her in her junk food colors, they're on the couch. Lizabeth Chipperfield's in the easy chair. That's her Caddy Escalade on the street. Next door is wall-to-wall Caddies and a trailer. Neighborhood's looking like Chipperfield's lot, only the cars are nicer.

"Buddy, why don't you have a seat," Martha says.

Meaning sit down before I fall down. It's quiet, like someone's died. I plop on a dinette chair and wait for the other shoe to drop. Smack-dab on top of my head.

Martha does the honors on Chipperfield's arrest and hands me a newspaper. Chick's making a face at the camera and his comb-over hair's like a bird's nest in a tornado. Martha, she sticks up for Lizabeth, telling me how bad she feels for her unintentional role in mixing me up in the car fraud mess.

Oughta be going through the roof. But I'm feeling ding-dong, like when Fatso landed that punch on the side of my noggin. All that's going through my mind is that I have my picture in the paper for the first time in my life.

"We knew something was rotten in Denmark," I say.

Melanie sighs. "Father."

"Chipperfield, the rancid son of a bitch." I nod at Lizabeth. "Sorry. Pardon my French."

"No apologies needed. I've called Daddy and my ex-husbands worse."

Dr. Dave and Melanie look at each other.

She looks at us. "Mother and Father, David and I feel you owe us an explanation. About everything."

Martha and me, we look at each other.

I have me a brainstorm. "What gets my goat, I didn't get any credit in that article."

Melanie asks, "For what?"

"That Randall Avery guy."

"The man your father warned," Martha says, our telepathics kicking in.

"In the horseflesh. Part of our routine, me tipping him off on the sick Beemer. Randy, as he introduced himself and his official capacity, took care of the rest."

"It was an ongoing sting operation, Dad," says my son in law. "That car was doubtlessly targeted in advance."

"Thanks for clarifying, Dave."

"Speaking of clarification, will somebody please clarify what you were doing involved with used cars in the first place?" Melanie asks.

"Long story," I say. "Long and complicated."

"An old friend wasn't it, Buddy?" Martha says, beaming her telepathics at me.

"Yep. Used to be at Boeing. Worked gate security. His brother-in-law is in law enforcement. He knew I was retired. Signed me on."

"For undercover support," Martha says as she rereads

the article.

"Really?" Melanie says.

"It's long and complicated."

"Can't talk about it or I might queer things for the trial."

Lizabeth's eyes are shining and I think she's biting her cheek.

My daughter sighs again. *"Everything's* long and complicated."

Lizabeth's telepathiced into us, saying, "This is the best for Daddy. He'll have his hand slapped before he can get in more serious trouble."

Martha pipes up, tapping the page, "Look. See right here. It says the investigation was aided by anonymous sources."

"There you go," I say. "Call me Buddy Whitacre Anonymous Source."

David says, "As I said, Dad, it's been an ongoing investigation."

"Dave, can we keep that article? It's suitable for framing."

Melanie says, "Mother says you have a job in insurance communications. Congratulations."

"Awesome," Lizabeth says.

"Thank you. First day. I'll keep you posted how it goes."

"How do you find the time for a full-time insurance job and undercover work?" asks my suspicious daughter.

"Multitasking," Martha says.

Melanie throws in the towel on the subject with, you guessed it, a sigh.

Martha's in her junk food uniform. I reckon the jig's up on that count. Melanie stares at her mother, then me, waiting for another dose of clarifying. How our retirement came to be what it's come to be and so forth.

I keep my yap shut. I'll let Martha lead us through this minefield. Except all she's doing is fussing with the doily on the end table.

Lizabeth stands, unpregnanting the silence. "I'll scoot. I just wanted to get things off my chest, for what good it'll do."

"No, wait. Stay for dinner. Everybody stay," Martha says, likewise on her feet. "Buddy, don't we have a package of bratwursts in the freezer?"

"Yep. Buns too. I'll nuke the sausage to thaw 'em and light the coals."

"I can whip up a salad," Martha says.

"Sounds fine to me," Dr. Snatchecologist says as I detect that his eyeballs haven't strayed far from the Lizabeth's pink duds, and not in an office-visit kind of way.

Neither has Melanie's eyes, narrowed on her lawfully wedded husband's. She's on her feet too. This powwow's aged my little girl five years.

"We can't stay. David, you said you had paperwork."

He's up too, finally unassing my recliner, slow and disappointed-like. "Indeed. Yes. So I did. So I do."

Lizabeth moves her rig so the kids can get out. She comes back in and says, "Martha, Buddy, no, I really can't stay."

"Yes you can, dear," Martha says. "We insist."

I've just stuck the frozen brats in the microwave and set it on defrost. "Yeah. C'mon. We're past the point of no return here."

We hear a loud muffler and big tires crunching our

gravel. For crying out loud, it's Grand Central Station around here. A tow truck's backing up to Lizabeth's Escalade, déjà vu for the second time.

Lizabeth clenches her fists. "Damn, damn, damn. Someday I'll be able to quit apologizing to you guys, but not today. They were pulling in when I left Daddy's. They followed me. I thought I'd lost them. We reached some pretty high speeds."

"Must've cruised through the complex till they spotted it," I say.

"Who is *they*?" Martha asks.

"Pencilneck the repo man," I say.

Sure enough, it's him stepping out. The other door slams. Pencilneck has got a sidekick, whose belly button's sticking out from under a T-shirt that may of fit him one hundred pounds ago.

"Buddy, please, it's okay, I'll handle this," Lizabeth says, zipping between me and the door and on outside.

Martha has me by the arm. "That young lady is perfectly capable of taking care of herself. If she isn't, there's nine-one-one. Buddy Whitacre is as of now retired from the superhero profession."

So we watch. My free hand's on the doorknob as Lizabeth and the boys have a conversation that is not totally cordial. I can read lips enough to know what some of the words coming out of her mouth are. I'm losing the circulation in the arm Martha has ahold of, but nothing develops. Lizabeth takes some suitcases and boxes out of her rig, forks over the keys, and away they go, Escalade on the hook. Like to think Pencilneck enlisted backup help on account of me.

She stacks her stuff off to a side and comes in.

"Heather and I had a blowup over Daddy," she explains. "When he phoned home from the slammer, my advice to her was to let him cool his heels for a few days to teach him a lesson. She goes, you're an expert on a life of crime, you and your crook husband, so don't you judge my Chickypoo. That's what she calls him, Martha. Chickypoo. Yuck. Barf. Puke.

"It went from there. I packed what I could carry and moved out. I'd worn out my welcome anyway. I was going to find a motel after I'd seen you guys. If I can use your phone, I'll call a cab."

"Bosh," Martha says. "You can't go out into the night without accommodations or transportation. We have a second bedroom that's gathering dust. You stay with us until you're settled. Isn't that okay, Buddy?"

I'm already headed out the door for her belongings.

~ ~ ~

In bed, Martha and me tell each other how our day went. I'm so pissed about her paycheck, I'm not gonna sleep more than 20 minutes at a stretch.

"The workers who work in that business, they work their butts off for peanuts," I tell her. "And then he goes and stiffs you! Selling out to Chinamen or not, you can't convince me that it's not a load of guano, your boss being unable to meet his payroll."

Martha orders me to calm down and after I kind of do, I recap my duties at Unity. That deathtrap pool car too. The claims guy, Frank Rambaugh, older than Methuselah. Last but not least, the Angel of Death cutting his swath, clipping the personnel lady who hired me in the process.

I don't understand all this downsizing," I say. "It's like the whole, entire economy's gone aerospace."

We smell cigarette smoke. Martha says it's Lizabeth out on the deck slaking a nicotine fit, the poor tormented child. When all's silent, I get up for a drink of water. I see a cell phone on top of the envelope from Stan. It's half the size of a pocket calculator. There's a user manual with it that's twice the size of the phone. Gotta wonder if Martha's making a statement with her placement of the gizmo. Figured she'd be getting an updated and modern one sooner or later.

Martha comes out, finger to her lips.

She sits next to me and whispers, "Fast asleep. Orange and Tangerine are curled up against her. She does have a way with the males of the species."

"Can't argue with that. The kids. What do they know for sure?"

"I blew it with my work uniform," Martha says. "They know too much, although the Murganzer Stable Fund cat isn't out of the bag."

"We're fine," I say. "Hunky dory."

"Are you okay with me and this, dear? I bought it today."

She's flipped up the lid of her baby telephone. The screen's twice the size of a postage stamp and as bright and blue as a swimming pool.

"I'm okay. How they keep getting smaller and smaller, maybe someday they'll disappear altogether. If we're lucky."

She laughs. "Dream on."

The envelope from Stan is suddenly on my mind. This

telepathicness of ours, it won't stop zapping between Martha and me. The curse of decades of marital bliss.

"Well," she says.

"Yeah," I say as I get up and go get it and climb back in the sack and tear an end off the envelope. "What the hell."

I lose my nerve and slide it to her. She can remove the contents, like it's the Oscars winner. And that's what she does, gazing at a five-by-seven photograph for the longest time.

She gives it to me and says, "Your mother? I don't recall seeing many pictures of her."

It is Mom, in black-and-white that's yellowing. The paper's shiny and curling at the corners. Mom's back is to the camera, her head turned slightly. There's no mistake who it is. She's smiling, like she's aware Dad's snuck up on her to take this picture. A window's directly in front of her. Either the flash is bouncing off the glass or the background's fuzzy. Dad probably snapped it with a Brownie box camera. I'll take Stan's word that it's the Copalis Beach cabin and the ocean out beyond.

Mom is kinda plump like *Girl*. She's older than *Girl*, naturally, and her hair's curled at the ends, how they wore it those days, 1957 or 1958 or thereabouts. She bears no resemblance whatsoever to *Girl* and I still don't remember this picture. Mom's in baggy jeans and has got an apron on over her jeans. I can't compare her exact shape, her figure, to *Girl*'s, not that I'd want to.

The kitchen sink's underneath that window and she's doing the dishes. Her hands are in the dishwater, so I can't see rings. I was too young then to remember any of this, Mom in the photo, the layout of the cabin, nothing, zilch.

This picture, like *Girl*, it brings back the murder, not my living, breathing mom.

I have me a sudden flashback of the first sergeant at Ord calling me out of the mess hall to the orderly room. That old first shirt had a helluva time spitting it out, why I had to go home. He was as nervous as if he was the recruit and I was the old Sarge.

"Do you think of her much, about what happened to her? You haven't spoken of her in ages."

Since Martha's holding my hands, I can't cross my fingers without being caught. I cross my toes. "Nah. It was a long time ago."

"You said it affected Stan even more deeply. He was at a vulnerable age."

"I hadn't been in the service long. We were closer then than we are now."

"I'm not implying it was easy for you," she says.

"I know you're not, Martha."

"Hmm. There's something else."

She fishes a note and a folded paper that looks like a brochure out of the envelope. I'm breathing easier as she hasn't added two plus two regarding *Girl*. My secret's gonna remain my secret.

"It's from Miriam. She did the mailing. No hello, how are you, we're fine, simply that she found this, which had been forgotten. That's Miriam for you. Your folks took a policy out on both you and Stan when you were youngsters."

Martha is none too partial to Miriam neither. Poor Stan and the sour, unfriendly gals he finds to marry. "Policy?"

It's a musty-smelling life insurance policy in my name to the tune of $1500. The outfit promising to pay that amount to my next of kin when I croak is The Old Indemnity Life Company.

"Sounds like a brand of cheap bourbon."

Martha checks in the phone book. "They aren't listed locally."

"Could of gone belly-up," I say. "I'll check with Rambaugh. He handled the claim for Custer's arrowhead poisoning."

Martha looks at me.

"Mother Unity humor," I say. "The company had life insurance on some of his troops. Honest Injun."

Martha lifts her eyebrows. "If you say so."

"Fifteen hundred's plenty to cremate me. That's what we said we wanted in our wills, didn't we?"

"We did."

"I want the mortician to get as little of our assets as possible. It's a goddamn racket."

Martha smiles. "You might have mentioned your opinion of funeral parlors five or six hundred times."

I look at myself in the paper again, me and Bruno hanging that banner while Chick talks himself into the jailhouse.

"Who's that artist, Norman Rockwell or one of them, who said everybody gets fifteen minutes of fame?"

"Andy Warhol," Martha says.

"Me as an anonymous source, even if I wasn't. You gotta take what flavor of fame you get. This Andy Warlock, he should've said that too."

Chapter 18

MARTHA

Saturday races by at the speed of light.

Despite wretched weather, never has a day off been so precious. We are treated to a ferocious summer rainstorm accompanied by thunder, a record downpour. We stay inside, we nest, a truly peculiar nuclear family, us and the widow of the man who very nearly ruined our lives. We make popcorn and watch baseball. Lizabeth and I collaborate on a crock-pot mulligan stew. Anything in the fridge and pantry is fair game.

Lizabeth scampers out to the deck for a puff whenever the rain lets up. Pavement steams and the out-of-doors smells like laundry. I do not attempt to count how many beers Buddy put away. Our day off is a sabbatical from serious conversation too. Our only serious effort at anything is Monopoly and Scrabble.

Suddenly, Saturday is over. It's dark and we're exhausted from inactivity. We sleep like logs.

~ ~ ~

I awake to a gorgeous morning. Yesterday's soggy blast has drifted into British Columbia.

Although the restaurant opens later on Sundays, I assumed I would be the first in the household to rise and shine. Not so. Lizabeth is at the dinette with her purse open, the contents strewn – cosmetics, billfold, pens, cigarettes, bobby pins, facial tissue. She has her bankbook out, poking away at a pocket calculator. I smell a pot of coffee brewing.

"Oh hi," she says. "I took the liberty with the coffeepot. I thought you guys would like some. How do you take yours?"

Indeed I would. Oddly, I'm not miffed. I should be, this exotic creature puttering about in *my* kitchen as if she owns it, but I am not. The coffee we serve at the restaurant meets neither minimum Seattle coffee standards nor ours. Buddy says fast food coffee will remove the gum from fuel lines. The premium beans we buy is a luxury we tenaciously cling to. I request milk and sugar. Lizabeth takes hers that way too.

She sips and holds up her bankbook. "I'm trying to figure what I have and don't have. It's an inactive account I didn't close, thank heavens. When Charles and I got married, he controlled the purse strings. I didn't lack for anything, but he doled the money in dribs and drabs. Martha, I feel like a jerk for playing along with that control freak. Now I'm glad I did. It was a blessing in disguise. I'm glad I didn't squirrel any money away. It'd be dirty money. Your money."

How could anything on earth be more ironic, more touching? "I appreciate that, Lizabeth, very much. I've also appreciated money in a different light lately. Money isn't important unless you don't have it."

She says, "Amen. If my arithmetic isn't too rotten, I have enough for first and last month's rent. I'll find a place near a bus line. I can always land a job. That's the advantage of being a food and hospitality professional. There's always an opening for somebody who's great at what they do and isn't afraid of work, people like you guys and me."

I say, "This job is temporary for me. I have no food service background. Buddy and his Army mess hall experience is better off in insurance. So is the general public."

We both think that's too funny. I hope our laughter doesn't awaken him.

"If you change your mind about work and want to stay in touch, I can help," Lizabeth says. "You'd make a great cashier and greeter at an upscale eatery."

Buddy said he had found himself opening up to her. Me too, to an extent. However, there will be no talk of banks losing their patience with us, delinquent paychecks, and a dreaded house payment growing further overdue with each passing day.

"Well, thanks. I'm hoping to get ahead enough to afford vocational training. You're never too old."

"No you're not. What interests you?"

"Aside from learning watercolor painting, nothing practical vocationally, I'd have to say technology.

"Cool."

"It's a new wrinkle that's just now been popping in my head. The field intrigues me, computers and such. What exactly, that's difficult to say. Certainly not a desk job. I wouldn't be able to sit still. I have no academic credentials and I'd be competing against zitfaced little nerd boys for IT jobs. Buddy's future plans are even less focused. I don't see insurance in the cards for him any more than I do used cars."

Lizabeth raises a fist. "Go for it, Martha."

Up goes mine in solidarity. "I will. Do you have long-range plans, Lizabeth?"

Lizabeth opens her palm in oath. "Only this. I swear on a stack of Bibles, no more husbands for this kid, Martha. Lizabeth Chipperfield Hollis Doherty Carnahan Smithson Murganzer is now plain old Chipperfield forever and ever. She has learned her lesson."

"Just one husband can be exhausting," I say.

"And he's a dandy too. Mine weren't." She ticks them off on ruby-red nails. "Kevin, my high school true love for all eternity. He was a quarterback, I was a yell queen. My legacy with him was a botched abortion and no chance for children. The last I heard he weighs three hundred pounds, has a ponytail, lives with his parents, and works in a warehouse. The next three, call them Tom, Dick and Harry, were handsome and charming bar customers. Duh. You'd think after the first drunk I'd learn. Last and least comes Charles. All rats, but Charles was the absolute pits. The others were bums, but they weren't in anyone's pockets, with the exception of the Three Stooges sneaking into my purse for booze money."

I sigh. "Love is blind."

"It's less or more complicated than that. I'm not sure which. I tried to explain to Buddy that falling in love to me is like catching a bad cold. It clobbers me, knocks me flat on my back, uh, literally."

I have to smile. "Then you get well."

"I experience the wellness that's the opposite of well. I recover to reality. Am I making any sense?"

"You are. The moral of the story is to get over that virus fast, before you walk down the aisle."

"I can't do anything stupid until Charles is declared legally dead. Then what, give myself a magic pill?"

"The pill is called *time*, Lizabeth. That is the chicken soup for what you catch."

"You and Buddy had a long courtship?"

"Do as I say, not what I do. Melanie thought she was born prematurely until she learned about the birds and the bees."

Lizabeth opens her mouth in mock shock.

"We'll be married forty years after next year. Perhaps we were an exception. We beat the odds or nobody else would have us."

"What you are is incredible. I'll have an apartment and be out of your hair by the end of the day."

I finish my coffee, get up, and wag a motherly finger.

"You take the time you need."

"Yes, ma'am."

As I back out en route to work, I see gaudy SOLD stickers plastered diagonally over the FOR SALE signs at Jim and Ellen's. They are preparing to roll. That tentative date of ours at the buffet came and went. I am not holding my breath that we'll reschedule. Farewell hugs would be nice.

That's when a man parked across the street gets out of his car. He gives me a little wave and smile. He has a haircut and is presentably dressed. He is carrying a clipboard and appears to be harmless. Buddy muttered some nonsensical, paranoid thing to me the other day about all the meter readers in the neighborhood. Perhaps this man is one, although it is Sunday.

I lower my window.

He looks at his clipboard and says, "Excuse me. Mrs. Whitacre?"

My knuckles whiten around the steering wheel. Is he leading the charge of the first wave of bill collectors?

"And who are you?"

He removes a thick envelope from his clipboard and asks, "Could you hold this for a moment?"

I foolishly do and he says, already backpedaling to his car, "Martha , you've been served. You have fifteen days to respond. Have a nice one."

I unfold a summons and complaint filed by a Chicago law firm in behalf of Nicky Cheshire. I recognize that name. He is Buddy's obese soccer hooligan assailant, the one he calls Fatso. On behalf of a British solicitor and their client, they are seeking the American equivalent of £2,500,000 from Buddy and Martha Whitacre. Legal writing has an illiteracy all its own. As far as I can determine, they are demanding this money from Buddy and me for their client's injuries and pain and suffering. This document uses words such as malicious and disabling and unprovoked.

How much is £2,500,000? I shall check how the pound is doing versus the dollar. Regardless and irrelevant, it is more than we have or ever will have.

Buddy has his crackpot theory that Charles Murganzer is alive. I am developing a crackpot theory of my own about these British lawyers and their American counterparts, first a New York City firm and now Chicago. This and his ordeal with the Spanish authorities. The harassment would be getting monotonous if it weren't so stressful. This is fishy. This is too pat. There is chumminess behind the scenes.

We have never been sued before. There is no good reason to inform Buddy yet. He would blow a gasket.

And I need to think.

~ ~ ~

The restaurant is dark and I have no keys. When I open up on weekdays, the janitorial service is inside, finishing up. They let me in. Perhaps they don't work Sundays. Perhaps they haven't been paid either. I wait in my car.

After 20 minutes, I'm ready to leave. Then Todd and Nicki pull into the lot in a small truck jacked up a mile high on knobby tires. I had a suspicion they were an item, the sidelong glances, how they would take their breaks together. We exchange waves. I go over to them and suggest we give it 20 minutes more. They ask if we'll be paid. I wish I had an answer.

Next is a carload of our senior citizen regulars. They wait patiently in a full-size sedan. It is not new, but it's in showroom condition. Their routine is to have a leisurely breakfast, cheap eats before walking at a mall. Time is not a problem. I refuse to envy them.

Shawn shows and hurriedly opens up. He apologizes and replies to my unspoken question with a sad headshake. Once we are up and running, he goes to his office to work the phone. I can't quit on Shawn. Cannot. He is trying so so so hard.

I complete my shift like a good soldier and change into civilian clothes I brought along. I shall not repeat that boo-boo.

~ ~ ~

I check email. Mr. Timkins has not replied. He must think I'm the world's biggest pest, not to mention crazy. I write him of this latest development. I write him that the dictionary defines conspiracy as an agreement to perform together an illegal act. I capitalize "conspiracy" and state my belief that this conspiracy (again capitalized) extends from the Spanish police to English lawyers to American lawyers. I ask for help. I capitalize "help."

~ ~ ~

I arrive home to another driveway surprise. Apparently, Driveway Surprise is going to be an everyday event, a signature of our new life. Next door, a Cadillac and the trailer are gone. Behind Buddy's pickup is a Mercedes-Benz, the E300 model. It is not big or new like David's. The paint has its share of scrapes and dings.

I hear laughter. I go around the side to Buddy and Lizabeth on the deck. On the table is an ashtray and a pitcher of lemonade.

"Martha, take a load off. This is tasty stuff," Buddy says and runs in for a glass.

I sit down and Lizabeth says, "We've had quite a day, Martha. How was yours?"

"I've had better and I've had worse. Whose car is that?"

"Long story," Buddy says, returning with a tumbler full of ice. He's red-faced and it isn't entirely sun exposure.

He pours. I taste and shudder. "I have a hunch this isn't conventional lemonade."

"Chock full of vitamins," Buddy says, hoisting his glass.

"Vodka for flavoring. I mix them weak," Lizabeth says.

"Mm." It is tart and has a delicious bite.

"The car," Buddy says. "Lizabeth needed wheels and I had me a brainstorm. We cruised past the lot."

"Don't tell me. Chipperfield's Preowned Automotive Elegance Superstore? That lot?"

"Yeah. Heather sprang the old boy, you know."

"I doubt if Daddy spent two hours behind bars," she

says sourly.

"He wouldn't return to his car lot, after what happened. Would he?"

"You know what they say about returning to the scene of the crime, Martha," Buddy says.

"We had to climb over that yellow police tape and go in a side door. Daddy was in his office. He almost wet his pants when he saw Buddy."

I look at my husband.

He throws up his arms, as if surrendering to a posse.

"Lizabeth made me go back and wait in the car. That's what I did. There was no violent action in any way, shape or form."

"Daddy gave me this old Mercedes to get rid of me. I don't know what he was doing, destroying papers they didn't confiscate or who knows what. He was in a tizzy. I see you're worried, Martha. Buddy was too. Don't be. This car is perfectly legal. Technically."

"Technically," I say, looking at him, then at her.

"Daddy gave it out as a loaner when Bruno worked on a customer's car. It wasn't posted for sale."

Buddy says to me, "Just in case, I recommended her to go easy when going over bumps and potholes. If it's a junk car Bruno and Bondo Boris and the Russkies slapped parts together to make, it could bust clean in two."

"I'm apartment hunting in the morning."

"I told her," Buddy says. "No point trying on a Sunday."

There is an odd and prolonged series of short horn honks out front. We go around the side. It is Ed (I think) piling out of their car saying, "Hey, guys. Sorry if I gave you an earache. It's a hassle to play *Here Comes the Bride* on a one-note horn."

Yes, it is Ed. For out of the back seat, Ted gallantly holding the door, steps Janine.

Janine and I squeal like schoolgirls and hug.

"I'm so glad you got out of Spain so quickly," she says.

"No small part to your help, dear. I'll forever be grateful. There are other issues, but I've asked Mr. Timkins at the embassy in Madrid for further assistance."

"If there's anything I can do," she says. "We're going back."

"To Spain? When?"

Janine is blushing. She is the same sweet Janine, a bit wide in the torso, hair hanging slightly limp. She's different too. It is her eyes. They were always a tad melancholy in Spain. No longer. There is a twinkly sparkle in them.

"Next week," she finally says. "We are."

"We?"

Ted's grin is as wide as his round face.

"Here comes the bride?" I ask Janine.

Ted has an arm around her.

Janine nods, beaming. "The agency has contacts in Spain. We're going to be married in an Andalusian white village in a centuries-old church. I'm switching with another director to lead this tour of the Andalusia region."

"Ted proposed on his knees, like they did it in the olden days," Ed says.

"Whatever works," Ted says, squeezing his fiancée's waist.

"Well, I'll be damned," Buddy says. "Everybody c'mon in."

Ed says, "First things first. Buddy, lend me a hand."

Ed, the poor man, he's so mesmerized by Lizabeth, he trips on the board we edge the driveway gravel with. He recovers and they bring from the trunk a case of beer and the biggest bucket of takeout fried chicken I have ever seen in my life.

"We barged in for dinner," Ted says. "It's only fair we bring it."

On the way inside, Janine says, "We're learning lifestyle compromises. Last night was candlelight, duck l'orange and a Napa Valley chardonnay."

"Any more art cinema?"

"If you regard the *Dirty Harry* movies as artsy."

We have a roaring good time. Ted and Janine are adorable, tender and considerate to each other. We make short work of the chicken and much of the beer. Lizabeth mixes pitchers of her high-octane vitamin drink. Ted is – what is the word? – courtly. He moves her chair for her when she gets up and down. I wonder if Buddy notices, I wonder if it might rub off.

The kids decide to continue partying, all four of them incidentally. Lizabeth knows a place with a jazz combo that has Sunday night jam sessions. I announce that the bar is closed. Janine, I suspect, is to be the designated driver, but she's taken to Lizabeth's favorite beverage. Ed is taken with Lizabeth, period. I think she's reciprocating to the extent that she seems flattered that he barely stops short of drooling when their eyes meet.

At the door, Janine takes me aside. "I'd love it if you and Buddy could attend our wedding."

"We'd love to, but it would be impossible on short notice. Retirement keeps us busy."

"Obligations coming out our ears," Buddy contributes.

They're gone and I'm depressed. We couldn't afford the trip if we hitchhiked.

With the exception of chicken bones that go into the garbage can, the cleanup can wait until tomorrow. Everybody's been tidy and I'm bushed. I'm on the couch, yawning. Buddy is beyond bushed, snoring like a locomotive in his recliner, oblivious to the tail end of a day-night doubleheader.

The bases are loaded. The Mariner pitcher walks in the winning run. It's just as well my Buddy is conked out. Plays like this do his blood pressure no good whatsoever. I shut the TV off and pull out that photograph of Buddy's mother. If I study it, it is Buddy's mother. If I look at it for the length of a blink, as if a flashcard, it is *Muchacha en la Ventana*.

I think I'm remembering the title correctly. I've already forgotten 90 percent of *mi español*. As they say, use it or lose it.

It is her, Ana Maria Dalí, age 18. I'm relieved. When this photograph came out of the envelope, my Buddy went into a trance. But it isn't a silly old man's sexual fantasy. *Muchacha* is his mother and he doesn't even realize it.

That shall be my second little secret of the day.

Chapter 19

BUDDY

Monday, Monday, so the old song goes. I'm remembering how much I hate and despise Mondays.

Didn't sleep worth a diddly shit neither. Tossed and turned all night long. Forget how many times Madrid Ricky pulled up out front of this house in a '57 De Soto Adventurer convertible, two-tone in gold and red. He's my Ricky, but Lucy's beside him, Fred and Ethel Mertz, their neighbors and best friends on the show, they're in back, dead ringers for Jim and Ellen. Get this, everybody's in black and white, even Lucy and her red hair and her necklace that's my mom's red one. Ricky, he'd honk and honk for me. By waking me up, Martha, she'd chase Ricky away. Off he'd go, peeling rubber.

I'm awake for good early, with a headache and a queasy tummy. I belch and taste chicken grease and grapefruit and beer. Maybe I got me a touch of the bug. It's going around this time of year.

I get up shortly after Martha heads off to work, which I wish she wouldn't do on account of her deadbeat boss, but she has got her mind made up. As for me, I can't just mope around the house my second day on a new job cuz I'm not 100-percent. So it's off to work I go. My window rolled down helps clear my head, but not enough.

I walk into the mailroom a half hour early to find Frank

Rambaugh sorting what mail was delivered on Saturday. Jesus, he's whistling, for crying out loud. Whistling while he works. On a Monday morning, no less.

Rambaugh's got 50 or 75 years seniority on me at this company, so I'm figuring there's no delicate way to ask him why the hell's he doing my job. He beats me to the punch. No good morning, no kiss my ass, no nothing.

"I am gleaning my correspondence. A day without fresh mail is like a day without sunshine. There could be signed proofs of loss. Therefore, claims I can pay and close. I love a closed file on a Monday."

I hop up and sit on the sorting table, on the other side of the postage meter. "I gotta say this for you, Frank, you're gung ho. How's it going with the character who made kindling out of the lobby chair?"

"The claimant has obtained the services of a chiropractor and an attorney. A chiropractor will treat a patient into eternity and the attorney will not present a demand until treatment is completed and bills have accumulated. I wished the claimant luck and informed him that he should receive his settlement in time to pay his great grandchildren's college tuition."

"How old is this claim claimer of yours?"

"Youthful and single."

I gotta smile. Don't know if Rambaugh's any more ethical than the shysters and quack doctors and the whiplash liars he's gotta deal with, but I like his moxie.

"I betcha you'll be there to sign him on the dotted line when he caves in."

"The claimant had best hope I am not. I regard Mother Unity's money as my own. A bloated claim is no different than a pickpocket's hand on my wallet."

"Lemme get personal for a minute, Frank. You allergic to retirement?"

He stops with his mail and looks at me over those antique glasses. "You are not a young man in your own right."

"So I been told."

"Yet you are gainfully employed and you moonlight."

"I gave up the moonlighting. This job is plenty. It's pin money, gravy over and above my regular retirement income."

"Didn't I see you on a television news story."

I answer with a shrug. I'm not admitting my appearance on that tape before or after the fact. Furthermore, as an anonymous source, I wasn't exactly lying to the kids about being a secret agent. I'm kind of liking this air of mystery I got.

He says, "I suffer from insomnia and channel-surf. I am addicted to Channel 81 and *Hawaii Five-o*. Wo Fat is a classic television villain, is he not? I enjoy those episodes, no matter how often I have seen them. He is reminiscent of claimants I have known."

"Wo Fat never had a bad hair day," I say.

"In light of Mr. Chipperfield's legal difficulties, I will not pry, Buddy, and I am not a gossip."

"I appreciate that, Frank."

In response to your question on retirement and myself, it has been asked frequently and rather aggressively over the past ten to fifteen years."

"I'm curious is all."

Rambaugh folds his arms and looks out into space,

thoughtful-like. He's got wrinkles galore and a turkey gobbler neck.

He says, "Idealized retirement is indolence and independence. Those are the desired components, are they not?"

"Sure."

"Irrespective of your age, if you were handed a sum of money that would permit you to live in comfort for the rest of your life, what would you do?"

"Like hitting a Powerball lotto? Well, I'd give notice to whoever I give notice to now that Bobbi Jo's gone. Cyndi?"

"Of course you would give your notice. The Take-This-Job-and-Shove-It Syndrome is human nature. You brought up an unfortunate sidebar. The bloodbath you witnessed Friday cost the jobs of one outstanding person and two individuals who will not be missed."

"Bobbi Jo, the personnel lady?"

"Top-notch," Rambaugh says, as he resumes his mail shuffling. "First rate. She gave twenty-three years of loyal and professional service to Mother Unity. Her release was unconscionable."

"The Tomb of the Unknown Regional manager. What was he like?"

Rambaugh looks off in that direction. "We hardly knew ye."

"The Angel of Death gave us a pass, Frank, you and me both. How come?"

"The Angel is irrationally frightened of older people."

"He won't downsize what you'd call your mature worker?"

"Yes and no. An employee under sixty seems not to

affect him thusly."

"I snuck in under the wire."

"He sees us and he sees his future. My theory is that he sees himself as Ebenezer Scrooge in it. That or a grandfather abused him when he was a child."

"We're scary, huh?"

"He witnesses his own mortality. The Angel is not a bad sort and he is only following orders. Back to your windfall. What would you do? Play golf around the clock?"

"I don't golf. I thought I'd take it up some day when I was too feeble to do anything else. What would I do? Let's see. What I feel like doing, I reckon."

"Which is, please?"

"Haven't thought about it. My next-door neighbor won the Oregon lottery to the tune of ten-plus million smackers. I don't think there's that kind of luck left in the neighborhood for me."

"We are speaking hypothetically. Get up as late as you like? Travel? Watch television all day? Volunteer? Build birdhouses and attempt to sell them at street fairs? Make a pest out of yourself visiting children and grandchildren?"

"Yeah. Some of the above. What I'd like to do, I'd like to check out Branson, Missouri. My rich neighbors will end up there. Maybe even buy the place."

"What if your fortune just as suddenly vanished? What if you were forced to subsist on Social Security and a niggardly pension?"

"If my cash flow gets constipated, Branson, Missouri is out. Branson would not make the cut. Anyway, if we had the loot, Martha'd veto it again and go for Spain since friends of ours are getting hitched there shortly."

"You would enjoy fewer leisure options and have more time to fret over money. I do not know your financial well-being, but most people at or near retirement age fall somewhere between moderate wealth and borderline poverty."

"You too, Frank?"

"While Mother Unity's retirement plan is abominable, retirement is financially feasible. I have no avocations, I have no interests outside of my work. I am a widower. My grown children live out of state. I make brief annual visits or vice versa. I cannot conceive myself parked on their davenports or in a recreational vehicle in their driveways for a protracted period of time."

It would be bad taste, considering Rambaugh's age, to remind him that somebody's probably gonna be stuck with the chore hauling him out of the office here on a stretcher.

I say instead, "I guess there's a moral to this story."

"Indeed. Do not create an artificial obligation to retire at an arbitrary date based on an age at which you have arbitrarily decided you deserve to be out of the laboring mainstream and/or you are no longer useful. Do not be resentful if you work beyond that date. Retire when you can comfortably and eagerly segue into new activities, new enthusiasms. You are old only when you look at yourself in the mirror and pronounce yourself so. What is the alternative?"

"Pushing up daisies."

"Precisely."

"Plop your butt in a rocking chair when you're not ready to, you're sticking one foot in a pine box. If there's no hopes, no dreams, you're royally screwed."

"Elegantly stated," he says, putting down the mail, *my* mail to sort.

This conversation has got me feeling a little more upbeat about Martha and me. These words of wisdom coming from a fella who makes Father Time seem like a squirt in diapers. My headache's almost gone too. I whip out that old life insurance policy.

"Frank, if you got a minute, gimme your take on this."

He reads it cover to cover, turning the pages careful so they don't flake apart, squinting at the fine print, even taking a sniff at the mustiness. Looks like he's looking over an artifact.

"Old Indemnity Life," he says. "Fascinating. I vaguely recall them as a minor and growing player in life and health. They were undercapitalized. They expanded too ambitiously and fell into grave financial condition. I do not recollect their fate."

"My folks bought these policies for my brother and me. When did you last hear of them?"

"Mid-nineteen-seventies." He gets this faraway look. "The years blend and blur."

"Think they're still in business?"

"Not in their present form. The Old Indemnity name disappeared."

"You're saying the company maybe didn't go belly-up?"

"In a sense, no. State insurance commissions are reluctant to allow companies to abandon their policyholders. Other carriers are continually bargain-hunting. I imagine that Old Indemnity's book of business was purchased at a distressed price. I will research it for you."

"I owe you one, Frank. Fifteen hundred bucks is no big deal. If it's there, though, I'd like Martha to be able to cash in if I croak first."

"Your wife?"

"Yeah."

"You have been married how long?"

"We joke that we need a calculator to do the math. Forty years before you know it. You said you were a widower."

"Cancer," Rambaugh says. "If you live long enough, you either die from it or with it. Helene and I were together forty-two years. She passed away five years ago."

"Sorry."

"A policyholder conducted the services."

"Everybody knows the funeral industry's a racket. Unity insures them, huh?"

"One of our unfortunate niches. I can relate substantiated examples of necrophilia and cannibalism."

"That's okay, Frank. Don't bother. As long as they reduce me down to a pile of ashes Martha can keep in an urn. That's the extent of the business I intend to do with those vultures. Gonna do your researching on the computer?"

Rambaugh shudders. "An overrated gadget. I will telephone some cronies."

I give him two thumbs up. I knew this guy was aces.

~ ~ ~

Rambaugh comes in the mailroom as I'm loading up for my afternoon run to the post office.

"Old Indemnity and its transformations have led a transient existence," Frank says.

He goes on with a bunch of gobblygook where big fish

eat little fish and some medium-sized fish bite chunks off the biggies. He must've rattled off a dozen companies, none of them I ever heard of. It's as complicated as this offshore money hanky-panky you read about.

"Your coverage has been transferred intact."

"So it is worth the paper it's wrote on?"

He taps the table and says, "Sit down, Buddy."

Chapter 20

MARTHA

Mr. Larionov materializes at mid-afternoon, a typical lull period.

Or should I say Comrade Larionov?

We have few customers and I am wiping down the counter.

Shawn said earlier that he would be by. He wouldn't swear that Mr. Larionov was bringing paychecks, but he was optimistic. Why else would he show his face? Mr. Larionov goes into Shawn's office with a plump manila envelope, a positive sign. He will not look me in the eye, however, even after I say hello. This is not a positive sign.

That Mr. Larionov is talking and Shawn is listening and looking forlorn is not a positive sign either. I am going to wipe a hole right through this plastic if I continue, but my vantage point is perfect. Shawn is talking now, talking so loudly I can hear, although not distinguish words because of the noise of the dishwasher.

Shawn is animated to say the least, shouting with his hands. Mr. Larionov is shaking his head. They are both on their feet and I fear they are going to come to blows, but Mr. Larionov leaves as Shawn is getting the last word (s) in, some of the four-letter variety.

Everyone in the restaurant is watching. Todd, Nicki, Josie, Steve, Barb and our three diners. Mr. Larionov strides by us and out the door as if we aren't there. I go on in to Shawn.

"The checks are through the middle of last week," he informs me. "The sale to the Chinese fell through and Corporate is taking over the restaurant. Larionov isn't sure if they want to keep it running or board it up. He told me to shut down tonight at normal closing. No way. We'll bag it as soon as I hand out the checks and talk to everybody and lock the doors. Piss on him."

I am at my wit's end. Two days pay, a mile-high stack of bills, and one week's fast-food experience to add to my pathetic résumé.

All I can do is hug Shawn. He is young with his life ahead of him, yes, but he is marginally educated and this is all he knows. I feel worse for him than I do for Buddy and myself. Shawn seems utterly lost. He is trembling with fear and anger.

A car with a stuck horn and squealing brakes diverts my attention. It's a small sedan, faded blue and dented. The noise stops and out of the driver's seat leaps my husband. Buddy has parked that thing next to Mr. Larionov's backed-in SUV. Their doors opened simultaneously, Mr. Larionov to enter, Buddy to exit. My husband is grinning at him, no doubt presuming who Mr. Larionov is from my description of the collective farm Communist and his giant vehicle.

Knowing my man, Mr. Larionov isn't out of the woods yet. Buddy has been as angry as he gets over my paycheck situation. Still, what on earth is he doing here in that strange car, wearing a demented smile? He should be at work. Has this something to do with Lizabeth and her disgusting father?

Mr. Larionov is pausing, foot on the running board, not

certain what to make of Buddy. I hurry for the exit. We already have all the trouble we need and much, much more.

Then the oddest thing happens. Buddy gives Mr. Larionov a congenial greeting, a "howdy" or some such. Mr. Larionov finds Buddy disconcerting and ignores him. He climbs into that monstrosity of his and slams the door. I have to admit he's justified. Buddy is acting deranged.

Then an even odder thing happens. Buddy blows Mr. Larionov a kiss as he pulls out. A normal Buddy would give him the finger or worse.

My Buddy is drunk or he's having a meltdown. Our problems have gotten the best of him and he's having a nervous collapse? His drinking and brooding, and his insomnia and his jabbering in his sleep. I should have seen it coming from a mile away.

"What on earth?" I say.

"Hey, kiddo, how's your day going?"

"I'm being paid a grand total of two days pay and I'm out of a job. Other than that, marvelous."

"What the hell. It's only money."

I step closer to smell his breath. I do not smell a thing.

"Untwitch your nostrils, Martha. Ain't touched a drop. That'll change later on after I'm off duty."

"What is wrong with you and where did you get this junker?"

"Mother Unity's pool car. Never ever stand in front of it. Thanks to Frank Rambaugh, I had me a pep talk on retirement philosophy and also what you'd call your basic windfall, two for the price of one," he says, flapping a folded paper in front of me as if it is a fan.

I take it out of his hand. "That old life insurance policy?"

"Rambaugh did some researching. Turns out this policy is what they call whole life where the premiums my mom and dad paid into it were put to work as investments. This insurance company that took over the policy says it's worth, get a load of this, Martha."

He hands me a slip of paper: $23,764.19.

"Goodness. They pay me that if you die?"

"Better yet. Pay now, croak later. We can cash it in for that amount. As of like two hours ago. The balance's more than that now. The meter, it just keeps running, like it has been for all these years."

I fall into his arms. "You're kidding."

"Call Janine up and reserve our places. Sweetie, you and me, we're going to Spain! Say goodbye to your double bacon cheese gutbomb shitburger. Say hello, *tapas*."

Chapter 21

MARTHA

Buddy asks me for the tenth time if I can hear his stomach growling. We have been stalling dinner, sitting out on the deck, savoring our newfound luck, sipping iced tea on this glorious early evening, keeping an eye out for Jim and Ellen. Things with them should not end on this note. If they come home, we'll casually invite them to our favorite buffet, our treat.

Except to complain of extreme hunger and malnutrition, Buddy has been quiet, how he is when he's mulling something over. Then he announces to me that he's has, and I quote, "a wild hair up his ass" and would I like to take a ride.

He adds, "We could wait up all night for Jim and Ellen. They're probably at Cadillac, buying out the showroom."

"A ride where?"

"Out to a lake. We'll enjoy the moonlight on the water."

"Lake Chester?"

"Bingo."

"Give it up."

"Hey, we can afford the gas now."

"Buddy."

"Martha, I been putting two and two together."

"Do they equal three or five?"

"No, listen. Number one, there's no 'FOR SALE' sign out."

"So you told me. The realtor may not be posting a sign because it's unoccupied. You invite vandalism."

"Nah, don't think there's a realtor. They'd have one of those lockboxes on the doorknob like realtors use to get in when it's vacant. Number two, there's an alarm company sign up that's phony. Number three's Chipperfield and his present tense. Number four is that it's not spiffed up, not even dusted, which you'd do if you were showing the place."

"You and Lizabeth went through it."

"In the daytime. You think Murganzer'd be sitting out on the porch in his bib overalls, watching the fish jump? He'd creep back in from the woods at night to sack out or whatnot."

There is no debating Buddy when he's like this. You can toss logic and reason out the window.

"Promise me, this is the end. The last I hear of Charles Murganzer in hiding. Ever."

I look at him until he raises his right hand, for what good it does, and says, "We can grab dinner on the way."

~ ~ ~

Buddy drives my Honda. It gets almost twice the mileage as his truck. We may have a gift from the gods, but we are hardly flush. His notion of dinner is whatever is available at a Tacoma convenience store. Two corn dogs for him as he drives and smears grease all over my steering wheel, a tub of yogurt for me, accompanied by a diet cola.

On the northbound Narrows Bridge, he points at the sidewalk and says, "Just about there. Splat. So they claim. Show me the body."

"Yes, yes."

That is quite enough. I spill the beans about the

summons I received yesterday morning. I attempt to jolt him to reality. I tell him twenty-three thousand dollars is not a fortune. I, after all, do the bills. My euphoria is wearing off. We should be giving Spain second thoughts. The money will hold our creditors at bay for a period. However, we are far from being out of the hole. We should stop chasing Charles Murganzer's ghost and hook up with one of those class action attorneys who have been hounding us.

"Goddamn shysters," Buddy says. "What you're saying makes sense, though. The conspiracy part. First Stringbean, now Fatso. Different English and U.S. lawyers splitting up the gravy. Ricky, that'd be right up his alley."

"Shall we call Janine with our regrets?

"Nope. She's booked our tickets by now."

"Perhaps not. We talked this afternoon."

Buddy is not listening. "Blood from a turnip is what they'll get. Fuck 'em. And if we spend a chunk of it on the trip, there'll be less for them to fight over and maybe they'll lose interest."

I roll my eyes, speechless, but I must admit that his rationale, such as it is, is appealing.

Buddy pats my knee. "You know that old beer commercial, kiddo. You only go around once, so grab for the gusto. That's us, gusto grabbing."

I groan.

It is getting dark and Buddy hunches forward as he drives. Perhaps this isn't the best time to remind him yet again to get his eyes checked. We arrive at Lake Chester at sunset, park on the shoulder of the road, and walk in.

In the twilight I can see the silhouettes of the trees. I

smell stagnant water and skunk cabbage. Hand in hand, we navigate the rutted cow path of a road and avoid stumbling. If a creature springs out of the brush, we may or may not be able to identify it as it eats us.

There is a full moon tonight, not necessarily a good omen. Oh, the surface of the water! The moon is plating it pure gold.

"Holy cow," Buddy mutters.

He is not exclaiming about the light on the lake, but a light inside the cabin. A car is parked beside it.

"A real estate agent and a prospect," I think out loud.

"You don't kick tires in the dark."

Buddy raises a palm and creeps ahead on his toes. He peeks inside and waves me forward. He tries the locked door, then pounds on it.

He yells, "Avon calling. Ding dong. Open the fuck up, Murganzer!"

Charles Murganzer does not open the door. Chick Chipperfield does. He is actually dressed like a human being for a change, in tan slacks and a pullover.

"We were in the neighborhood," Buddy says.

Chipperfield is cool, calm and collected. "Small world."

"Sprucing up for the sale?" Buddy asks.

"As a matter of fact."

"Don't forget to sweep up that money I saw on the table."

"Money?" I say.

"Two bundles he had apart counting, when I looked in the window," Buddy says to me.

"And you are Mrs. Whitacre," he says to me with a pained facsimile of a car salesman's smile.

"Mrs. Martha Whitacre to you. Should we be made aware of this money my husband mentioned?"

"This thing, it ain't going away, Chick."

"Lizzie told you where this is, Buddy? Are you interested in the cabin? I'll give you an employee discount."

"What you need to do is cut the crapola and talk to us about Charlie Murganzer."

Chipperfield steps aside and says, "Welcome to my humble secondary abode. You aren't armed, are you?"

We go in and Buddy says, "Martha won't let me keep a gun in the house."

The interior décor is what one might expect – Dusty Primitive. I never yearned for a vacation home. The water and the summer sun might be nice, but you are essentially doubling your household chores, and it is traditionally the womenfolk who clean the fish if the men manage to catch any.

"Lizzie let it slip you're clinging to your hunch that Chaz is among the living," Chipperfield says. "Let it go, my man. Chazbo was slippery but not slippery enough to come back from the dead."

"Mr. Chipperfield, I am now a convert to my husband's theory. He has legitimate reasons for believing Charles Murganzer is alive, so don't you patronize him. Don't you dare!"

My tone startles all three of us.

Buddy jabs a finger. "And don't go and tell us that that pile of cash is none of our beeswax neither. Three guesses where it came from."

I know it's a cliché, but the air seems to go out of Chick Chipperfield. He says, "You nice folks wanna join me for a cold one. I have the juice on to power the fridge."

We sit at the table and drink icy longnecks out of the bottle, and allow Mr. Chipperfield to proceed at his own pace.

"You hit the nail on the head, Buddy. Me and Chaz made us a hasty arrangement. When the heat came down on him, he came to me. We weren't bosom buddies, but business is business. Question. Is what I'm saying to you leaving this room?"

Buddy looks at me.

"Your call, dear."

Buddy lifts a shoulder. "Depends. Keep talking."

"You're sure you don't have a gun? You old people all have a houseful of them. I've had unhappy customers of a certain age confront —"

I interrupt, "Mr. Chipperfield, you are making me rethink my personal firearms policy and my opinion of those Second Amendment loons. Why don't you start with the money? I presume it is those unseemly lumps in your back pockets."

"Ninety-nine hundred smackers."

"An odd amount," I say.

"You can't deposit more than ten grand at a clip without the IRS nosing around, thinking you're a dope dealer," Chick Chipperfield says. "I gotta deposit it to pay my bills, to keep the superstore afloat."

"How much did Murganzer pay you to hide him out here?" Buddy asks.

"Irrelevant and immaterial. I've been making daily trips and this is the last of it. You can look. I stashed it in a loose floorboard between the sink and stove. Go on. Look. You want, you can tear the dump apart."

"It doesn't take a genius to figure where Murganzer got the money to pay you. Is this property really up for sale?"

Chipperfield shakes his head. "There'd be nothing in it for me. It's remortgaged to the hilt. Heather knew I was coming out here and let it slip to Lizzie. I had to tell her something."

"Lying to your daughter who loves you very much," I say.

He will not look me in the eye.

Buddy asks, "So the sixty-four gazillion dollar question is, where's the rancid son of a bitch?"

"Chaz's game plan was that he'd lay low while the fuzz scoured airports and exotic locales. When things cooled off, he'd've grown a beard. He'd complete the disguise with fake glasses, a hair dye job, new clothes. Using fake ID, he'd head off into the horizon."

"Aha," Buddy says. "Murganzer's got more loot elsewheres."

"Hey, don't overrun the story. I'm getting there. Chaz pays me and I follow him to the bridge where he'll fake suicide. He'd already written the note and taped it to the dash."

Chipperfield sighs. "The Aston Martin he was driving. Aluminum skin, twelve cylinders, zero to sixty in a heartbeat. It'd dress up my lot something fierce. I tried to talk him into one of my units instead and –"

"For crying out loud, Mr. Chipperfield."

"Okay, okay. We stop at mid-span. It's the middle of the night and foggy. There's no traffic. It's ideal. He gets out of the car but doesn't move. I get out and say, come on, man, we can't stand here all night. Then he says that there's no more money to speak of that he can get his hands on. They came down on him too fast, took him by surprise. He says they'll arrest him sooner or later and throw away the key. He says, 'Six hundred and some counts. They'll send me up forever. I won't be eligible for parole until the sun goes into nova.' His exact words."

Chick Chipperfield pauses and makes an arcing motion with his beer bottle. "That was all she wrote."

Buddy and I look at him, waiting.

Chipperfield rubs an eye with a knuckle. A tear?

"He jumped for real. I may be a sleazeball, but that doesn't mean I don't have half a heart," he says. "It's my subconscious in denial."

Chapter 22

BUDDY & MARTHA
BUDDY:

Martha and me, we're sardined in the cattle car section of a 747 I may of riveted belly skin onto at Boeing. She's snoozing, her pillow pressed into my shoulder. I'm looking out at the twilight over Greenland. Nothing down there except ice and snow. It's beyond me how the polar bears get by.

Some things, they never change.

Janine's handing out more of her informational handouts. Some things do change. Like who she's handing her handouts to. Niles and Breece, Martha's pointy-heads, they're not along. Neither are the other total strangers from last time. We have got us another complete bunch.

The wedding party's filled a goodly share of the slots on this cultural tour of Spain's Andalusia region. Seated directly behind us are Janine's folks, Marvin and Julia. Janine has two younger sisters who are gonna be maid of honors. Martha says cuz they're married they're co-matrons of honor. Whatever, they're catching up with us later on.

Julia's a schoolteacher nearing retirement her ownself. She's hardly had a dry eye since we boarded. Martha says they're tears of relief and joy. And other issues too, she strongly believes.

While Mom Julia's relieved that Janine's finally tying the knot, the concern is her choice of beau and the whirlwind courtship. But happiness seems to be overruling worry, irregardless of her son-in-law-to-be's drawbacks in their minds.

Marvin's a college professor, a real one who teaches a real subject. Aeronautical engineering, not philosophy. Waiting to board in Seattle, we had us a nice chat. Marvin and me, we have lots in common. Before he left Boeing for the University of Washington to teach, he worked as an engineer on the 747. Marvin helped design access door pockets and wheel wells I assembled in the nineteen eighties. Small world.

In the middle of the center section is Buck and Flo, Ted's folks. They are not small people and are unhappy being squeezed in there. But the plane's full, so there's no choice. Buck's a meat cutter and Flo's a wrapper. This clan of Ted's, they got supermarkets in their blood. They're not warming to Janine's folks and the feeling's mutual, as there's not a whole helluva lot in common.

When Janine's not doing her tour leader job, she sits in the opposite window row with Ted. Martha went to the can and came back and said they were holding hands and that they're adorable. This is good. Janine has got other interests than cathedrals and museums. Maybe she'll go a little lighter on the culture this trip. Fewer sculptures in squares that pigeons use as honey buckets, more *tapas*.

Ed and Lizabeth are snuggled up in the row ahead of them. They're doing more than holding hands. Ed's gonna be Ted's best man. Him and Lizabeth are having themselves a pre-honeymoon without benefit of clergy. Everybody agrees that this is smart, given Lizabeth's marital track record.

Those two hit it off from the git-go, if you'll recollect. Lizabeth found herself an apartment the next day. Ed's there constantly, though they deny they're officially cohabitating. Lizabeth got herself a job in the deli of their supermarket, Ed's and Ted's. She says you meet a better class of people there than behind the bar.

The weirdest members of our merry band are Chick and Heather, six or seven rows in front of Ed and Lizabeth. Lizabeth says her daddy jumped bail. Heather says her Chickypoo's being driven into political exile. Everything's kinda patched up between everybody for the sake of the betrothed, though the air's frosty when Heather and Lizabeth are in snarling range. As for Chick and me, he keeps his fucking distance.

This section of the aircraft, the hormones in the air are so thick, you can cut 'em with a knife. Martha's stroking my leg, whispering in my ear that they're contagious.

Enough said.

~ ~ ~

We're stopping over in Amsterdam's Schiphol Airport instead of London. The clock says eight in the morning. My aching head and butt say my body has no clue what time it is.

Ed and Ted and me, we're aware that the Dutch brew tasty beer. I make the mistake of mentioning this to Martha. Ed and Ted make a production of deciding against a libation. Those boys are so pussywhipped as to be almost unrecognizable.

Short hop from Amsterdam to Madrid. We're not staying. We're hopping a bus from the airport directly to the train station. We're riding this high-speed bullet train to

Seville, the main burg in Andalusia. The train's called the *AVE*, which is Spanish for Train That Goes Faster'n a Bat Outta Hell.

The bus takes the street that goes by the Prado, which, uh oh, is coming up on the left, so the Reina Sofia will be coming off to our right. Martha hasn't put two and two together about *Girl*, who's pretty much out of my system anyways. I have not had a goofy dream since the night before that big fat day when Frank gave me the news on the insurance policy and we had it out with Chick and learned the true fate of Charles Murganzer. Martha calls it closure.

When we're within view of the Reina Sofia, for crying out loud, I'm seeing Ricky Ricardo and his finger-waving sidekick on every street corner. I bend down and pretend to tie my shoelace till we stop at the train station. The Reina Sofia's catty-corner from the station, so I do not waste time getting on inside. I ain't paranoid, I'm careful.

Day before yesterday, Martha got an encouraging reply from Thimblekins to her inquiries. These latest legal eagles that're suing us for £2,500,000, I looked up the pound on the business page and it is serious money, to the tune of $4,300,000 or thereabouts.

Martha says not to worry. Thimblekins said he's started a documentation process for us and asked Martha to follow up on e-mail while in Spain.

We called brother Stan to say Merry Early Christmas and that he's got more than $23,773.56 (which is what is was to the penny when we cashed in the policy) at his fingertips, him and me and Martha and Miriam are on friendlier terms. They have a home computer too. Naturally Miriam's the major user. Martha promised to write them from Spain, and I don't mean postcards.

A thought popped in my head after we hung up with Stan and Miriam. Through *Girl* and the picture Stan sent and the insurance policy Miriam sent with it and me connecting up with insurance expert Frank Rambaugh, has Mom been playing me like a puppet from the grave? This is hogwash, but hogwash I'm gonna believe till my dying breath. This is a thought I'm gonna keep private.

The *AVE* is smooth as silk. It's a rolling rocket. There are cute, young stewardii, like on airplanes. Julia, Janine's ma, she speaks Spanish. She asks a stew how fast we're going. She says 280 kilometers per hours. In plain English, that's nearly 174 MPH. We make the 300-plus-miles to Seville in two-and-a half-hours including stops. A couple of zillion olive trees blur by. There's a teenage girl aboard wearing a *Girl* T-shirt. She's with her family, Spanish tourists going home from Madrid. Am glad they walked through to the next car. I'd be getting into trouble eyeballing her, wondering if she reminded me of anybody.

Mom, I think.

Enough already.

~ ~ ~

Next day, it's still sinking in that we're here. In Spain.

I'll tell you what, it was a mad frantic scramble to get ourselves and our gear organized in time to go. Melanie's looking after Orange and Tangerine and the house. This trip has laid to rest any prying on poverty and related areas. Betcha Dr. Dave's scratching his noggin over how we came up with the bucks. The house payment's been made, and various and sundry creditors fended off. When we get home we'll be damn near broke again. But that's then, this is now.

Getting a leave of absence at Unity was as easy as pie. I called up the Angel of Death and he says, what, you've been with the company one week. But he gave it to me. My job'll be waiting. I'm sticking to Frank's theory on the Angel that besides the Scrooge hang-up, he fears and respects his elders on account of his grandpappy used a switch on him when he was a kid.

Janine, I swear she's immune to jet lag. She's got us culturizing soon after breakfast. There's this art museum with a mix of stuff that looks like stuff, and stuff that doesn't. Then we take a boat ride on the big river that cuts through Seville. We see sights that're old and new and in-between. Martha nudges my ribs to encourage me to keep my eyes open.

The Seville Cathedral's next. Woozy or not, it snags my attention. To give you an idea of the size, it's got an orange grove inside the walls, 25 separate chapels, and a tower 300-feet tall. A stroll around the perimeter burns off half a mile of shoe leather.

What really grabs me is that Chris Columbus's bones are supposed to be in the Cathedral. Four statues are holding up this whachamacallit that looks like a big breadbox made of dark wood and leather. Martha has to drag me off, calling me a ghoul.

Everybody takes an afternoon siesta, like the natives do. Ted and Janine, they have got separate rooms. This settles a popular topic of gossip. We're all going out to a traditional and formal Spanish dinner. No doubt it's gonna include that soup they can't bother heating up.

During my snooze, *tapas* bars dance through my head like sugarplums. When we get up, I tell Martha I got a killer headache. I gulp down an aspirin I don't need to prove it. She cuts me some slack and pretends to believe me, and says don't get into any mischief here by myself.

I was paging through Martha's guidebook on the *AVE* train and came upon El Rinconcillo. This is a Seville *tapas* bar not two blocks from our hotel. El Rinconcillo is said to date to 1670 and to be the world's first *tapas* bar. The book's skeptical but, like Columbus's bones really being Columbus's bones, you gotta have faith. I got faith.

El Rinconcillo therefore is a holy site.

After the gang's gone to dinner, I beeline it to what you probably wouldn't call a shrine when you see it up close and personal. El Rinconcillo is an ordinary old saloon. Guys behind the bar are friendly and serve up ice-cold beer and *tapas* mostly in the cholesterol family. Chorizo, Serrano ham, cheese. Yum and double yum.

Joint's filling up with a combo of tourists and locals. You order a beer and they make a chalk mark on the bar in front of you, a system dating to who knows when.

I'm standing at the bar when I hear, "Buddy Whitacre."

He's appeared on my left. Through the cigarette smoke, I can smell cologne and hairspray.

"Chipperfield," I say, eyes straight ahead, "You're spoiling the moment."

"I don't blame you for hating my guts. I'm a rat. Lizzie must've told you I'm incorrigible."

"Nobody's arguing."

"Buy you a beer and another plate of the goodies you're eating?"

His color scheme's toned down some, but he's wearing the white patent leather belt and shoes they triple-checked at the airports when we went through security. I am too jet-lagged and mellowed out to be overly antagonistical and pissed off.

"Sure. Why not?"

Chick orders a beer, which goes down in a gulp. "Hey, you could sympathize a tad for a man who's being persecuted."

"Ain't the word 'prosecuted'?"

He stares at his beer and shakes his head. "When you trust your right-hand man and he betrays you – et tu Bruno."

"I gotta agree, that boy is a piece of work."

"There are extenuating factors to my expatriate status. We can't go home with the group. Heather's expecting."

"A baby?"

"We phoned home to her obstetrician today for the test results. Heather throttled a rabbit."

"Congratulations, Dad."

I signal the barkeep that the next round's on me.

"You're the first person to hear the news. Lizzie doesn't even know. She's been acting pissy toward us."

I nod, flattered.

"I'm worried that Heather's exposed to an overdose of airport X-rays carrying our child. Fetuses are sensitive to radiation, you know. Our baby'll be glowing in the dark."

"That's a legit concern."

"What do you think of Lizzie's new flame, Buddy? That boy doesn't strike me as having much get up and go. Jesus, a supermarket checker."

I look at Chick hard. "Ed would walk into a fucking blast furnace for your daughter."

He raises his palms. "No offense."

"Cut Ed some slack, okay? Treat him with a little respect. If they're what each other wants, don't queer it. There's already plenty of folks in our merry band looking down at him."

"Not a problem."

"I'll make you a deal, Chipperfield."

He makes a production of sucking in his breath. "Name it."

"Martha and me, we haven't spoke a peep about you and Murganzer."

"I mailed the cash to the bankruptcy court like you said."

"I know. We were there to see you lick the envelope and drop it in the mailbox."

"A nice gesture, though that money divided up to the victims won't amount to much."

"Believe me, Chick. That wasn't easy for us to do neither, given our cash flow situation."

"Do you believe me, Buddy, that Chaz is fish food?"

"Martha and me, we agreed that your story's too much of a whopper, even for you."

He extends a hand. "We're square?"

I shake it. "Square."

"Hey, great. I'll toss in a bonus. Brady Hardcastle?"

My stomach knots. "Yeah?"

"Phoned a gink I knew who also mentored under Maniac Monahan. He knew a guy who knew a guy who knew a guy who knew Hardcastle. He wasn't easy to forget."

Gotta play dumb. "What do you mean?"

"Long time ago, he killed his girl friend and himself

because his wife wouldn't give him a divorce so he could marry the girl. This was back when divorces were tougher to get. You couldn't just put your moccasins outside the teepee."

I thank Chick. He buys a round. I buy a round. He doesn't ask what Hardcastle is to me and doesn't let on if he knows. Me, I'm flabbergasted and astounded. Hardcastle, the rancid son of a bitch, he killed my mom out of love.

~ ~ ~

We got further touristing to do before the wedding in the white village. Next stop's a nifty oceanside town called Chipiona. You wanna find it on your map, good luck. You'll need a magnifying glass. It has got miles of great beaches and we're the only Americans I've seen. This neck of the woods is known for sherry and other potent sweet wines. We spend three days kicked back. Me, personally, I spend many an hour at seaside cafés, partaking of *tapas* and careful sips of the local elixir, gazing out at the sea, absolutely zilch on my mind.

The bus route follows the south coast. We stop at breezy little Tarifa, which is noted for windsurfing. We're there as kind of a staging area for day trips to Gibraltar and to Tangier, across the Mediterranean in Tangieria, North Africa. It's mostly the strangers who go. Us family and friends, we hang out.

Last stop before the knot is tied: Ronda. You take this winding road up from the coast. Scenery's incredible. Hills, mountains, rolling fields, forests, et cetera. We make the bus driver stop I don't know how often for pictures.

Ronda is your basic photo op in its own right. There's a 330-foot-deep gorge running smack-dab through the middle of town. Ronda's connected by three bridges. The New Bridge was built in the seventeenth century. The Old Bridge is older than the New Bridge. The A-rab Bridge's older than both of them combined.

Our hotel's the usual mix of old and new. The swimming pool was installed just a few years ago. Martha says the bathroom plumbing dates to the Inquisition. She's excited cuz they have a computer set up so guests can get on the Internet.

Martha drags me to it, prior to lunch. She says business before *tapas*, so what are you gonna do?

What she does is log on with her account and checks her mail. There's this deal she calls an attachment from Thimblekins. She clicks her clicker more and a letter appears in actual letterform on the screen. Martha says that Mr. Timkins scanned it and loaded the file from a CD.

This documentation's a letter from the Barcelona East Injun boy who I intersected in behalf of. He's written to the police in perfect English what really and truly happened and how grateful he is to me and how he'll swear to his story in a court of law. There's a P.S. on the bottom that he's mailing me a sword of the scimitar persuasion, free gratis.

Thimblekins's letter is likewise good news. Seems that there's a minor league scandal brewing in the Spanish police. There's a very small element of them in cahoots with local *abogados*.

"*Abogado* means lawyer," Martha says.

"I know, I got other names for them."

We read on that these sideways cops would sell the *abogados* reports of incidents involving foreign tourists that had civil damage potential. The reports were "prone to exaggeration", making the subjects appear to have more assets than they do and/or in more trouble than they were, therefore more likely to cave in to monetary demands. The *abogados* would then sell the information to lawyers in the homelands of the alleged victims and/or perpetrators.

"I'll be damned," I say.

"They are the ones who should be damned. Damned to hell," says my unreligious Martha.

He closes by saying that the police ringleader has been suspended without pay. He says our complaint was instrumental in the ongoing investigation.

"Gotta be Madrid Ricky. Ricky's a slicky boy," I say. "He's as smooth as Murganzer. They'll never pin anything on him. He'll walk."

"Think of his career, Buddy. What will be left of it?"

I smile, picturing Ricky directing traffic in the middle of Madrid's busiest boulevard, kamikaze drivers zipping by to and fro.

Martha types in the computer addresses of the New York City shyster and Chicago shyster, copies the London barrister shysters, and sends them the attachment and Thimblekins letter, along with a go-piss-up-a-rope note she writes in much nicer language than I would.

My head doesn't stop spinning until I've sampled half the *tapas* on the menu and the second pitcher of sangria. Martha and her e-mailing, she's solved this thing and got us out of our jam and saved our bacon. When she drags me computer shopping for a modern unit, I'll have no defense.

~ ~ ~

Today's the day.

Can't for the life of me remember the name of the white

village, except it's Italian sounding, Rocky Graziano or something like that. Makes me think of Martha. Before our trouble, she'd been hinting at Italy for next year. Italy, birthplace of Charles Ponzi, by the way, who was known there in the old country as Carlo.

The bride and groom and their parents have gone ahead in rental cars. The rest of us are on the bus. The strangers on the tour too. They're not strangers any longer. They're really getting into this holy matrimony event. Our non-wedding gang on the tour's been invited, as well as to the reception that promises *cerveza* and *vino* and *tapas* coming out our ears.

A lady our age traveling with her brother asks me, "Is there always a wedding on these tours to Spain? It's a lovely touch."

"Every other tour," I answer her. "They alternate."

Where we're going – Grazalema, the name of it is – but it's an hour from Ronda on a crooked road that looks a foot narrower than our bus. You'd think, the closer you get to a white village, the less white it'd get, but it's fairly white when you see it perched up on a hillside.

It's white when you're there too, walking around. There's red tile roofs and cobblestones and streets as wide as sidewalks. Many of the houses have got potted flowers on hooks dug into the stucco walls and on the ground

The wedding ceremony's at high noon in a church that's, you guessed it, white. It's got a bell tower, arches, statues carved into niches, the full nine yards.

I got a secret. Weddings make me cry. Irregardless who's getting hitched, they flat-out do. Don't ask me why.

There's suspense whether this will come off, despite

travel and arrangements. There's a discussion regarding the bridegroom. Janine's been a faithful Catholic all her life. Ted, on the other hand, does not belong to any particular parish of any denomination.

Chick Chipperfield involves himself. Him and somebody connected to the church, not the priest, but an important fella, step aside to a corner. The hold-up's fixed, like Ted's been blessed and validated. My hunch is that Chick promised a contribution to their building whitewash fund. Good luck collecting.

This is a small wedding by Spanish standards, which everybody and his brother attends, so I'm told. Curious locals are looking in the door. Now I know what they feel like when we're snooping inside their cathedrals, camera flashes going off like fireflies.

The organ's playing and the ceremony begins.

Ed and Ted are up front in their tuxes, looking like penguins on steroids.

Janine and her daddy walk up the aisle. She's in white, as we're all certain she's entitled to be. Janine and her sisters are built the same. Sturdy peasant girls from the waist down, semi-petite and flat-chested north of there. Ted looks like he wants to jump Janine on the spot.

I lock my mind on other topics so there'll be no waterworks.

Jim and Ellen. You know, we never did see them again. Could of knocked on our door. Just once. And vice versa. We're no more or less than fifty percent to blame. Frank Rambaugh and his attitude that you're only old when you think you are and dead whenever your time comes kinda turns on the light bulb in my head.

The priest is saying his words in Spanish or Latin, can't tell which. Everybody gets the general idea.

Martha and me, we're holding hands.

I sniffle and whisper, "Damn allergies."

She gives me her hanky.

~ ~ ~

MARTHA:

Well, it is not prudery or my imagination. Buddy confirms this by wolf whistling under his breath. Ted and Janine's kiss *is* that long and steamy.

As if a boxing referee, the embarrassed priest is poised to separate them. They finally break and walk down the aisle to cheers and organ music. Janine is gorgeous and radiant in white. Ted is beet-faced from desire and being choked by his tie.

I have read that traditional Andalusian weddings are wild, colorful, lavish affairs that evolve into nightlong parties. The entire village turnouts. In days of yore, the bride and her entourage rode to the church on horseback.

This ceremony is not large or authentically Spanish. There was no time for pomp and circumstance. Distance and logistics made excess impossible. It is no Vegas quickie either. The experience is heartfelt and lovely.

The church was built before Washington crossed the Delaware. Dark wood pews glisten and floorboards creak. The wedding is illuminated by candles and sunlight through the stained glass. I can almost hear the clippety-clop of the bride's mount in the front courtyard. The flowers are fresh and local, the summer annuals Grazalema people hang in pots.

We guests are in our tourist finery, if slightly

disheveled. I haven't worn this skirt and blouse since interviewing with Mr. Larionov. My husband is dapper in white shirt and string tie.

While Buddy pretends not to cry, I look around at those close to this couple who are now wed till death or divorce do them part.

Lizabeth and Ed are scrunched together ahead of us. I trust she is heeding my advice, her and her oath on a stack of Bibles. Buddy says Ted says Ed's already pressuring her for a commitment, wanting to pick out a ring. Until Charles Murganzer is declared legally dead, the bigamy laws will save Lizabeth from herself. Not that I am critical of Ed. Lizabeth must consider her track record, her chronic falling-in-love affliction.

However, the pre-honeymoon, as Buddy terms it, is not under duress. They do appear blissful, an odd couple if there ever was one. Lizabeth tells me that the attraction is that she has never felt so genuinely worshipped for herself, not just her looks.

The Chipperfields. I suppress a sigh. Chickypoo and his child bride. Buddy told me about Heather's baby. We are both skeptical. As far as I know, they do not have to kill rabbits these days to determine pregnancy. Even if this isn't a Chick Chipperfield con job, the airport X-rays should be utterly harmless unless Heather travels as checked luggage.

Marvin and Julia are getting up on one end of the front row, Buck and Flo on the other. One set of parents is in lightweight suit and cocktail dress. The other is wearing matching satiny blue shirts, that could be bowling shirts without the lettering.

The reception is at a little restaurant around the corner.

Grazalema has few dining options, but the kids wanted the whole shebang done here in this picturesque white village. I suspect that the banquet room is customarily a card room. There is a permanent tobacco odor and bullfight posters on the walls. Ted has been trying to coax Janine out since the minute they sliced the wedding cake.

Perhaps the occasion and the wine is making us giddy. That or the wedding signals the beginning of the end of this glorious bonus trip. After a stop in Córdoba, it's off to Madrid and home and reality.

Buddy and I are having a partial meeting of the minds regarding our future. We've moseyed outside with our drinks. Between loud recorded Spanish guitar in the banquet room and a soccer game on the bar television, our ears are ringing.

I announce that since I am unemployed and we have a little money, I am going to take a crack at studying IT.

"That's the information whatchamacallit?"

"Information technology. The college's certificate program on hardware networking and troubleshooting. The course lasts six weeks and is cheap enough. It's part-time, so I can work too."

"Okay."

"Successful grads have gone on to advanced courses, although temp work is more up my alley. During a company's move or expansion or systems changeover, multiple hookups and setups need to be done quickly. As long as my limbs and joints hold up, I'm game."

"If Mother Unity and me part ways, I'll find a Spanish restaurant to work in. I already know *tapas* inside and out. I'm maybe Seattle's leading authority."

Buddy remains serious about culinary arts. This from a man the Army taught to cook meatloaf you have to cut with a chainsaw. But far be it from me to rain on his parade.

Janine and Ted are long gone when the reception ends. They went to their room for the night at a hotel on the Grazalema outskirts. Somebody said Ted was handling the rental sedan like a Formula One racer.

We don't get back to Ronda until dark. I am exhausted, but I tell Buddy I'm checking e-mail before coming to the room.

"Be my guest," he says.

There is one message, from Melanie.

It is giddy and full of exclamation marks. She and David are expecting in late January. So that is the hormone wackiness I detected! They have been hopeful for a couple of weeks, but didn't want to make an announcement until they were absolutely certain.

I notice there is no printer. Well, usage of the machine is free, so how can I complain? I leave my mail on the screen and hurry to the room and Buddy, as fast as I can without tripping and making a fool of myself.

I shall sit him down at the keyboard and watch his expression.

I shall ask him to peck out congratulations with his own two index fingers and tell Melanie how much we love them.

❄ ❄ ❄

Thank you for reading.
Please review this book. Reviews help others find
Absolutely Amazing eBooks and inspire us to keep
providing these marvelous tales.

If you would like to be put on our email list to receive
updates on new releases, contests, and promotions, please
go to AbsolutelyAmazingEbooks.com and sign up.

About the Author

Gary Alexander has written 16 novels, including *Loot,* fourth in the mystery series featuring comic Buster Hightower. *Disappeared*, the first in the series, has been optioned to Universal Studios.

He's written 150+ short stories and sold travel articles to 6 major dailies. One story appeared in *Best American Mystery Stories 2010*, another in *Ice Cold*, last year's Mystery Writers of America anthology.

Alexander is a nonsmoking, nondrinking vegetarian. He does, however, abuse caffeine and chocolate.

His website is www.garyralexander.net.

The New
Atlantian Library

NewAtlantianLibrary.com

or AbsolutelyAmazingEbooks.com

or AA-eBooks.com

www.ingramcontent.com/pod-product-compliance
Lightning Source LLC
Chambersburg PA
CBHW070447030726
47503CB00004B/927